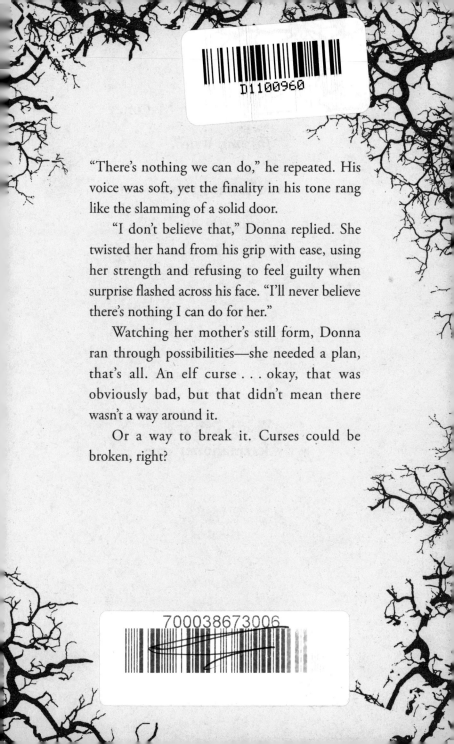

"There's nothing we can do," he repeated. His voice was soft, yet the finality in his tone rang like the slamming of a solid door.

"I don't believe that," Donna replied. She twisted her hand from his grip with ease, using her strength and refusing to feel guilty when surprise flashed across his face. "I'll never believe there's nothing I can do for her."

Watching her mother's still form, Donna ran through possibilities—she needed a plan, that's all. An elf curse . . . okay, that was obviously bad, but that didn't mean there wasn't a way around it.

Or a way to break it. Curses could be broken, right?

Also available by Karen Mahoney

The Iron Witch

And coming soon

Falling To Ash

Visit Karen at
www.**kazmahoney**.com

The Wood Queen

KAREN MAHONEY

CORGI BOOKS

THE WOOD QUEEN
A CORGI BOOK
978 0 552 56382 6

Published in Great Britain by Corgi Books,
an imprint of Random House Children's Books
A Random House Company

This edition published 2012

1 3 5 7 9 10 8 6 4 2

The Random House Group Limited supports The Forest Stewardship Council®
(FSC®), the leading international forest certification organisation. All our titles that
are printed on Greenpeace approved FSC® certified paper carry the FSC® logo. Our
paper procurement policy can be found at www.randomhouse.co.uk/environment.

MIX
Paper from
responsible sources
FSC® C016897

Corgi Books are published by Random House Children's Books,
61–63 Uxbridge Road, London W5 5SA

www.kidsatrandomhouse.co.uk
www.totallyrandombooks.co.uk
www.randomhouse.co.uk

Addresses for companies within The Random House Group Limited can be found
at: www.randomhouse.co.uk/offices.htm

THE RANDOM HOUSE GROUP Limited Reg. No. 954009

A CIP catalogue record for this book is available from the British Library.

Printed and bound by CPI Group (UK) Ltd, Croydon, CR0 4YY

For Mum, who reads everything I write but still always asks, "When will you have the next thing finished?"

The Wood Monster is dead.

I know this is true because I killed it. And yet my dreams are still full of fear and pain, even though it is a different sort of fear and a new kind of pain.

This morning I woke at dawn with the covers thrown off, pajamas sticking to my body and sweat-soaked hair in my eyes. My hands and arms ached and I knew that, if I looked at them, the familiar silver markings would be writhing around my wrists like living tattoos. Sometimes it feels as though my tattoos really are alive, but that's just the magic talking. Being marked by alchemical magic messes with your head at the best of times—and right now is just about as far as I've ever been from the best of times.

After I came to and switched on the light to chase away the shadows, I tried to recall what I'd been dreaming of—what nightmare had woken me this time—but the sights and sounds and twisted images were already gone. Melted away like the frost outside my bedroom window.

If only I could remember the nightmare more clearly. I'm sure there's something important in it—something I'm supposed to know or do. It feels like a warning, but how can I heed a warning that arrives so fleetingly and disappears just as quickly? The only memory I'm left with is of my mother sitting beneath a dying tree in an otherwise empty wasteland. Her face, half concealed behind her tangle of red hair, is white as bone. The white streak in the front of her hair is braided into a bizarre plait, and the thread that runs through it is bright green.

And the crows; so many of them. A murder of crows? Circling round and round in an indigo sky, shedding oily feathers that look like black petals.

Maybe I'm just having anxiety dreams ahead of the trial. Aunt Paige gets mad when I call it that—my "trial"—but isn't that what it is? She said it's just an "internal investigation", nothing more than routine after something serious happens. But really, what's the difference? Representatives from the three other Orders will pass judgment on me when the hearing begins today, and if that's not a "trial" then I don't know what is.

My first thought, when I woke, was to talk to Nav about my dream; to tell him what I could remember of those fading images and ask him to help me figure it all out. But I sank back against the pillows as sharp reality hit me: Navin is hardly speaking to me. After what happened to him so recently, I can't really blame him.

He still hasn't told me the details of his abduction by the wood elves. He won't open up to me the way that he used to. And I know I deserve this, given all the secrets I kept from him for the entire three years of our friendship. He's right not to trust me. How can we truly be friends when I hid so much? How can he ever forgive me, after the magical realities of my stupid life dragged him into something so terrible that he can't even bring himself to talk about it?

Xan says to give him time. Even Aunt Paige says to give him time; like she really cares. But as each day passes I can feel him slipping away . . .

I miss my best friend.

One

Donna sat up straight in her chair and tried not to look as though the last half-hour hadn't already nailed up her coffin good and tight. Listening to Simon Gaunt drone on as he listed her "crimes" was almost as bad as being forced to listen to a lecture on Hermetic literature.

Almost.

Her fingers curled inside the long velvet gloves that she always wore. Ten years of wearing them to hide the truth of what she was, and yet all she'd ever really wanted was something normal to hold on to; a regular existence. Recently, however, she'd begun to accept the idea that you don't always get what you want; making the best of things was often the only practical option. But that didn't mean she had to like it.

Her life seemed to have become an endless roller-coaster of crazy, and it was really starting to piss her off.

Everything she knew—or thought she knew—was based on a finely spun web of secrets and lies, yet what choice did she have other than to go along with it? At just seventeen, Donna wouldn't truly be free of the Order's influence for another year, as much as she wished things were different.

Biting her lip, she looked around the makeshift courtroom; really, it was just an old dining room that had been converted into a meeting space some years ago. Dust motes glittered in the air and the sickly sweet scent of furniture polish made her feel vaguely sick. The room seemed to be full of crusty old men, apart from one young guy—a tall Asian dude wearing awesomely inappropriate Goth-style makeup. She couldn't help feeling curious about him. And, of course, there was Paige Underwood, sitting quietly at the back looking pale and composed. But apart from that, the representatives from the four alchemical Orders were for the most part over sixty, white, and male. Donna let her eyes rest for a moment on the one other woman in the room, a perite blonde who looked about the same age as her aunt and who seemed to know Goth Dude.

Donna glanced at the gathered officials before meeting her aunt's eyes and mouthing the question that had been bugging her ever since she'd watched each alchemist take his place: *Where's Maker?*

For one moment, it looked as though Aunt Paige was going to either ignore the question or pretend she couldn't understand, but then she pointed to her watch as her lips formed the silent word, *Later.*

Later? What was that supposed to mean? Scanning the room again, Donna couldn't help feeling worried about Maker's absence from the crowd of alchemists. He'd been her only real source of support leading up to this hearing, and it was something she was intensely grateful for. So it seemed more than a little important that he should be here now, especially considering that he was—oh, you know, nothing major—supposed to act as her freaking *defense*.

Of course, she wanted to count her aunt as on her side too, but, if she were brutally honest, Donna had to acknowledge that Paige hadn't really spoken up for her at all. She hadn't been supportive about the trial, either. It hurt to admit it, but Donna was nothing if not realistic: Aunt Paige was still furious with her for sneaking around behind her back.

Simon was supposedly the Order of the Dragon's official secretary—sort of like an administrator—although

Donna's recent discovery of his hidden laboratory led her to suspect that there was a lot more to him than she'd always believed. Only a full-fledged magus would have a lab like that, one that the Order had obviously gone to great pains to conceal. Which begged the question: if it was true that Simon was a magus, why would they want to cover up the fact that there was such a powerful magic-user living within their diminishing ranks? It didn't make any sense.

Pushing conspiracy theories out of her head, Donna was torn between thinking how ridiculous this whole thing was and feeling terrified about what an alchemist trial might involve. She'd cost the Order something valuable—maybe even priceless—and she'd also given up their secrets to a "commoner". Not to mention befriended a guy with fey blood running through his veins.

Oh, I am so screwed.

She sighed and made an effort to tune back in to what was going on around her. Glancing at Quentin Frost, the Archmaster of the Order of the Dragon, she noticed that he looked tired—even more so than usual. He was old, it was true, but a new aura of exhaustion had settled around him like a thick gray cloud.

Simon had switched to using a more impressive inflection in his delivery, which was vaguely entertaining, at least. It was like he was on stage delivering a Shakespearean soliloquy, hands linked loosely behind his back as he paced up and down the nasty, patterned brown carpet. He cut an unassuming figure—average height and skinny, with thinning brown hair and plain wire glasses that caught the light each time he moved. He seemed to be taking great pleasure in recounting every single one of Donna's transgressions.

When it came to the part about "fraternizing with the enemy", she had to resist the urge to stand up and shout, *I object!* It probably wouldn't go down too well, and this wasn't a criminal trial—as Aunt Paige liked to remind her. A "hearing" was simply that: an opportunity for representatives from all the Orders to hear what Donna had done, and to decide on an appropriate punishment. Of course, according to the alchemists, Donna had betrayed them in just about every way imaginable. There wasn't much room for compassionate consideration of her actual motives, though she could hardly be surprised.

Two weeks ago, Donna had stolen a vial—containing the final drops of the supposedly mythical elixir of life— from the alchemists, to give to Aliette, the Wood Queen, in exchange for Navin's life. But as they fled from the Ironwood, she'd broken the vial and thrown it as far as she could into the trees, beyond Aliette's grasp. True, she had destroyed the only hope the wood elves had of lengthening their fading existence, but what the alchemists cared about was that she had destroyed the elixir of life itself.

She'd spent the intervening days grounded by Aunt Paige and agonizing *not* about her impending trial, as her aunt no doubt expected, but about what sort of revenge the Wood Queen might be planning for the girl who'd tricked her. Aliette wasn't the sort of creature to take betrayal lightly.

Yet Donna felt fully justified in her actions. She'd had to save Navin, but she also couldn't just give away everything the Order had fought for over the centuries. Even though she had doubts about the work some of the alchemists were doing—and whether or not she was truly on the side of "good", as she'd always believed—she still couldn't actually hand the Wood Queen the elixir, betraying the people who were, for better or worse, her family.

Of course, it didn't seem to matter how many times she tried to reassure everybody of this, and it hadn't made a bit of difference when Maker spoke up on her behalf. In the eyes of the Order, she was a traitor—no matter how good the reasons had been for her actions.

Donna suspected that the alchemists were all secretly more worried about the fact that she'd gotten involved with a half-fey guy, someone who already knew far too much about the conflict between the wood elves and the Order of the Dragon. As the child of a human woman and a father who had long ago returned to the faerie realm, Alexander Grayson's halfblood status made him something even worse than a commoner in the eyes of the Order—since alchemists immediately classified anyone with even a hint of fey blood as dangerous.

Every time she thought too much about it, Donna felt like her head might explode.

Yet despite the sickening anger that had come with this realization, it also somewhat explained why Simon was so disapproving of her: not only was her best friend, Navin Sharma, just a commoner, but her maybe-sort-of-boyfriend was, by the very nature of his birth, their enemy.

She rested her chin on her cupped hand and waited for a break in Simon's oratory; she was dying to go to the bathroom.

Simon was now describing the schedule for the coming days. Donna fought the urge to roll her eyes; there was so much pointless ritual involved. It seemed that the members of this emergency meeting of the Council would stay at the Frost Estate until a final verdict about her punishment was reached. The matter was set to be resolved within the next few days.

She knew she should be paying more attention, but it was difficult when her mind kept wandering. Back when she'd been allowed to attend Ironbridge High School (before getting kicked out for trashing school property and threatening a fellow student), her class had studied the horrific witch trials that took place in seventeenth century New England . . . perhaps the alchemists would take a page from Massachusetts history and dunk her in the local river to test for demonic influences. *And knowing my luck, all the iron in my body will mean I'll sink without a trace.*

Smiling ruefully at the gallows humor she would normally share with Nav, she realized that Simon might actually be winding things up. Donna almost breathed an audible sigh of relief, but just managed to check herself in time.

But then he rubbed his hands together in a horribly familiar gesture, the sound of his dry palms suddenly too loud in the small room, and said, "Next, we will hear from the representatives from the Order of the Lion. If you could—"

"Simon." It was Quentin who spoke. His voice was low but implacable. Just speaking Simon's name was enough; everyone knew, in that moment, who was Archmaster and who was the Order's secretary.

At least in name, Donna couldn't help thinking.

Quentin stood slowly and faced the room's occupants: the Council of alchemists. Simon, the slimy bastard, smiled thinly and perched dutifully on his chair. Watching this unappealing man with his watering eyes that always seemed too big in his narrow face, Donna honestly wondered—and not for the first time—what on earth Quentin saw in him. She also found it hard to imagine Simon as potentially more powerful than the Archmaster himself. Maybe even more powerful than Maker. Not that she knew any of that for sure. It was just a growing suspicion, but she was becoming more aware of how listening to her intuition could be such an important thing. It had certainly gotten her out of more than one tight spot during the race to save Navin.

The Archmaster took a few steps forward, his long crimson robe swirling behind him. "The Order of the Dragon speaks for all the alchemists gathered in this room. Are you in agreement?"

A murmur passed around from alchemist to alchemist, as each representative nodded.

Quentin gripped the carved wooden lectern in front of him, only the whites of his knuckles betraying the fact that he was holding on for support rather than just to make him look more official. He always reminded Donna of Santa Claus, and he sort of had the right personality to go with the image. He had never been anything but kind to her, and she had fond memories of him reading to her while she was recovering from the magical operations that had created her tattoos and saved her arms and hands. Quentin had been ill for several months last winter, and he hadn't been quite the same since—he'd seemed to age several years in the space of weeks, and the alchemists had feared for his life. Donna remembered how worried Aunt Paige had been, and there had even been talk of choosing a new leader in case the worst happened.

But now the Archmaster cleared his throat authoritatively and let his blue eyes meet Donna's for a moment. She felt her spine automatically straighten, and tried desperately to detect something—some sign of hope or forgiveness—but then his gaze swept past her, over the rest of the gathering.

"As Archmaster of the Dragon alchemists, and as the duly appointed spokesperson of this Council assembled here today, it is my duty to guide us toward a verdict in the matter of Donna Underwood's recent actions. This judgment will be reached by the representatives from the Orders of the Dragon, Crow, Lion, and Rose."

Get on with it, Donna thought, wishing she could be anywhere but here. She noticed a middle-aged man from the Order of the Rose tapping continually on a computer keyboard, only lifting his head when there was a pause in the proceedings. The Rose alchemists were glorified record-keepers, in Donna's opinion, but all the other alchemists seemed to hold them in high regard.

Her cheeks flushed as Quentin talked briefly about the loss of the elixir and what that could mean for all four Orders. She tapped her foot and wondered if her black-sequinned sneakers could be magicked to work the same way as Dorothy's ruby slippers. Strangely, just as she was wondering that, a warm feeling flooded her chest and her stomach tightened in an unfamiliar way. The tips of her fingers tingled and her wrists began to ache.

Donna shook her hands and tried to will the odd sensation away, just as Quentin's even tones reached her again. Sometimes her tattoos *did* pull some weird crap, but now wasn't a good time for them to start acting up.

"Before we continue with Simon's rather impressive schedule, there is someone I need to officially introduce." Quentin lifted one hand from the dragon-carved lectern.

"Miranda Backhouse, the newly appointed first-level alchemist of the Order of the Crow, would like to say a few words."

The petite woman Donna had wondered about earlier rose and joined the Archmaster by the lectern. Quentin sank almost gratefully into his chair, and Donna couldn't help noticing that the normally cold and distant Simon Gaunt laid a steadying hand on his partner's shoulder.

And then Miranda was speaking, filling the space with her gentle voice. Despite how soft-spoken she was, there was an undeniable thread of power running through each word, and Donna let herself imagine what it might be like to have someone like this working within the ranks of the aging Order of the Dragon. There had always been a shortage of women around her. Apart from her aunt and her tutor—the rigid though well-meaning Alma Kensington—Donna had lacked female mentors in her life among the alchemists.

Then Miranda Backhouse turned to face her, her intelligent blue eyes missing nothing. "It's nice to meet you properly, Donna, despite the difficult circumstances. I knew your parents, back when they were stationed in England for a short while not long after you were born."

Clearly, she was waiting for some kind of a response, but Donna wasn't sure if she was even supposed to be speaking at this point. *But when has protocol ever stopped me before?* "I don't remember ever being in London . . ."

"Oh, you were just a baby. I have lovely memories

of Patrick and Rachel, though." Miranda stopped for a moment and smiled, a genuine expression that filled her heart-shaped face with warmth. "It was truly a pleasure spending time with them."

"Thank you," Donna said. "I miss them." A simple truth, but one that made her feel stronger after sharing it with this stranger. Glancing at Simon and noting his pinched brow, Donna was pleased to have taken the spotlight off him for a moment.

Miranda nodded and the moment passed. Simon took over once again, and events moved on.

Donna sighed. What the hell had happened to the recess? She was sure she'd heard something about a scheduled morning break, but it was hard to remember amid all the other tedious pronouncements.

It was going to be a long day.

Two

Clouds filled the late morning sky, stealing the light, and Donna kept her head down, watching her step on the icy path. The cold air was sharp against her cheeks and she blew out a breath, idly watching the white mist slowly drift away. She tried not to think about all the official crap going on inside the house, simply glad to be free for a few precious minutes. The recess had finally been called, and the moment Simon had rung that stupid ceremonial bell, she was *out* of there.

She needed to breathe, and out here, on the sprawling grounds of the Frost Estate, was as good a place as any. Miranda Backhouse's gentle words had prompted memories that Donna believed to be long buried, and she suddenly felt terribly alone.

A lone, tall tree with winter-stripped branches cutting the sky brought her up short, and she shivered in the chill breeze. The dream-image of her mother seemed to taunt her. Her mother . . . permanently institutionalized, yet with startling moments of clarity that still gave Donna a cruel sort of hope. Knowing her father was dead was a pain she carried almost daily—though of course it was a pain that had faded over time. But with Mom, it was completely different. She wasn't exactly *gone,* and yet . . . you could hardly call her presence a nurturing influence. Not any more.

Much as she missed Navin, the person Donna wished she could talk to right now was Xan. On the one hand, it felt good to have someone care for her the way that Xan seemed to—she could hardly deny it now, after all they'd shared in such a short space of time. But on the other . . . well, if she was honest, she felt nervous whenever she thought about Xan and their intense connection.

No, it was more than that. The real problem came down to this: Donna didn't know whether she could let down her guard enough to *allow* herself to be protected, by Xan or anyone else. She was so used to looking out for herself; a large part of that was because she'd been taught to be independent by the Order. Sometimes she found it difficult to allow herself to truly have faith in another person. Navin had been that person for the last few years, but even then their friendship had lived in the shadow of all the secrets she'd been forced to keep.

Trees reared up on Donna's left, one of the little copses that had been relocated from Ironwood Forest a couple of years back after part of the woods had been torn down to make way for a new road. Simon had insisted that some of the trees be brought to the Frost Estate for replanting—trophies of a sort, marking how the wood elves' last home was slowly being destroyed.

Shivering, Donna couldn't shake the feeling that someone was watching her from the trees. She tried to persuade herself that it must just be her imagination; it wasn't as though the estate was short of protective wards, after all.

But when she passed another cluster of Ironwood trees, with their wintering branches like sharp knives, looking suspiciously similar to the ones she remembered, Donna came to a dead stop and bit her lip. This was sort of disturbing. It could just be coincidence, but she was almost certain she'd already been this way. Sure, the grounds were huge, but were they big enough for her to get turned around so quickly?

She walked a slow circle, trying to pinpoint her location and get the main building back in view, but stopped again when the air between two of the largest trees in the copse began to shimmer. With her heart beating hard enough to make her dizzy, Donna took a hasty step back and cursed as her foot hit a fallen branch, tripping her; she ended up on her backside on the hard earth.

A humanoid shape, small and slightly built, seemed to *flow* out of the foliage, and Donna gave up any hope of reaching help before the new arrival reached her. There weren't many things that could move that fast and that . . . inhumanly.

Except wood elves.

She scrambled to her feet, trying not to focus on how much the bones in her arms had begun to throb, and stood frozen in place as the fey creature approached.

If it was a wood elf, it had to be wearing a glamour, although it wasn't the strongest elfskin Donna had ever seen. The form this one had taken could pass for human at a glance, but it was undeniably strange-looking. As with all alchemists-in-training, Donna was beginning to learn how to see the sometimes-blurred edges of weaker glamours. She gazed at the creature, suddenly wondering if it could be something *other* than an elf. Fascination bloomed within her, helping to keep terror at bay.

The wild-looking teenage girl—because that was what she looked like—seemed to scamper rather than walk, her green hair glowing in the morning mist and shedding eerie light on the rest of her appearance. It was as if the creature had tried to assume the shape of a slender, emo kind of girl, but had only gotten things partly right. The features were all human, but her skin was emerald tinted and her eyes were huge and viridian-bright. She was clothed in camouflage pants designed for combat and a tight khaki tank top. She was all skin and bone, with autumn leaves in her green hair.

Donna swallowed and glared at this imposter. How *dare* she just walk into the home of alchemists, and how had she even managed it? Was she solitary fey, or did she have something to do with the Wood Queen? And if that was true, how had the wood elves known where to find her? This thought almost wiped the bravado from Donna's face, but she squashed her fears about Aliette's revenge and raised her chin defiantly. The ethereal creature stood before her, watching her with a bold sort of curiosity.

Then the strange girl spoke. "Donna Underwood of the alchemists, I offer you greetings. My queen requests your presence."

Her voice was one of the creepiest things Donna had ever heard—and she'd seen and heard a lot of weird stuff. The fey girl sounded like she was speaking from very far away. Her voice whispered and rustled, and every word seemed to be accompanied by the sigh of a cold wind.

Donna raised her eyebrows, unable to keep the cynicism out of her voice. "She *requests*, does she? Really? I wasn't aware that *Her Majesty* made such polite things as requests. Isn't she above all that?"

The girl's face contorted into an expression that Donna interpreted as confusion. "My queen has a message for you."

Taking a steadying breath, Donna wondered if she could expect help from anyone inside the mansion. Maybe she should play for time, at least see what Aliette wanted. It wasn't as if she didn't have her own strengths.

"Do you have a name?"

Again, that near-comical expression of confusion crossed the creature's face. "A . . . name?"

"Yes. Like, you called me Donna Underwood. That's my name. What's yours?"

"Oh. I'm Ivy." The creature nodded as though confirming something to herself, and dislodged a small pile of leaves from her hair.

"Ivy. Okay, good." This was freaking surreal, but Donna could hardly walk away without finding out why this girl had been sent to her. And anyway, the Wood Queen was a cunning being—with the potential for immense cruelty. It might not be so smart to disrespect her messenger and, by extension, the queen herself. At least not until she'd heard what she had to say.

"So, come on then; what does she want?"

Ivy's huge green eyes widened even further. "The Queen of the Wood, she whom you know as Aliette Winterthorn, has a proposition for you. She asks that you meet with her."

Donna's mind was racing. Aliette "Winterthorn"?

That part was news to her. She knew of the queen's chosen first name, of course—the one she gave to humans so they could pronounce it—but she didn't know that the Wood Queen had a last name. Was it information she gave freely, or had Ivy slipped up somehow?

In any case, it was interesting. Donna filed the name away for future reference and squared her shoulders.

"Her *Majesty* is mistaken if she believes I will ever set foot in the Elflands again," she replied. "And anyway, I was forbidden to return and told that the Old Path we used to gain access last time would be moved. How does she expect me to visit when I won't be able to find a way in?"

Ivy jigged from one foot to the other. She either needed to go to the bathroom really badly, or she was uncomfortable standing in the open wearing such a weak glamour. *Was that even a glamour?* Maybe this was what she really looked like.

"No, no, you misunderstand." The fey girl stopped moving and clutched her hands before her as though imploring Donna for something. "The queen comes to the city—she will be here tomorrow."

She was coming *here*? Whoa. Donna felt her whole body flush with heat as shock threatened to short-circuit her already struggling brain. How could Aliette come here, to the human realm? Didn't the Wood Queen have to stay with her people in the Elflands, hidden away in the Ironwood?

Donna didn't know all that much about the specifics, but her understanding was that Aliette's power was the only thing keeping the elves alive, stuck as they were between dimensions and stranded on the outskirts of the human world. The entrance to their temporary home could only be found through the dwindling remains of Ironwood Forest, with the Elflands sort of running adjacent to it but not visible to the human eye. The only way to gain access to it was by using one of the Old Paths and crossing the magical barrier between realms.

Finding an Old Path was, of course, the real trick—which is where Xan had come in, last time.

Xan . . . She had to give herself a mental shake; no time to get sidetracked by thoughts of the new guy in her life, and what he might mean to her.

How could the queen leave her people, then, and enter Ironbridge? Perhaps with the same power that allowed her to send a messenger to the Frost Estate . . .

If Ivy noticed or understood Donna's silence, she gave no sign of it. She just stood there still as a stone, all her fidgeting gone in an instant. Waiting.

Donna needed to snap out of it, and fast. She had to do something—say something. "Tell Her Majesty that I need to know more about this meeting. How do I know she's not setting me up?"

Ivy fixed her with that disturbing gaze. "My queen expected you to be afraid, which is why she offered to meet you on your own territory. She will take human form—something she hasn't done for almost a century —and is prepared to meet you in a public venue of your choosing." Ivy's expression turned sly. "My queen says that she has something you desire, and that you will go to her in the end."

Donna scowled, all fear momentarily forgotten as she fought the temptation to say something cutting and just walk away. Why risk getting caught up in Aliette's games again? But there was something in Ivy's bright expression that Donna couldn't quite bring herself to ignore, no matter how crazy she was to listen to the twisted words of her enemy.

Of course, the queen *would* dangle a potentially tempting morsel in front of her, but surely it was a trap— this had to be a lame attempt to draw her out.

But if it wasn't a trap, what on earth did she have that Aliette could possibly want?

"Listen, Ivy," she said, making the only sane decision there was. "I don't care about what your queen wants from me. We did a deal, and it's over now. Tell her that this time I won't hesitate to go to the Order. Whatever she's really after, it can't possibly be worth starting a war over."

"You might be surprised." The fey girl nodded before heading back into the mist-covered trees. "She said you would refuse her."

Relief made Donna light-headed. "Is that it? You're leaving—just like that?"

Ivy stopped and looked over her shoulder. "But she also said that you will not refuse her a second time."

♻

Minutes later, Donna found the right path and headed back toward the main part of the estate. She knew that if she uncovered her tattoos right now, the iron markings would be flashing with their own inner light and power. Pins and needles filled her arms and hands, buzzing like angry wasps.

Something in her chest felt heavy and restricted—as though a metal band was being slowly wrapped around her chest and squeezed. Donna gasped and tried to breathe through the strange sensation. Pain in her arms and hands was hardly a new experience, but this pain was entirely different.

This new feeling seemed to affect the *whole* of her.

Breathing through the pain, Donna forced herself to be calm. At least she knew enough to be sure that whatever this sensation was, it had something to do with the tattoos, with the iron that laced her skin and bones and held her together in ways she couldn't even begin to understand. Probably it was something triggered by Ivy's presence.

Maker had fixed her before, which meant he could do it again.

Even though it must be getting close to midday, it

seemed to be getting colder. She picked up her pace, knowing that her aunt was going to be angry she'd been gone for so long. They'd probably already sent out a search party.

Donna remembered a story her father used to tell, about a totally kick-ass princess held prisoner at the top of a tower in a strange country far from home. But this princess didn't need to be rescued by the handsome prince. No, the princess in Patrick Underwood's tale was more than able to take care of herself—which was lucky, considering that the prince she'd been expecting never did arrive in time to save her. She tore her prison's moth-eaten velvet curtains into strips and tied them together to make a rope long enough to climb all the way down, then escaped back to her own land. She had many perilous adventures on the long journey home, but of course she kicked everyone's ass with her superior martial arts skills.

When the handsome prince finally rode into town and asked for her hand in marriage, the princess told him to get lost; she was quite happy by herself and, anyway, what use did she have for a husband who was afraid of heights?

Donna smiled as she remembered her father's face and the laughter that crinkled his eyes. Sometimes she couldn't help wishing that there was more of Dad in his younger sister. Aunt Paige did her best, but she wasn't really cut from the same cloth; it was strange to think of them being brought up together.

As that thought crossed Donna's mind, she caught sight of her aunt striding toward her, her pale face pinched with barely repressed fury.

"Where have you been? You were told to take ten minutes—not half an hour!"

Donna almost rolled her eyes at the blatant exaggeration. "It was hardly that long. I was just—"

"You were just trying to test everybody's patience." It was a cold statement.

Cheeks flushing, Donna resisted the impulse to clench her fists. Aunt Paige had no idea what she'd been doing out here, and she wondered if now was the time to come clean and tell her about Ivy. Perhaps telling her the truth would do something to start repairing the broken trust between them.

But seeing the open hostility in her aunt's eyes shocked her, and made her resolve fade before it could even get started. "Aunt Paige, I really was just getting some air."

Pursing her lips, her aunt glanced back at the house. "I thought you might have done something silly."

Donna raised her eyebrows and tried to look innocent. "Like what? You thought I was going to try and make a break for it—really?"

"These days, Donna, I really don't know what to think when it comes to your behavior."

Donna tried to get a grip on the sudden flash of anger that hit her, intentionally ignoring how tired her aunt sounded. "You talk like I'm just a kid."

"You're not eighteen yet, Donna. Not for quite some time. Until then, you're my responsibility."

"So when I reach eighteen, I can leave home?" Donna made it a challenge, knowing full well what her aunt's response would be but unable to resist baiting her.

"Leaving home doesn't equal leaving the Order, and you know it. Your life belongs to us—with the alchemists—wherever you might one day move to." Aunt Paige's expression softened. "You know how important you are to us, how important you are to Quentin."

Donna had heard it all before. Young alchemists were in short supply as more and more of the older generation died without passing on their genes. Not to mention the huge investment of resources that had gone into saving her life—she was under no illusions about the money and time spent on her recovery.

Paige waited impatiently, pulling her tailored jacket more tightly around herself and tossing her shiny dark hair. "Come on. We need to get back inside."

Donna fixed her with a determined expression. "You're really going to make me go through with this?"

Genuine surprise slackened her aunt's face. "Of course. What did you expect? That I could just wave a magic wand and make it all go away?"

"Honestly? I was hoping that maybe you could show a little trust in me. Can't you do that, just this once?"

Aunt Paige's eyes became guarded. "How can I trust

you? After everything you did . . ." Her voice trailed off, but not before Donna heard the thread of uncertainty running through it.

"What I did, I did to save Navin. And *Maker*. Why can't you understand that?"

"I do understand, Donna." She took a hesitant step forward. "That's just it. It's not that I don't understand; the problem is that I think you were wrong."

It was as if her aunt had slapped her. Shocked, Donna tried to rally herself. "How can you say that? They would have died!"

"Then so be it. If that's what was meant to be."

Donna's whole body stiffened. "Even Maker?"

"Even him." There was no doubt in Aunt Paige's voice now; her faith in the greater good—of whatever freaky higher consciousness the alchemists believed in—was absolute. And absolutely unshakeable.

Barely able to catch her breath, Donna slowly shook her head. "Then I feel sorry for you," she whispered, feeling like she might cry.

Before Aunt Paige could reply, the shrill tones of a ringing phone cut through the frigid air between them. At the same moment, Simon emerged and stood on the steps of the main entrance, looking like he was about to implode. Paige held up a hand to him and pulled out her cell phone.

"Underwood."

Donna gritted her teeth. Her aunt was all business

now, no doubt expecting a call from the Mayor's office.

Aunt Paige suddenly looked at her, her face drained of color. *Now what?*

"I understand. Thank you." She tucked the phone back into her pocket and took a deep breath.

"Well?" Donna asked, feeling sick. Fear clawed at her throat and she wanted to grab her aunt's arms and shake her. "What is it?"

Somehow, even before Paige spoke, Donna knew exactly what she was going to say. She didn't fully understand *how* she knew, but she suspected it had a lot to do with the crazy dreams that had been haunting her.

"I'm sorry, Donna," Paige said, all signs of anger deflated. "That was the Institute—I'm afraid it's your mother."

Three

Donna was running by the time she reached the glass doors of Ironbridge General's privately fund-ed Special Care Unit. Her mother had been rushed there from the Institute just this morning, as soon as her cond-ition had turned "critical."

"Wait," Aunt Paige called, struggling to keep up in her high heels. "Slow down!"

Ignoring her, with all thoughts of the trial scattered behind her somewhere back in the parking lot, Donna scanned the waiting area and fixed her attention on a group of nurses who didn't seem to have much to do. Everything looked calm and quiet; surely Mom couldn't be so sick in a place as tranquil as this?

She marched toward them, only vaguely aware of her aunt's footsteps clattering just behind. "I need to see Rachel Underwood."

One of the nurses—Nurse Valderrama, according to her nametag—raised dark eyebrows. "And you would be . . . ?"

"I'm her daughter." Donna tried to look composed and in control, but her heart was hammering almost painfully and she knew she must look young and scared.

The nurses exchanged a look that she couldn't quite interpret, but it certainly didn't indicate anything good. Aunt Paige appeared at her side, acting all official, and showed them some identification. Things moved along more smoothly after that, especially given *how* the SCU came by their funds—Quentin was a significant bene-factor, which granted the alchemists privileged access to the facilities. It never ceased to amaze Donna how the four Orders had fingers in so many different pies throughout the world. Wherever they operated, you could pretty much guarantee their influence was working behind the scenes in a variety of institutions.

Within minutes they were standing at the foot of her mother's bed. The room felt chilly but was pleasant enough. Sort of peaceful. There were actually two beds, and an intimidating collection of hospital equipment that Donna didn't want to examine too closely. All she cared about was seeing Mom.

Rachel Underwood had once been a striking woman. Not traditionally beautiful in the way you might expect a model or an actress to look, but she had almost regal features: creamy skin, without a freckle in sight despite her long red hair, and unusual silver-gray eyes that had been dulled by drugs in recent years. She was thin, too, with bones sticking out in ways that made Donna wonder if they'd been feeding her properly at the Institute—the secure mental facility where Mom had spent the better part of the last ten years. Ever since that night in the Ironwood.

The night her father had been killed by the Skriker and Donna's hands and arms had almost been destroyed.

She tried not to breathe the sterile air; something about it made her feel lightheaded and sick. Maybe if she took really shallow breaths, just through her mouth, she'd be okay.

She asked, "Can she hear us?"

Nurse Valderrama had been bustling around her mother's still form, but glanced up with unmistakeable kindness on her pretty face. Her skin was a little darker than Nav's, Donna couldn't help noticing, feeling a sudden pang of longing for her best friend. She wished he was standing beside her instead of her taciturn aunt.

The nurse's expression shifted to something more like

regret. "She probably won't hear much of anything right now. She's heavily sedated."

Donna licked her lips, realizing how dry they were. "Why did you have to do that? Sedate her, I mean."

"Mrs Underwood was very unwell when she was admitted."

"I know *that*," Donna replied, unable to keep the impatience out of her voice. "But what's wrong with her? What kind of 'unwell' are we talking about?"

Aunt Paige shifted slightly behind her. "The staff are very busy, dear. You've seen your mother now—let's leave them to do their jobs."

Turning on her, Donna released some of the fear and frustration she'd been holding on to. "But nobody's told us anything!"

"Donna—" There was no mistaking the warning in Aunt Paige's voice.

Not that she cared about that. "So Mom collapsed, but not a single person can tell me anything else?"

Nurse Valderrama smoothed her uniform with slender brown fingers. "The doctor will be along soon." She made as though to leave the room.

Donna moved to block the doorway. "What aren't you telling me?"

Aunt Paige rested a hand on her shoulder. "Donna! What on *earth's* gotten into you?"

"Into *me*?" She almost laughed in her aunt's face. "Why even bring me here if you're not going to tell me

35

what happened? So, Mom 'collapsed' and that's it? *That's* all I get?"

The nurse pursed her lips and eyed the door nervously. For a moment it looked as though she might be weighing something up as she glanced between the two visitors, but then she squared her shoulders and faced Donna. "Your mother has been experiencing seizures that the doctors haven't been able to figure out the cause of yet. We're keeping her sedated for her own safety."

Aunt Paige let out a sigh of exasperation. "And the safety of everyone else, apparently. She's been quite violent."

"Oh my God!" Donna turned on her aunt with fury. "You knew! You knew why they brought her in and you didn't tell me."

There was no missing the scowl that Paige threw in Nurse Valderrama's direction, but she quickly focused her attention back on her niece. "Well, of course I knew. I also knew how upset you'd be, and there was no point in telling you anything when we don't yet know the cause."

Trying to get her temper back under control, Donna tuned out her aunt's excuses and appealed to the nurse. "Can you tell me anything else, *please*? What kind of seizures? Do you mean like an epileptic fit?"

"We should really wait for Doctor—"

But Donna didn't find out the doctor's name, because her mother chose that moment to sit up in bed. It was as though something had violently propelled her into a sitting position, like a rubber band snapping, the movement was so sudden and shocking. She opened her eyes and stared directly at Paige, her expression filled with something like terror and pain all mixed together. "You!"

Then Rachel threw back her head and screamed.

The room was suddenly full of other people. At least it seemed that way to Donna; too many people, so many that she couldn't fight her way through them. Nausea made her stomach churn, but she tried to reach the bed—if she could just help them hold Mom down, maybe it would all be okay. The way Rachel was thrashing and screaming, it almost seemed impossible that even the two orderlies and the second nurse who'd arrived could keep her mother from hurting herself.

Straps came out, as though conjured from nowhere, and they began securing the patient to the bed. A syringe that the taller of the two orderlies had brandished was kicked out of his hand by a flailing leg.

Aunt Paige was speaking in Donna's ear, urgently, almost desperately. "We need to leave them to do their work. Donna, can you hear me?" She had Donna's upper arm in a tight grip but one look from her niece was all it took to make her let go.

A small Indian woman ran through the door, her white coat flapping around her legs. She spared the spectators—Aunt Paige and Donna—a glance. "What are these civilians doing here? Nurse Valderrama, get them outside where they belong; I don't care who they are!"

Translation: *I don't care if they are paying my salary.* Donna would have normally smiled at this, but she was too busy craning her neck, trying to see over the bodies crowding the bed. Mom was in there somewhere, her voice cracking under the strain of so much screaming—a horrifying sound filled with black despair.

Another nurse entered the fray, and it seemed almost as though each person had one of Rachel's limbs in a death-grip as the doctor nimbly scooped up the fallen syringe and ducked under all the bodies to reach her patient.

And then Mom seemed to . . . deflate . . . as though the prick of the needle had punctured more than just her flesh, releasing all the crazy fight in a rush. She fell back against the scattered pillows, long hair matted around her face, the ragged white streak seeming almost to blend in with the putty color of her cheeks.

One of the other nurses was shaking her head as she straightened a blanket and stepped aside, allowing the orderlies to finish securing Rachel's arms and legs. "I don't understand how this could have happened, Doctor Gupta. She was heavily sedated. It doesn't make any sense . . ."

Doctor Gupta looked just as perplexed. She was still holding the syringe, gazing at it as though she was holding something dangerous. "She may have been sedated earlier, but she isn't now."

Donna's eyes widened and she shook off Aunt Paige's hand. "What do you mean?"

The doctor's face was pinched with confusion. "I pierced her skin, but I didn't have time to actually administer the sedative. She collapsed, and I could see she was unconscious so I didn't hit the plunger. It might not have been safe when we don't know yet—"

Then Doctor Gupta shook her head, as if only now realizing who she was speaking to. "I'm sorry, you both need to leave. Let us examine Mrs. Underwood and try to get some answers."

"But—"

"I'll find you afterwards," Doctor Gupta said, her tone brisk but not unkind.

To Donna, watching her mother being strapped to a bed, it all looked barbaric. She gritted her teeth to keep from protesting, knowing they were just trying to help; wishing there was something she could *do*.

She suddenly remembered her dream again: the image of her mother's plaited hair, and the vivid green thread that reminded her of Xan's eyes. And then Ivy's warning—that Donna wouldn't refuse the Wood Queen's request for an audience a second time. She'd hardly given it a thought, what with worrying about getting back to the hearing, and of course the phone call from the Institute. But maybe all these things were linked—the dream, Aliette's message, and now Mom's seriously whacked illness. Surely it was obvious, if she actually used her brain and put the pieces together.

But how could she find out whether or not she was

right? She needed to find a way to test her theory: that Rachel Underwood was under some kind of fey attack.

Aunt Paige helped the wide-eyed Nurse Valderrama herd Donna out of the room, and this time she didn't put up any resistance. Not because she wasn't worried about Mom any more, but because she was busy formulating a plan.

A plan that involved a certain half-fey guy who might be able to tell her what the hell had just happened to her mother, and whether her darkly growing suspicions were right.

~

Telling Aunt Paige that she needed to use the bathroom seemed the simplest way of giving her aunt the slip for a few minutes, but Donna was still surprised that she'd been allowed to go to the restroom alone.

She walked directly to the hospital's main entrance dragging anxiety like a long shadow behind her. She tried to look like she wasn't flicking guilty glances all around the gleaming waiting room, checking to see if Paige had followed her after all.

Keeping her head down, Donna made for the three public phone booths on the far wall. Ducking behind a chaotic plant display that had grown to epic proportions, she reached for the nearest phone, squeezing her fingers inside the red velvet gloves. She found herself wishing she wasn't wearing such an obscenely bright color; this little act of rebellion for her trial seemed petty in the face of everything that had just happened.

She hoped she could remember Xan's number. Her cell phone had been confiscated two weeks ago, and Simon's voice still rang in her ears: "Who does she need to call? Her only friend lives next door to her. Everything she needs is right here within the Order." His mocking tone was about as subtle as his aftershave.

Thankful to find a few coins in her jeans pocket, Donna made the call. Her heart pounded as she waited to hear Xan's voice for the first time in way too long. If she weren't sick with worry over Mom's condition, she might have been nervous in that annoying, giddy-girly way she seemed to develop around this guy who'd turned her world upside down even though they'd only recently met. But she had no time for nervousness now. Xan was probably the only one who could tell her if her mother's condition was a result of something the Wood Queen had done.

She couldn't reach him at home—the townhouse he lived in alone while his adoptive father was traveling—and how the hell she was able to remember his cell number she would never know. But she did, and almost crumbled with relief. He sounded distracted when he finally answered.

She could hardly believe how much she'd missed him. "It's me."

"Donna!" Xan quickly lowered his voice. "Where are you? I've been calling you for the past two weeks—I don't think your aunt's been giving you my messages."

"I know," she replied, trying and failing to stop the tears that were already running down her face. "I knew you would be. But listen to me, Xan; I need your help."

"Anything. Anything I can do, you know that."

"I'm at Ironbridge General; you have to get here now, *please*. Ask for the Special Care Unit."

"What happened?"

"It's my mom. She's . . . I think she's really sick and I don't think they'll be able to help us here. Not somewhere like *this*."

He didn't ask anything else; he didn't need to. Xan would know exactly what she meant, and once again she felt gratitude that she'd met someone who understood such things without needing endless explanations. Which made her feel guilty about Navin, but, well . . . that's just the way it was. Magic did that to your life: filled everything with secrets and shadows, so that it was almost impossible to have a normal friendship.

Sometimes it almost got your best friend killed, too.

"Donna? You still there?"

She shook herself and clutched the receiver more tightly, quickly easing up when she heard the plastic crack. *Oops*. "Yeah, I'm here. Sorry . . . I should get back. Aunt Paige will be wondering what happened to me."

"Okay, I'll be there as soon as I can," he said. And then, "I've missed you."

Despite her growing nerves at what her aunt would do, Donna couldn't stop the surge of elation as she ran to the nearest staircase.

Xan was on his way!

❧

Aunt Paige looked her over, suspicion flashing in her sharp eyes. "Where have you been?"

"The bathroom. I already told you that."

"What took you so long? I was about to come looking for you."

"I didn't feel good. I've just seen my mom having a seizure—excuse me for freaking out. I was feeling kind of sick . . ."

Pursing her lips in distaste, Paige glanced at the nearby nurses and lowered her voice. "I'm trying to trust you, but I keep expecting you to disappear."

Donna simply raised her eyebrows and tried to look innocent, wondering how long it would take for Xan to get there. She'd been so relieved to hear his voice she hadn't even thought to ask where he was.

"Anyway," her aunt continued, "you missed the doctor."

Crap. "What did she say?"

"They need to do more tests." Paige gave her a rare, wry smile. "Isn't that what doctors always say?"

Donna almost smiled in return, but just managed to stop herself in time. "So Mom's unconscious? Sleeping?"

"I'm afraid they suspect she could have sunk into some kind of coma."

"*What*?! Why didn't you tell me that in the first place? I have to speak to the doctor for myself."

Paige shook her head. "Donna, let them do their jobs and stop bothering them, for goodness sake. Rachel is stable—all her vitals are completely normal, that's why they're so mystified by all this. I wouldn't be surprised if that Doctor Gupta was secretly hoping to get some kind of paper out of this . . ."

Trust Aunt Paige to think of something like that. "I want to see Mom again."

Her aunt stopped, coat half on, impatience darkening her face. "We need to get back to the estate so that the hearing can resume. Everybody is waiting for us. There's nothing we can do for her at the moment; she's in the best possible place, you know that."

Do I? Donna tried to keep her expression neutral. "Please, Aunt Paige. It was so awful to see her like that. I really want to see her before we go—when she's not having a full-blown fit. Please?"

Paige pressed her lips together but nodded, shrugging back out of her smart wool coat and sitting down again. "I'll wait for you here."

"Thank you," Donna breathed, practically running

back to her mother's room before Aunt Paige changed her mind.

The room seemed larger this time, though that was probably due to the fact that there was no longer a whole group of people crammed in there trying to get Mom sedated. She couldn't help feeling curious about the second bed, though. This was a private hospital wing, and the rooms were meant to be for one patient only.

Nurse Valderrama walked briskly through the door, offering her a tentative smile as she followed Donna's gaze. "That bed's for family, in case they want to stay the night."

"Oh." Donna ran her gloved hand over the pristine sheets. "I didn't know you could do that."

The nurse turned to what looked like a heart monitor and wrote some unintelligible figures onto a chart that she tossed back into the wire tray at the foot of the bed. "It's not normal hospital policy. But then, this isn't a 'normal' part of the hospital." She gave Donna an unreadable look, nodded, and left the room before she could get tagged with any more questions.

Donna pulled the only chair up to the edge of Mom's bed, laying her coat carefully over the back first. She felt nervous, as if Rachel might sit up and start babbling nonsense any minute. Like when she'd looked right at Aunt Paige in that accusing but terrified way. Had Mom even been *seeing* her sister-in-law? Her eyes had seemed very far away.

Now, Rachel's face was a smooth mask. Her skin was so white it was almost translucent, and it looked thin and stretched across her prominent cheekbones. There were tubes coming out from her body, under the covers, and leading to various machines and plastic bags.

Donna thought her mother looked dead. An image flashed into her exhausted mind: Dad lying cold and still on the ground of Ironwood Forest after he'd saved her from the Skriker.

The Wood Monster is dead, she reminded herself fiercely. *I killed it.*

But that fleeting memory of her father . . . was it even real? She wasn't sure—she could never be entirely certain of the things that had happened to her ten years' ago. She honestly didn't know what to believe anymore, especially when it came to her own memories. The only person she felt she could trust to tell her the complete truth was right here in front of her, in a coma state that was anything but normal. If Donna could be sure of anything, she could be sure of that.

She shivered and pushed away the morbid thoughts. Mom was *not* going to die. She wouldn't allow it. Now wasn't the time to go chasing nightmares. Instead, she tried to focus on her mother's face, searching for signs of life—any glimmer of hope. She remembered reading that coma patients sometimes responded to the voice of loved ones. *Anything's worth a try, right?*

Feeling vaguely self-conscious, she cleared her throat. "Mom, it's me . . . Donna. I don't know if you can hear me, but I just wanted you to know that I'm here and I won't give up on you. I never have, and I promise you that I never will."

The tight knot of tension in her chest eased a little. Maybe this whole theory of talking to people in comas was more for the benefit of the family left behind; but either way, just telling her mother how she felt seemed to help. She didn't want Mom to feel alone—that suddenly seemed very important.

Rachel Underwood had spent the best part of a decade fighting. Something awful was tormenting her; something the hospital staff and the doctors at the Institute could have no hope of truly understanding. She was slipping further into madness, and there didn't seem to be a damn thing anyone could do about it. Donna swallowed. Not yet, anyway.

Even though Rachel Underwood wasn't exactly "well" at the best of times, it had always been a manageable condition, an unspecified form of mental illness that nobody could really diagnose but treated as something like a combination of schizophrenia and early onset dementia. Very early onset. Her mother wasn't yet forty, so the alchemists had quietly installed her at the Institute just a couple of miles from Ironbridge General. Traditional doctors were stumped, and the Order didn't want questions asked. Money had been donated to the Special Care

Unit at the hospital, and her mother had been smoothly admitted to the permanent residential Institute with the minimum of red tape.

Donna had a sudden thought and removed the glove from her left hand so she could reach the charm bracelet tucked down inside it, against her tattooed wrist. She'd been wearing it ever since Simon had found and returned it to her with a knowing smile. Mom had given it to her just a couple of weeks ago, in a rare, half-lucid moment at the Institute, and Donna was sure that there was some significance to the delicate silver bracelet beyond its six magically warded charms. Maker had soldered the dagger charm back onto it for her and confirmed that there was protective magic on the bracelet—alchemical protection, which had faded since the wards were first placed on it many years ago.

Donna quickly unclasped the bracelet and wrapped it around her mother's thin wrist, then tucked her motionless arm back underneath the covers. She didn't know what good it would do—if any—but just knowing it was there made her feel a little better.

She pulled her glove back on and whispered, "I'll stay with you for as long as you need me to, okay?"

Not really expecting a reply—but sighing when there wasn't one, anyway—she shuffled her chair closer to the edge of the bed, crossed her arms next to her mother's still body, and rested her head for a moment. The scratchy velvet of her gloves was warm against her cheek.

The gloves looked like splashes of blood against the white blanket.

She stifled a yawn and wondered how long it would be before the nurse returned to find her fast asleep.

Four

Donna's eyes had just begun to drift closed when the sound of angry voices reached her through the gray mist of emotional exhaustion. *Xan.* She immediately stood up and ran for the door. Her hand was already on the door handle before she stopped and caught her breath, listening to her aunt's raised voice, suspicion radiating neon-bright from every word.

"How did you know she was here? You need to leave *now*, young man."

Xan's measured tones replied, but Donna knew his anger was bubbling, barely held in check out of reluctant respect for her aunt. Well, more like out of consideration for Donna, but either way he was doing a pretty good job of keeping his cool.

"I'd appreciate it if you didn't speak to me as though I was still a child, Ms. Underwood," she heard him say in that haughty, cut-glass voice he could mimic. He was good at that, when he wanted to put it on—his adoptive mother was British and currently living back home in England.

"You're a teenager," Aunt Paige said.

"I'm nineteen. I'm responsible for myself and have been for a long time. Please do me the courtesy of showing me the same respect I'm giving you."

Holy crap, score one for Xan! Donna thought, with a highly inappropriate level of glee.

She thought about the owner of that voice for a moment, allowing herself to remember his warmth and the touch of his lips against hers. Admittedly, finding Xan had been pretty tough to handle at first, but only because in her worldview—the worldview she'd been raised with as a trainee alchemist—the half-human children of solitary fey were assumed to be easily hidden in society. She'd been taught that they had no real power or deep magic—certainly nothing that would mark them as different in a physical sense.

The fact that Alexander Grayson had been born with

fledgling wings—wings that were ripped from his back in a beyond-cruel gesture of hatred by the wood elves, who had captured him as a baby—made Donna realize that a lot of things weren't quite as she'd been brought up to believe.

The door opened, forcing her to take a couple of shuffling steps back, and a harried-looking Nurse Valderrama appeared. "Excuse me, Miss Underwood? There's another visitor for your mother out here." She spoke briskly, but she looked over her shoulder and then gave Donna a conspiratorial wink. "I thought you'd like to know, before your aunt succeeds in getting him thrown out."

The young nurse tucked a strand of shiny black hair behind her ear and left, ninja-style, on silent-soled shoes.

Donna had no choice but to follow, heading down the corridor to the waiting room. Her pace increased, almost of its own accord, as Xan's voice grew closer. Despite the crappy reason for them all being here in the first place, her stomach was still filled with a fluttering sensation of anticipation.

Rounding the corner, her eyes fixed on the achingly familiar young man in the long black coat. He seemed even taller than she remembered, and his amber hair shone under the ugly bright lights—making it look for a bizarre moment as though there was a halo around his head.

But his eyes were the same striking forest green that made her heart beat faster, and his unseasonably tanned face broke into a smile at the sight of her running toward him. Screw being cool; she was so happy to see him that she didn't care if she was acting like an over-eager puppy.

"Donna!" He swept her into a hug, lifting her off the ground and squeezing her tightly enough to make her ribs ache.

Not that she minded. In that moment, reunited with the one person who seemed to understand everything about her and her crazy life, nothing else mattered at all. Not her furious aunt. Not the half-smiling nurses and orderlies in the corridor. And not even her mother lying pale and still, back in the room that felt too much like a mausoleum.

She breathed in his familiar scent of tobacco and pears—along with the gum he'd obviously been chewing in a poor attempt at hiding the fact that he'd been smoking again. But even that couldn't spoil her pleasure at being held by him once more.

He set her down gently and held her at arms length to study her. "It's so good to see you. I really fucking missed you, Donna."

The simple sincerity of his words made her heart soar, and her mind flashed back to their first date—when they'd been ambushed by a wood elf on Ironbridge Common who had taken on the form of a wiry homeless guy. Xan had been badly bitten, and that was the night they each recognized the other for what they truly were: soulmates. Not soulmates in an icky romantic sense, but in the sense of the powerful connection they felt due to shared history and painful knowledge. The terrible injuries they'd both suffered at the hands of the fey bound them closer and more quickly than mere physical attraction ever could.

Although, by most general measures of such things, Xan *was* pretty hot. Donna tried to tell herself that this was simply a bonus.

"Xan," she breathed, glancing over his shoulder and wishing that Aunt Paige would just disappear. *Like I'd ever get that lucky,* she thought nastily.

Her aunt stalked toward them, business-like heels clicking on the floor. "I won't ask you again, young—" She stopped and corrected herself. "*Alexander.* This is a private area. I don't even know how you got in here."

As if on cue, Nurse Valderrama volunteered her neck for the noose. "That would be my fault, Ms. Underwood. I apologize. I thought he was a member of the family."

Aunt Paige raised perfectly plucked brows, two bright spots of color appearing on her pale cheeks. "And whatever gave you the idea that we are related to . . . him?"

Donna felt anger burn inside her as she realized that her aunt had been about to say "that" instead of "him." *How dare she?*

She spoke quickly. "Aunt Paige, Xan is my friend and I asked him to be here."

Paige turned away from Nurse Valderrama—who looked relieved to have an opportunity to escape—and blasted Donna with almost palpable vibes of hot disapproval. "You had no right to invite yet another outsider into our lives."

Her aunt had met Xan only once before, when she, Xan, Navin, and Maker had returned from the Ironwood in his car. The expression "the shit hit the fan" had been invented for moments like that.

Donna shuddered as she remembered the chaos, the raised voices and accusations, the dawn phone call to the Frost Estate to inform Quentin of Donna's actions. But through all of it Paige had barely looked at Xan, almost as though to do so might soil her in some way. Xan had extended his hand and introduced himself, but her aunt had actually taken a *step back*. Paige Underwood, the professional woman who worked a day job as the Mayor of Ironbridge's Personal Assistant, was unable to keep up a polite mask when faced with a child of Faerie. Well, he was only half fey, but perhaps to her aunt it was all the same.

Donna was learning more and more about the way things worked within the Order, and with each new discovery she became more certain than ever that she wanted out. Like, as soon as freaking possible.

Trying not to think about the things she couldn't change—at least, not quite yet—Donna curved her arm through Xan's in a blatant show of defiance that made her feel a little better. Yeah, it was petty, but she couldn't help herself. Xan, meanwhile, was still trying to keep his temper and treat Aunt Paige as though she wasn't a bigoted relic from another world.

"Ms. Underwood, I know this is a family matter, but when Donna called I didn't have any choice." He glanced down at her, warmth in his eyes, before returning his gaze to Paige's rigid expression. "As you know, I went with her into the Ironwood." He took a stop forward, forcing Donna to step with him, and lowered his voice. "I faced down the queen and helped rescue Navin and Maker. You may not give a crap about the human boy, but Maker is one of your own."

Paige's face was frozen somewhere between disgust and fury. "We thanked you for your aid, but it was not *our* request that took you into the Ironwood."

"Still, I went. And Maker is safe, in part because of me." Xan narrowed his eyes until only slits of green fire showed. "You owe me. The *Order* owes me."

Donna was shocked at the conviction in Xan's voice. She hadn't expected this. Was Xan just playing Aunt Paige, trying to manipulate her sympathy, or did he truly want to use his role in the rescue mission as a bargaining chip? She turned to him, questions on the tip of her tongue, but his hand reached down for hers and gave it a gentle squeeze.

She bit her lip and resolved to keep her mouth shut. For now. Her questions could wait—especially considering why she'd asked him to come in the first place—but perhaps she and Alexander Grayson needed to have a talk about why, exactly, he'd been so willing to charge into the Elflands with her to save two people he didn't even know. Sure, she believed he genuinely had feelings for her (whatever the hell that even meant), but she also knew he'd taken one look at her iron tattoos—magically crafted by Maker—and had immediately started wondering whether the talented alchemist could do anything to help him with the loss of his wings. She liked Xan; maybe she even liked him a *lot*. But she wasn't an idiot.

Xan turned and gazed at her, the intense green eyes that marked him as "other" unblinking. "So, take me to your mom."

Donna flicked a nervous glance at Aunt Paige, but what could she really do to them? In front of all the hospital staff? Her aunt's position as assistant to a high-profile public figure might actually work in their favor here.

"Come on, it's this way," she told Xan.

Aunt Paige followed them. "If you do this, I will never forgive you."

Donna stopped, putting a gentle hand on Xan's arm to signal that he wait a moment. She took a shaking breath and gathered herself, feeling something inside her loosen. It was the strangest sensation, almost as though a tight belt had been moved to a slightly more comfortable setting. She could breathe more easily than she'd been able to in weeks.

"Aunt Paige, I appreciate everything you've done

for me in my life—and I'm grateful that you brought me here to see Mom—but I asked Xan to help me for a reason, and I'm not going to let you stop me."

She turned away and walked on trembling legs toward her mother's room, not even bothering to check whether Xan was following her.

❧

Donna closed the door on the corridor outside and leaned against it. They couldn't risk someone coming in while Xan did what she'd asked him here for in the first place. Or at least, while he attempted to do it.

As usual, he was trying to tell her how weak and unpracticed his damaged magical abilities were, but this time Donna was having none of it. She believed he must have his reasons for hiding things, even from her, and that would normally be good enough for her. But now wasn't the time to tread gently around his trust issues; she needed him to figure out if her mother's current state was elf-induced and, if so, what they could do to help her.

If anything *could* be done. No, Donna thought, clamping down on the cold hopelessness that threatened to overwhelm her. She refused to believe that her mother was beyond hope.

Xan pulled a chair up to the edge of the bed and took her mother's hand gently in his. A strange emotion filled Donna, something she couldn't quite put a name to. Seeing them there, together . . . it was almost as though her past and her future had come together in a surprising moment of harmony. Her throat tightened as she watched him close his eyes and do whatever the hell it was he was doing.

He began to *glow*.

Donna stifled a gasp as she saw that the radiance wasn't so much coming from Xan's skin as it was from *within*. It wasn't a surface sort of glow—it was more like a pulse of energy, like someone had switched on a light inside him. Where Xan and her mother's hands met, that strange inner light spread from his golden skin to her waxen flesh, lending her the warmth and vitality she so badly needed.

Taking a step nearer, unable to stop herself, Donna gazed with fascination at the emerald-brightness spilling from beneath Xan's eyelids like otherworldly tears. She wondered what his eyes would look like if he opened them and met her shocked gaze, and whether he would be able to see right inside her—right down to the bone.

But when Xan finally opened his eyes, they were just green again. Regular green eyes—although "regular" in his case meant a striking viridian brightness that didn't belong on the human color-palette. Still, the ethereal glow had gone, and his golden skin was merely tan once more; he no longer looked as if he were lit up from inside like the beautiful Christmas trees already filling the local mall.

The expression on his face was difficult to read, but whatever he was feeling, it certainly wasn't positive. "Donna," he said, releasing her mother's hand and reaching out to her instead. "Come here."

Foreboding made her stomach cramp, and all thoughts of Xan's magical ability *that shouldn't even exist* were forgotten. She wrapped her gloved fingers around Xan's and swallowed her fear. "Tell me."

"She's under an elf curse. I'm sorry. There's nothing I can do for her."

Her heart pounding, Donna tried to let go of him, but Xan's fingers curved around hers and kept her where she was.

"Let me go," she whispered, wanting to go to her mom. Fear spun its threads through her mind, glistening like a black spider's web. It was one thing to suspect that Rachel was under some kind of otherworldly attack, but to have it confirmed like this . . . and given a name. That made it seem too real. Elf curse. She shivered

"There's nothing we can do," he repeated. His voice was soft, yet the finality in his tone rang like the slamming of a solid door.

"I don't believe that," Donna replied. She twisted her hand from his grip with ease, using her strength and refusing to feel guilty when surprise flashed across his face. "I'll never believe there's nothing I can do for her."

Watching her mother's still form, Donna ran

through possibilities—she needed a plan, that's all. An elf curse . . . okay, that was obviously bad, but that didn't mean there wasn't a way around it.

Or a way to break it. Curses could be broken, right?

Xan put his arm around her shoulders, drawing her against the warmth of his body. His thumb moved against her upper arm, an absent-minded caress that felt both natural and comforting. Donna leaned her head against his chest and listened to the steady beating of his heart. She took a deep breath and pulled away.

"So, what exactly *is* an elf curse? I always thought that's what was wrong with her. I mean, I didn't know for sure and I didn't know what to call it, but it was clearly something fey-related."

Xan gave her shoulder a squeeze. "Assuming that we won't talk too much about how I can divine fey curses . . ." He let his voice trail off and offered her a crooked, apologetic smile. "Yeah, I suspect your mother's under the influence of an elflock. That's how Aliette keeps her people alive."

"Wait . . . *what?*" Donna resisted the urge to glare at him. *This wasn't his fault*, she reminded herself. "What do you mean?"

Xan actually looked surprised; surprised that she didn't know something that was clearly so obvious to him. "You know that Aliette's sort of a succubus, right? I mean, not so much with the sex part, just the part where she uses human souls to keep the elves alive in the iron world. I thought that was why you were so worried about Navin when they took him."

"But what does Aliette need the elflocks *for*?" Donna pressed. "There were a lot of them on that belt she was wearing." She shuddered at the memory.

"Her power is the only thing keeping the elves alive," Xan replied. "Remember what she said in the Ironwood when we rescued Navin and Maker? Her people are dying, cut off from the Elflands' true home within Faerie. The wood elves are gradually turning into something like wraiths—that's why she wanted the elixir. She was hoping it might help in some way."

Horror was making Donna dizzy, but she forced herself to focus on what Xan was saying. "Do the alchemists know about this?"

Oh, who was she kidding? Of course they knew. They knew all about the dark elves and about the Wood Queen. It was just *Donna* who didn't know anything. She was such an idiot.

Xan held both her shoulders and shook her. "Hey, you didn't ask to belong to a group of liars. You can't control what those bastards choose to tell you—"

This time she pushed him away so hard he stumbled. She threw a quick glance at her mother and tried to keep the panic at bay. "Don't turn this into an 'us against them' thing. This is about my mom!"

"I know that." A muscle flickered in his jaw, but to his credit he didn't betray any other reaction to her outburst. He held up his hands as though calming a potentially dangerous animal. "I know. We're on the same side, Donna."

"Stop making it about sides."

"Stop being so fucking childish," he snapped.

So much for not reacting, Donna thought nastily.

They glared at each other, and in the growing silence between them all Donna could hear was the beep of hospital machinery and, above that, the sound of blood rushing in her ears. She felt the tattoos shift beneath her gloves, almost as though they were alive and reacting to her emotions.

What on earth put *that* thought in her head? She shook herself and was relieved to feel her tattoos settle down.

Her shoulders slumped. "I'm sorry. God, I don't mean to be such a bitch . . ."

Xan's lips curved into a comforting half-smile. "You're pretty good at it, though, so that's something to smile about."

"Shut up," she said, but without any real conviction. She met his eyes, grateful that he was giving her an easy out. He deserved better than her unloading her fear and frustration all over him.

Xan gave her a speculative look, but all he said was, "The elves can't really survive in the iron world; not for long periods of time, anyway. It's Aliette's power that helps them hold their glamour when they *do* venture across the border from the Elflands." His expression was serious. "So the queen must have an elflock for your mom attached to that belt she wears."

Donna was filled with an exhilarating mixture of anxiety and excitement. This gave her something to focus on other than her anger; anger at the elves, sure, but also at the Order for keeping yet more secrets from her. But if there was something she could *do*—no matter how scary it might be—if she could take action of some kind, to help Mom, then she wouldn't feel so useless.

"Can we get it back, do you think? The elflock, I mean."

Xan was shaking his head. "I don't know. Aliette wears that disgusting thing all the time."

Donna shivered. She knew what Xan meant: she'd caught sight of the Wood Queen's belt back when they had been negotiating for Maker and Navin's release. It reminded her of history lessons where she'd seen pictures of vodoun practioners in Africa—and in the deep South—with voodoo dolls that had real human hair. Except that the Wood Queen's belt was strung tightly around her narrow waist and had locks of hair hanging from it like a decorative fringe made of human remains. Something about it also reminded Donna of scalping, gross as that was to think about—though Aliette at least only collected hanks of hair, braided thickly and tied with pieces of woodland vines.

Rachel stirred slightly, turning her head away so that the white streak in the front was hidden.

Donna fought the urge to touch her mother's face, wondering if Mom was fighting the curse even now. There was nothing she could do for her at the moment, of course, but that didn't mean she had to sit on her hands and just hope for a miracle.

There may not be such things as miracles, but magic, of a sort, certainly existed. And although each of the four alchemical Orders had a different approach to magic, there was one basic rule: real magic was transformation. It was the energy you put into a project—intention, or the will of the individual alchemist—combined with preparation and ritual. The results were dependent on how strong the alchemist's determination was. If there was something that Donna wasn't short of, it was determination. Or stubbornness, as Navin would probably prefer to call it.

Just thinking of Nav made her smile. Even though he'd withdrawn from her since his rescue from the Ironwood, Donna still couldn't think of him without her heart lifting. And anyway, it wasn't exactly easy for him to stay in touch with her—not when Aunt Paige had her shut away in the house, grounded until the hearing.

She pulled her attention back to the room. She needed to find out as much as she could from Xan while she had the chance. "So, the elflock taken from Mom caused her condition?"

Xan nodded slowly. "I can't be certain, of course, but

the original magic must have caused her to slip into a state of . . ." He trailed off.

"It's okay," Donna said, her voice flat. "You can say it. Madness. She's been going crazy for the better part of ten years."

Xan grimaced. "Sorry. Yeah, the elflocks take away a piece of the victim's soul. It's like a slice cut out and attached to the hair—because it's something personal and organic. Your mother would have been vulnerable after that."

"But this time, for Mom, it's different. It's much worse, I mean—that's why they brought her to the hospital."

"That's the curse," Xan said. His eyes wandered to the still figure beneath the stark blankets. "Aliette must have done something to your mother's lock of hair, something that fully activated an elf curse."

"She's sending a message." Donna suddenly knew it was true as her mind formed a picture of the strange fey girl, Ivy. She should really tell Xan about Ivy, but right now all she wanted to think about was Mom and how they could help.

"What would Aliette want from you now, though?" Xan asked. "The elixir is gone; she can't use you to get that anymore."

Donna swallowed, trying not to let the fear take hold. "I don't know, but I'm going to have to find out. How else can I help Mom?"

Footsteps clattered to a halt outside the closed door, making her jump nervously. There was no way it was Nurse Valderrama, or any other nurse or doctor. They didn't wear heels that sounded like that.

Someone tried the door and, on instinct, Donna grabbed the handle and held it so that whoever was on the other side couldn't get in.

"Donna?" Aunt Paige's voice was filled with irritation. "Open this door right now."

Xan watched her at the door, an amused expression crossing his face like a flickering shadow—there one moment, gone the next.

Aunt Paige knocked on the door. "What are you doing in there?" Now she was trying to rattle the handle, but there was no way she'd be able to move it with Donna squeezing it in a death-grip. "We have to get to the Frost Estate; we're going to be late. We can still fit in the final session of the day."

Sighing dramatically, Donna stepped away from the door and almost laughed when her aunt fell into the room.

Pulling herself up to her full height, and trying to regain some of her lost dignity, Paige straightened her jacket and brushed invisible pieces of lint from the material. "What on *earth* were you two up to?"

"Nothing, Aunt Paige." Donna glanced back at her mother, wondering if she really was in a coma or just sleeping. She *looked* like she was asleep, a fairy-tale princess waiting for a handsome prince to come and wake her from her magically induced slumber. Hadn't Sleeping Beauty been cursed, too, and by a wicked witch? The Wood Queen was perfectly cast in that role.

Once again, Donna remembered her father's versions of those tales—in which a prince was pretty useless. It was always the women who fought battles and won wars in Patrick Underwood's bedtime stories.

Aunt Paige was watching her with an expression of barely suppressed annoyance. "We need to leave. Now."

Xan touched Donna's shoulder and she gratefully turned her back on Aunt Paige. He smiled a crooked sort of smile, an expression that had become familiar to her during the few short days that she'd spent with him before that final night in the Ironwood.

"I'll see you soon, Donna," he said, his voice filled with certainty.

Sadness gripped her chest as she tried to smile back at him. "Sure. I'll let you know what happens at the trial."

Her aunt snorted. "I wish you'd stop calling it that. It's just a hearing."

Donna spun to face her. "What's the difference?"

"You're not on 'trial', Donna, and you know it. The alchemists simply need to be made aware of what happened, and why what remained of the elixir is no longer in the Order of the Dragon's care."

Donna and Xan exchanged a guilty look, and she tried hard not to look at the faint scar on his forehead.

Instead, she fiddled with one of the cuffs of her ruby-bright gloves. "You're conveniently leaving out the part where representatives from the other Orders will decide on my *sentence*."

Shaking her hair out of her face, Aunt Paige put her hands on her hips. "It's not a sentence, it's a punishment. There's a difference."

"I keep trying to tell you, Aunt Paige," Donna said, raising her chin. "I'm not a child any more. As you said yourself, I'll be eighteen next year. You can't keep treating me like this, grounding me and *punishing* me—"

"You're not an adult yet," her aunt cut in sharply. "And the more you argue with me, the more you're simply proving my point."

Xan shifted uncomfortably, but kept his mouth shut when Donna shot him a fierce glance. This was nothing to do with him, and she certainly didn't need him to fight her battles for her.

Paige turned stiffly toward the door. "Come along. I've brought the car around front."

Donna's stomach twisted, dread filling her as she realized this was it: they really were going to continue with this stupid hearing today. The alchemists were obviously so keen to punish her, they couldn't even adjourn the proceedings until tomorrow—the fact that Mom was so sick didn't mean anything.

Aunt Paige walked out of the room, not even bothering to check on her sister-in-law before she left.

Donna was tempted to stay where she was, but she knew she was only delaying the inevitable. And what could she really do, anyway? She could refuse to go with her aunt, but she was still a minor. Where would she even go? She let out a frustrated breath. Her aunt—or, more specifically, *Simon*—would somehow manage to stop her from seeing Mom if she refused to follow the rules.

Donna looked through the open door and saw her aunt's shoulders relax as she talked to Nurse Valderrama in the corridor. No doubt the nurse was on the Order's payroll in some way, although she had seemed pretty cool earlier.

Xan placed a warm hand on the small of her back and pulled her around to face him. "It'll be okay."

But Donna knew they were just words; there was a long way to go before things could really be okay. "How do you know?" she asked, keeping her voice soft.

"Honestly?" Xan's eyes shone.

She frowned. That wasn't exactly the response she'd been expecting. "Yeah, honestly. How do you know that things will be okay?"

He pulled her into his arms and kissed her forehead. "Because," he said, pushing her away and holding her at arm's length, "you're Donna Underwood, and you won't let anything—or anyone—get in the way of you saving someone you love."

Her eyes felt hot; more tears threatening, just beneath the surface. "I hope you're right."

Xan gave her a gentle shake. "You don't sound so sure, but trust me when I tell you this: you *will* save your mother. And I'll help you."

"Even though the Order has me shut away like a criminal?"

"Like that's going to stop you?" He smiled briefly and pulled her against him one last time.

Donna wrapped her arms around his back and took in the musky pine scent of him. He was right. No matter how afraid she was for her mom and what might become of her, she knew that nothing would get in her way once she'd made up her mind about something. It didn't matter how many lies the alchemists—and her aunt—told her.

Rachel Underwood might be under an elf curse, fighting for consciousness and in danger of losing her very soul, but that wouldn't stop Donna from doing whatever needed to be done. She closed her eyes and allowed Xan's arms to give her the comfort she was so badly lacking.

Finally pulling away, she wiped her eyes on her gloved hands. "I'll be back, Mom, I promise," she said, not caring that the words were probably wasted.

But, just for a moment, Donna was almost certain that she saw the ghost of a smile on her mother's pale face.

Five

Lunch—if it could even be *called* lunch considering how late it was getting—was a snatched sandwich and hastily gulped apple juice. Donna had hardly had time to freshen up before it was time to return to the hearing.

She pushed open the bathroom door only to find herself facing a stranger—although, after a brief examination, she realized that he'd been at the opening session of the hearing that morning. It was Goth Dude, the young guy who had taken a seat next to Miranda Backhouse. If he was from the Order of the Crow, as she suspected, he certainly *looked* the part.

Under the bright hallway lighting, she saw that he couldn't be more than a few years older than her. He was tall and skinny, with shoulder-length black hair that looked like it hadn't seen a comb—or a haircut—in way too long, though the heavy layering of blue highlights more than made up for that. He was sort of nice looking, despite rather thin lips, and his dark eyes had an angular, Asian look to them. He also had ridiculously long lashes; it looked like he might as well be wearing mascara. Actually, Donna could now see that he *was* wearing makeup—black eyeliner was smudged into his lower lashes, and, combined with his black clothing and silver lip ring, it made him look like he was doing a bad impression of a skinny rock singer.

This guy was an alchemist? She couldn't help wondering how he got away with dressing like this; there was no way they'd let him do it if he were part of the Order of the Dragon.

And he was still standing there, completely and utterly silent. *What a freak.*

Suddenly angry, she glared at him. "Are you *trying* to give me the creeps? Standing there like a big, dumb jerk and staring at me like you've never seen a girl before?"

For a moment she wondered if he might be laughing at her, but the quirk at the corner of his mouth was gone so fast Donna thought she must have imagined it.

He gestured with his head, clearly indicating that she should follow him, and turned away before she had a chance to say anything else.

Donna was beginning to feel increasingly nervous about the next stage of her trial—things were moving too fast. Still, she followed him because, right now, she didn't have much of a choice, and she needed time to figure out what she was going to do about Mom. And the Wood Queen.

"It'll be over soon. I'm sure you've got nothing to worry about," he said, surprising her. He had a pleasant voice, sort of quiet with a British accent.

Donna raised her eyebrows and glanced around the hallway. They were waiting for the ancient elevator to arrive, but for some reason the dial was stuck on "one" and didn't look like it would be moving anytime soon.

She forced a laugh. "So you *can* speak. I thought you might have taken a vow of silence, just to increase the dramatic tension." She knew she was being childish, but she couldn't help it—not when her heart was suddenly pounding hard enough to make her chest hurt.

Her companion barely looked at her. "This is taking too long. Let's take the stairs," was all he said.

He headed back toward the staircase and increased his pace, forcing her to run to catch up. *Long-legged bastard.*

Despite her growing annoyance, Donna decided to

try a more friendly approach. "What did you say your name was?"

"I didn't," he replied calmly. But at least he slowed down again. "My name's Robert Lee. I'm an adept with the Order of the Crow."

"Are you based in London, with Miranda?" She tried not to sound too interested. But Miranda had seemed cool, for an alchemist—totally different from the female alchemists she was used to. "What do you do there?"

Robert regarded her thoughtfully for a moment before looking away again. "You ask a lot of questions, Miss Underwood."

Miss Underwood? She almost laughed at that. "Call me Donna."

"It's probably for the best if I don't . . . Miss Underwood."

She rolled her eyes. Was this just him being polite, or had someone told him to keep her at arm's length? "Come on, *Mr. Lee*; you look like you've broken a few rules in your time."

His thin mouth curved into a real smile. "Maybe. But maybe I'm not supposed to be talking to you."

Donna fixed a mock-serious expression on her face. "*Really?*" She dragged the word out. "I think you're the one who started the whole talking thing, reassuring me that things are going to be okay. Remember?"

His cheeks flushed, but he refused to look at her.

"Oh, *please*," she said, genuinely exasperated. "What

are you afraid of—that I'll use my so-called magical powers to brainwash you into letting me escape?"

Robert led her into a short passageway, waiting for her to draw level with him before glancing at her. His expression was completely serious. "I sincerely doubt your magic could out-class mine, Miss Underwood."

This time she really did laugh. "You think?" He was definitely messing with her, but there was no way he'd admit it. She kind of liked that about him; that in his own strange way, Robert Lee was trying to take her mind off the hearing. At least, she thought that was what he was doing.

"So, you're really not supposed to talk to me? They told you that, huh?"

He shrugged. "I'm just following orders."

Of course you are, she thought tiredly, but what she said was, "Fine. But it's not like I can get out of a mansion filled with alchemists, is it? There's no harm in talking to me until we get there; I'm not planning anything. Nothing, you know, *dodgy*." She grinned as she said the last word.

For a moment he looked like he was going to laugh. "Did you just say 'dodgy' to me? Where did you get that from?"

"Isn't that the sort of thing you guys say?"

An expression she couldn't read crossed his face. "What guys?"

Donna frowned, genuinely confused. "Um . . . British

people. You know? It's not like I've never heard an English person speak before."

His gaze slid toward her and their eyes met for a moment. "Oh. Right."

"So?" she said, unable to keep the impatience out of her voice. "Are you going to answer any of my *totally harmless* and not-at-all-dodgy questions?"

He nodded slowly, as though uncertain of how much he should be telling her. "Yes, I'm based in London, although I won't be working with Miranda now. They'll assign me to an adept's duties when we get home. I only recently passed the final tests, so I shouldn't really be out here, but Miranda wanted me to meet Quentin."

If Robert was a newly qualified adept, having completed the initiate's standard magical tests and grueling exams, that meant he must be about twenty-one. He looked younger than that, though, with his scruffy hair and long skinny legs. Donna wondered what "duties" they would assign him once he returned to London. The Order of the Dragon might be the most magically active of the alchemists, but the Order of the Crow was supposed to be run by alchemists dedicated to finding—or remaking—the Philosopher's Stone, given that they were based in England, one of the historical homes of alchemy.

The stairwell narrowed and they had to descend in single file; Donna felt the walls pressing in on her and was glad when the winding stairs came to an end. Robert held open the door at the bottom and gestured for her to follow. She glanced at his long fingers on the smeared brass handle, noticing that his short nails were painted emo-black.

"Nice paint job." Donna smiled in what she hoped was an encouraging way. "They let you get away with that in the Order of the Crow?"

"It's not *school*, Donna," he replied. "There's not exactly a dress code."

Her cheeks flushed. "Sorry, I just meant—"

"Forget it," he said. His tone had turned unfriendly, and she wondered what she'd said to upset him. *Sensitive, much?* Thank God she hadn't mentioned the guyliner.

He led her into one of the many color-coded sitting rooms in the Frost Estate. This room was very . . . brown. The Brown Room. She couldn't hold back a sneer—it was just so appropriate. There was something deeply symbolic about walking into a room entirely decorated in shades of excrement; maybe Simon had developed a sense of humor?

"Sit down; they're not quite ready for us," Robert said, gesturing at the crap-colored couch.

Sighing, Donna perched on the edge of the scratchy material covering the seat. She wondered what was causing the delay. Aunt Paige had been in a crazy rush to get back here, almost begrudging the short recess needed for that snack, and now everyone seemed to have disappeared.

Robert watched her like she was a particularly fascinating alien species, reminding her that she wasn't alone. At least, not in a physical sense.

He cleared his throat as their eyes met. "You're not what I expected."

She scowled. "Why, what did you expect? A criminal mastermind?"

"Hardly. Although the Magus did tell me that you'd try to talk me into letting you leave."

"The Magus? Who the hell are you talking about?"

He closed his eyes briefly, dramatically, as though something had genuinely caused him pain. "Please don't invoke the name of the Demon realm. Even behind the mansion's wards, who knows what could be listening . . ."

"Are you for real?"

"What do you mean?" His tone had shifted from pained to defensive. "Miss Underwood you, of all people, should know the rules."

Donna felt like she was trapped in one of those nightmares—the ones where you know you're dreaming but you still can't wake yourself up no matter how hard you try.

"I already told you once: please call me Donna. And then please explain what you mean by 'the Magus'."

"Miss—" Robert stopped and smiled. He really did have a nice smile, and the laughter lines around his eyes made it clear he did it a lot more than his moody exterior currently let on. "Donna, you must know who I'm talking about."

She had a Very Bad Feeling, but the stubborn part of her didn't want to have it officially confirmed. "You mean Quentin, right? Our Archmaster."

"If I'd meant the Archmaster, that's what I would have said." The young alchemist gave her a look that clearly communicated his fears for her sanity. "I'm talking about Simon Gaunt—the guy who looks like a ferret."

Any other time, Donna would have enjoyed Robert's description of the man she'd grown to hate—but now was not that time. Her suspicions were correct: ever since she and Xan had found Simon's lab, hidden behind an old clock in the Blue Room, she'd been pretty certain that the Order's so-called "secretary" was in fact more than that. A lot more. The term "magus" had first snuck into her mind while they'd been stealing the elixir and trying to avoid capture, and she'd been finding it nearly impossible to shake those misgivings.

Perhaps it was the screaming bronze statue in Simon's lab that had been the final straw, for who else but a magus could animate lifeless matter with the consciousness of a spirit? She didn't really know *what* had been going on with that creepy statue, but it hadn't just raised the alarm; she'd heard it talking to Simon while she and Xan were hiding. It had been alive . . . in some way. Or, at the very least, there was something alive *inside* it.

She shuddered, and Robert reached out as though

to steady her. Donna realized that she had stood up without being fully aware of it. Her hands were clenched and her breath was coming out in short bursts. It was as though everything she thought she knew about her life was slowly unravelling. She wanted so badly to go back to simpler times—even if that meant returning to the misery of Ironbridge High and Melanie Swan's vindictive attentions.

"Donna, please sit down." Robert held her elbow and guided her back to the seat with surprising gentleness. "Come on, you're not looking well."

Donna allowed him to press her onto the dull brown couch. If Simon truly was a magus, did that mean he was the only one? Were there more? How had he kept something as huge as that hidden from her all these years? She'd heard talk of there being an actual magus in London, and possibly one in Prague, but the identities of those men (because they were always men) were kept a closely guarded secret.

She closed her eyes for a moment, trying desperately to calm herself, not caring that Robert was probably freaking out. Her head was pounding and the pain in her arms, beneath the tattoos, felt like it could crush the breath from her lungs. Her chest ached and a strange sensation began to fill her, reminding her of what had happened out on the grounds after meeting Ivy. Something was wrong, something new and scary—and it only seemed to be getting worse.

And then other thoughts pushed aside the worry about her rebuilt arms and hands. Why hadn't her aunt ever *told* her about Simon? In Donna's presence, the alchemists had only ever referred to him as the Order's secretary—or as Quentin's partner and lover—never as a potentially more powerful alchemist than the Archmaster.

Shouldn't Simon himself hold the title of Archmaster, if he really was a magus? Quentin had been a talented alchemist in his youth, but he was certainly no magus; she knew that because of a story he'd once told her about how he flunked some kind of important alchemical trial. It had been one of the many stories he'd told her while sitting at her bedside during her long recovery as a trau-matized child.

None of this made any sense.

But there wasn't any time left to unravel things as the inner door opened and Aunt Paige walked into the room, closely followed by "the Magus" himself.

Donna tried to stand, but her legs still felt strange. Instead, she shifted to the edge of the seat and looked up into her aunt's eyes. She was searching for some kind of signal; something she could hold onto during whatever was to come next.

But making eye contact with Paige Underwood caused any last drops of hope to slip through her fingers. Her aunt seemed as hard and unrelenting as the trees of Ironwood Forest.

"Donna, are you ready?" Aunt Paige asked.

"Yes," she replied. What else could she say? "I suppose I am."

Simon Gaunt was rubbing his hands together in the familiar gesture that grated on her nerves. The dry scraping of his skin made her feel sick all over again.

"It's time," he said, in his typically pompous voice.

Donna felt her heart speed up, and wished that she wouldn't always feel so afraid of the alchemists lately.

But she was made of tougher stuff than that. She was Patrick and Rachel Underwood's daughter. She had magically forged iron embedded in her flesh and wrapped around her bones. She had almost died in the Wood Monster's fiery jaws—twice. No way was Donna Underwood going to let an outdated secret society get the better of her.

Screw them, she thought to herself, unable to stop the slight smile that twisted her lips as she rose to follow her aunt through the doors to the meeting room.

She didn't even care when she figured that Robert had caught the unpleasant expression on her face.

Screw them all.

❧

Maker stood with the help of his cane, leaning heavily on it so that Donna could see the whites of his knuckles pressing against papery skin.

"There is a new witness I would like to introduce, Archmaster," he said.

The inner chamber was once again filled with alchemists, all sitting around the room in a semi-circle. This time, Donna had been ushered to a sturdy table on one side. There were two chairs behind the table, one of which was for her. The occupant of the other chair caused her to forget herself for a moment—*Maker*. Donna had been so relieved to see the old alchemist that she'd embarrassed them both by pushing the table effortlessly aside and hugging him. At least her "defense" was putting in an appearance for the second session of the day.

At the sound of Maker's proclamation, Quentin raised his head and met the alchemist's eyes. A look passed between them—a look that Donna immediately knew she was not meant to have seen. Something was going on, and it seemed that both Maker and Quentin were in on it. From the expression of outrage on Simon's face, it was clear that one of the old guard in the room *wasn't* aware of what was going on.

"And who might that be, Maker?" Quentin asked.

"Let me introduce you to—"

"This is highly irregular," Simon huffed, pushing thinning strands of hair back from his sweating forehead and cutting Maker off before he could go any further. "We have heard the case presented at this hearing. The Council is only expected to be here for a few days. I really think we should move on to—"

"Simon," Quentin said, "you know quite well that all our representatives will stay for as long as needed. Even beyond the weekend, *if* that becomes appropriate."

Simon blustered for a few moments, but soon ran out of steam.

Quentin's tone remained mild. "We will hear from this witness."

Donna swivelled in her seat so she could see her aunt, trying to figure out what the hell was going on—whether, in fact, everyone knew what was happening. But Aunt Paige looked as confused as she herself felt.

Maker nodded at Robert, who moved silently across the room and opened one of the panelled doors.

A slender figure of medium height stepped into the makeshift courtroom. His black hair shone in the flickering ceremonial candlelight, and his normally smooth brown face looked pale and drawn. His cheekbones protruded a little more than Donna remembered, giving him an older look that suited him.

Navin Sharma stood under the scrutiny of the representatives from four alchemical Orders, his red and black biker jacket completely out of place and marking him as *other*.

A commoner.

The expression on his face—the determination in his dark brown eyes—let Donna know that her best friend wasn't going to allow himself to be treated as anything other than an equal. In that moment she felt so unbearably proud, her heart swelling in her chest as she squashed the urge to run to him. If she could somehow let him know how glad she was to see him, how relieved, maybe she wouldn't lose him after all. And this wasn't just for her sake, but for his. She'd been so worried about him when the wood elves took him, and now she had to make sure he was okay.

The truth was, she blamed herself every single day for what had happened to Nav. There wasn't a day that went by when she didn't think about the queen's blade at his throat. His life had been under threat because of Donna—because of their friendship. She could only hope that he didn't feel the same way. He possessed so many amazing qualities, and she felt lucky to call him her friend.

And even though the last two weeks apart had been tough, perhaps it had done their friendship some good. Navin had discovered so many crazy truths about her, and, more than that, he'd learned that the world isn't the non-magical place he'd once believed it to be. He must have needed time to process everything. But he was here today, as part of her defense. Donna was dying to know how Maker had arranged that with Quentin—and right under Simon's nose, too!

It was just like Navin had come for her, in the same way that she'd gone in search of him in the Ironwood. In stealing the elixir from the alchemists, she'd been willing to give up everything—and now she knew it hadn't been for nothing. Donna wanted to cry; she wanted to throw her arms around Navin and ignore the watching alchemists. She needed him to know how grateful she was, how much she still cared about him.

But Navin wouldn't look at her—not even once, no matter how hard she willed him to glance her way.

Swallowing a rush of bitter disappointment, she watched Navin as he studied the gathered alchemists with an expression of curiosity. *Stop being so selfish*, she told herself sharply. Nav was here, that's all that mattered. Maybe if they spoke—or even made eye contact—it would put him off.

Simon was staring at Navin like he was something particularly unpleasant. His almost non-existent top lip curled upwards in a sneer as he turned back to address Maker. "Why have you brought a *commoner* before our Council?"

Donna had to bite the inside of her cheek to stop herself from calling Simon Gaunt something a lot worse than "commoner". She was quite impressed with her restraint.

Maker frowned. "I thought it prudent that we hear *all* the evidence—and that includes listening to Mr. Sharma's experience and his account of why Donna was in Ironwood Forest in the first place."

There was a pulse beating in Simon's temple, and for a very pleasant moment Donna wondered if he might have an aneurism. She immediately felt guilty for having

th a nasty thought, even though she was pretty sure
le man hadn't done much good in his life. Well, apart
from apparently making Quentin happy... *but was the
Archmaster happy?* He didn't seem particularly filled with
joy lately, but maybe that was more due to ill health.

Simon was still droning on about rule-breaking, or
something equally boring. "Not to mention the fact that
you have exposed our secrets to someone who has no
right to be admitted to our inner circle of knowledge.
This *boy* is not worthy. He—"

Maker cut in. "This *boy*, as you insist on referring to
him, almost became a casualty of our war with the fey.
We owe him the courtesy of listening to what he has to
tell us."

"Rubbish!" Simon was practically shouting. "We
have heard all the evidence against Underwood. This is
outrageous! Who authorized this?"

"I did."

Everyone turned to look at the speaker. Quentin
Frost had stood and was moving slowly into the center
of the room. There was no denying the man's presence,
despite his ill health. Even Simon stopped talking and
looked chastised—at least for a moment.

Quentin cleared his throat. "I believe it is in the
interests of the alchemists to hear the full story behind
Donna's actions. Surely we cannot stand in judgment based
only on the consequences of those actions; it is important
to know *why* she took the elixir in the first place."

Simon risked his partner's anger. His face was set in determined lines as he said, "But we have heard this already; we know that Underwood went after the Sharma boy."

"But," Quentin replied, more firmly this time, "there are *some* in this room who doubt the truth of the abduction in the first place. Now we can hear from Navin himself, and the alchemists can draw their own conclusions."

Donna risked another glance at her friend, fully expecting him to be as entranced by the Archmaster's sudden activity as she had been. But Navin wasn't looking in the same direction as everybody else.

Navin was looking right at her.

The cliché "time seemed to stand still" was invented for moments like this, Donna would later think. But right then, *in* that moment, it really did feel as though every thing slowed down. She met Navin's eyes, and she was almost certain that the two of them were communicating without words, no matter how stupid that might sound. Not that she seriously believed they'd suddenly developed psychic powers—although that would be cool—but the connection between them was so strong and clear that it made her sit up straighter in her chair as she tried to read the expression on his face.

As they locked eyes, and the room and everyone in it dropped away, she tried to tell him how sorry she was and how much she still cared; how much she hoped that *he* still cared about her. She hoped he knew how grateful she was that he was here, now, when she most needed him.

The moment passed—as all moments do, no matter how magical—and finally, something began happening around them. The room came back into focus and it appeared as though Quentin's intervention had silenced Simon's complaints. Simon was blatantly unhappy, but he was done arguing. For now.

Maker indicated that Navin should sit in the uncomfortable chair positioned in the center of the room.

"Don't worry," the old alchemist said, placing a deceptively gnarled hand on Navin's shoulder. Donna knew the true strength of those hands, after months and years of iron-forged operations. "Just tell the truth—that's all you need to do."

Navin tried to smile, but then Simon was standing in front of him and the questions began.

In fact, it was the answer to the very first question that made Donna's heart sing. "Why on *earth*," began Simon, with an expression of theatrical disbelief on his face, "did you agree to come here today?"

Navin glanced over at Donna one more time. Very slowly and very deliberately, he winked at her. She almost burst out laughing, but was glad she hadn't so that she could hear his reply. His voice didn't shake in the slightest as he turned back to Simon.

"I didn't have to agree to anything—I *wanted* to

come. She's my best friend. When my mom died—and all through her fight with cancer—Donna was there for me. When the wood elves took me. Donna came and found me. That's why I'm here today. This is my job, dammit. To support her; to protect *her*. To be there for her in the same way that she always is for me."

Navin stared at Simon, his expression a good imitation of the disdain on the older man's face. He raised an eyebrow and leaned back in his chair as though he didn't have a care in the world. "Next question, please."

Six

Donna never thought she'd be so happy to see her own bedroom again.

She all but collapsed onto the bed and stripped off her gloves, clenching and unclenching her fingers to ease the sudden shooting pains in them. She was exhausted. So much had happened: the opening session of the hearing; Ivy's message from the Wood Queen; Mom's collapse; seeing Xan again after all this time; and then finally, miraculously, Navin's appearance. It was a lot to take in.

The timely dismissal of the afternoon session was a bonus Donna hadn't expected, but Quentin needed to rest and everyone had seemed more than happy to take a break. She had been relieved when Aunt Paige said they could finally go home.

Donna kicked off her sneakers and crawled under the comforter fully clothed, hoping that her aunt wouldn't bother her for the next twelve hours. At least. In fact, Maker had told them that the schedule for the next day wouldn't include her again until the afternoon; during the morning session, each of the representatives from the other Orders would have their say. Donna had been too tired to even be pissed off that it was a "closed session." As in: closed to her. *I'm only the accused*, she thought bitterly, but really couldn't work up the energy to worry about it no matter how hard she tried.

Whatever happened now, she felt a little more able to handle it. As long as Navin was by her side.

She breathed a sigh of relief, trying to chase the day's tension away, though all she could really think about was how sick her mother was—and what could be done to save her. Rachel Underwood had been attacked by magic; the darkest, most insidious sort of magic imaginable. Perhaps there really wasn't anything you could use to fight that.

No, there was *always* a way. Her father had taught her that.

She finally managed to fall into a fitful sort of half-sleep. It was strange—she knew she wasn't fully asleep, and yet somehow she was dreaming. She had heard the term "lucid dreaming" before, and although she didn't know much about it, there was a part of her that wondered if this was it. It was like being "in" the dream and yet . . . not. Dreaming, but also watching the dream at the same time . . . a dream that unfolded in the same too-real way that most of her nightmares had lately:

> She is running in a field. No, a forest. No. Neither of those. She is at least aware that she's running on grass, and the only visible boundary is the night sky. There aren't any stars at all, not a single point of light in the unfathomable indigo-blackness. She hears a sudden sound, sharp and clattering like the sound of birds— lots of birds—taking flight together. Or perhaps it isn't birds at all, but snakes. Snakes made of flickering shadows, hissing as they slide toward her. And then she isn't running anymore because she's lying flat on her back on the hard ground. The darkness, like hundreds of cold hands, is pressing down on her. She can't breathe. She will drown in all this blackness if she can't get back on her feet. Her mother's voice says, from somewhere out there, "There's a storm coming. Can't you feel it? Make your choice and then live with the consequences."

Donna woke with a start.

For a moment, the bedroom's darkness got all tangled up in her head with the darkness from her dream, but then she remembered where she was, and that she was awake, and that she was safe.

A cold hand closed over her mouth. "You won't make a sound," a voice whispered in her ear.

Instinct took over and Donna wrenched her body to one side, flailing out with her right arm and making contact with something soft. Whoever had hold of her loosened their grip in a hurry, and she heard them gasp. Hopefully in pain.

Donna slid onto the floor and crouched with her back to the wall, trying to see through the thick blackness of the room. It seemed impossibly dark, especially considering she hadn't bothered to close the curtains before sleeping. It shouldn't be this dark.

She opened her mouth to call for help—

But nothing happened. No sound came out and she coughed silently, sort of choking as she tried to push something out from between her lips. *Anything*—any sound at all to reassure herself that she wasn't going crazy, or that she wasn't still dreaming.

She thought of those whispered words, strange words chosen with care: *You won't make a sound.*

Shit. It was magic, it had to be. She tried again to yell, just to be sure, but she couldn't speak a single word; couldn't scream or even cough. Her mouth opened but nothing came out. Panic threatened to overwhelm her, just as the suffocating darkness made her feel trapped like an insect in amber.

Movement, then, in front of her—she could sense it even if she couldn't see it.

Come on, Underwood, Donna told herself. *Just because you can't see or speak doesn't mean you can't still fight.*

Whoever was in the room ran at her. Donna heard soft footsteps and felt something brush past her knee; she kicked out, using her hands for leverage against the floor. Being abnormally strong had its benefits, even though she hated to use that physical strength. But now wasn't the time to think about past mistakes.

She missed her target. But it seemed she'd deterred them enough that they'd backed off, at least for a moment.

Going on the offensive now, Donna scrambled to her feet, still keeping the wall at her back so nobody could come up from behind. She clenched her fists and held her hands in front of her, elbows bent, sort of like a boxer or a martial artist. Feeling only slightly ridiculous, considering that she didn't know the first thing about martial arts, Donna strained her ears for any sign of her attacker.

And that was when a tentative voice, speaking more clearly now, said, "Donna Underwood, why are you attacking me?"

Ivy! How had she gotten inside the bedroom? Did the Wood Queen's supposedly weak power really stretch so far?

Donna wished she could say something in reply, but her voice still wasn't working. Whatever the hell Ivy—or Aliette—had done, it clearly only affected *her* and not anyone else in the room.

"If I release the charm," Ivy whispered tentatively, "will you call your aunt?"

Shaking her head, Donna wondered if the fey girl could see the movement. Perhaps she had night vision.

Something tightened her throat from the inside out, and then the sensation was gone. Donna coughed, experimentally, and was relieved to hear the sound cut through the quiet. At the same time, the unnatural blackness lifted, and by the light of the window she could see it was already past dawn—though early enough that Aunt Paige would still be sleeping.

"Thanks," Donna muttered. God, that had been too weird. "What did you have to that for, anyway? I would have talked to you without raising the alarm; there was no need to throw Aliette's magic at me."

Because now that she knew the truth—thanks to Xan—she would do pretty much whatever it took to save Mom.

"I expected you to give me trouble. The queen prepared me," Ivy said. She had an expression suspiciously close to embarrassment on her strangely pretty face.

Donna tried to glare at her, but she still felt too tired to bother.

Ivy was wearing all black this time: black leggings

and some kind of stretchy tunic, as though this was her ninja outfit for special operations. Her feet were bare.

Donna shook her head. "How can you walk around like that?"

"Like what?"

"You're not wearing shoes."

Ivy looked genuinely puzzled. "This is quieter."

"But it's *winter*. Aren't you cold?"

The strange girl shrugged her thin shoulders. "I am fey—I do not feel the cold."

Making a mental note of that, Donna moved to sit on the edge of the bed. Ivy folded her legs beneath her and sat on the floor.

"You're not a wood elf, though," Donna ventured.

"No," Ivy said.

"So?"

The fey girl's already huge eyes grew even wider. "I . . . don't understand."

Donna sighed. "I'm asking what kind of faery you are, I guess. I'm sorry if that seems rude . . ." *Was it rude?* It probably was.

But before she could feel too bad, Ivy actually smiled. Her white teeth made a startling contrast against her pale green skin. "You are curious about me?"

"Yeah, seems that I am." Almost smiling in return, Donna shrugged. "Sorry."

"I am a changeling."

Oh. She hadn't been expecting an answer at all, and,

honestly, that hadn't been the one she thought she'd get in any case. "There are adult changelings? Well, *young* adult, anyway."

"We grow to adulthood, yes. Sometimes." Ivy wasn't looking her in the eye any more, and Donna wondered whether she should push her luck and ask for more information.

But then she thought of her mother lying in the hospital, and all curiosity about what the hell a changeling was doing working for the Wood Queen slipped from her mind.

"So, Ivy. What brings you here?" *And how did you get through Aunt Paige's wards?*

Ivy crossed her legs and sat up straight. "Her Majesty requests that you meet with her—this is the second time of asking."

"Okay," Donna said, keeping her voice level. "Where does she want to meet?"

Victory flashed across the changeling's expressive face. "You will go to her?"

"If she's the one behind my mother's curse, I hardly have much of a choice, do I?" Anger was only a breath away, but Donna held it together. "The Wood Queen could have chosen a different kind of message—my mom isn't her plaything."

"'Plaything'? I believe the word Her Majesty used was . . . 'insurance'."

Insurance. Donna swallowed, wishing she could

let her fury off the tight leash she had on it. Just for a moment.

They sat in silence, and Donna half-imagined she could hear her aunt breathing from the other side of the wall.

"How did you get into the house?" she asked Ivy suddenly.

The changeling seemed surprised. "The window."

"And that didn't wake my aunt? Why didn't the wards break?"

Ivy's gaze slid away. "There were no wards."

Donna shifted her position on the bed. "Of course there are wards. The whole house is surrounded by various magical protections—they alert Aunt Paige to intruders."

The petite girl seemed to deflate. "I have an . . . ability."

"You can pass through wards without breaking them?"

"Some," she whispered.

That was a pretty cool "ability" to be in possession of. Donna gave the changeling an appraising look. She could certainly see why Ivy would be useful to the Wood Queen, and it also explained how the girl had entered the Frost Estate's grounds undetected earlier today. It was also interesting that, when pressed, she seemed reluctant—or perhaps unable—to lie.

Ivy met her eyes again. "My queen said you may

choose the meeting place within Ironbridge, as a sign of good faith."

How very kind of her, Donna thought snarkily, but resisted the temptation to take out her frustration on Ivy. Whatever the girl's involvement, she wasn't a dark elf and she didn't seem . . . bad. If anything, she seemed simply lost. Donna couldn't help feeling sympathy for her, even though she didn't exactly know why.

"Mildred's Café will do well enough. It's just off the main—"

"She will know where to find you," Ivy cut in.

"But—"

"She didn't ask for directions. Just the location."

Donna scowled. "Fine."

Ivy nodded as if nothing was wrong. "I will leave you now."

"You do that."

"I enjoyed our conversation."

Was this girl for real? "I'm afraid I can't say the same," Donna muttered. "But I appreciate you bringing me Aliette's message."

Ivy looked flustered. "She is my mistress. I do what I must."

Donna studied her. "She's got you too, right? In her power, I mean. Somehow."

For a long moment, it seemed as though Ivy might not reply. Then, in a small voice, she said, "Somehow, yes. Not in the same way as it is for your mother, though."

Nodding, Donna tried to squash the rising sympathy she was beginning to feel. "Can't you run away?"

"It is . . ." Ivy shook her head, dislodging a few leaves onto the carpet. "It is not as simple as that."

"No," Donna said, thinking of the alchemists. "It never is."

Seven

Donna pushed open the door to Mildred's. She thought she'd be a lot more scared than she actually was; perhaps she'd reached breaking point, and this was the stage before a full-blown nervous breakdown.

She thought of her mother's bone-white face as she lay in the hospital bed, hooked up to machines and pumped full of drugs that were probably useless. What was the point of belonging to a group of powerful magic users, Donna wondered, if there was nothing they could do for one of their own? And, honestly, was the Order even *trying* to do anything for Rachel Underwood? Aunt Paige had attempted to reassure her that they were, but Donna felt sure that was just bullshit to stop her from leaving the house this morning.

The story she'd told her aunt was that she was going to visit Mom during the morning session at the estate. Surprisingly, Aunt Paige hadn't offered much resistance to this plan. All she'd had to do to gain her aunt's blessing was agree to have the Order's car pick her up from the hospital at lunchtime. That seemed easy enough, and it left Donna free to meet Aliette at Mildred's before going to see her mother at Ironbridge General.

Honestly, Donna half expected Aunt Paige to have her followed, but she couldn't let herself worry about it. It wasn't important, not in the face of meeting the queen of the freaking wood elves. Certainly not when compared to the potential for saving her mother's life.

She took a deep breath and looked around, trying to remember that just because the meeting was happening in a public place didn't mean she was *safe*. In fact, she might need all the protection she could get from Aliette. Donna dug in her jeans pocket, grateful to find a scrunched-up hair band, and quickly tied her shoulder-length chestnut hair into a ponytail—just in case. She wished she had a hat with her. Although she didn't know how elflocks were gathered, it couldn't hurt to take extra precautions.

It had crossed her mind to call Xan, but she'd

immediately discarded that notion. She didn't intend for anybody else she cared about to be put in danger on her behalf—not again.

Looking around the café, Donna tried to spot an elf queen among the regular patrons. She had no idea what form Aliette would take out here, how her glamour would manifest in the Iron World.

Then she noticed a woman watching her from a seat in the corner of the room; her table was jammed against the side of the counter, almost as an afterthought. It seemed . . . separate from everything else going on in the busy café. The woman's red-painted lips curved into a wicked smile the moment she laid eyes on Donna. A cruel smile, and certainly not the sort of expression you would hope to see on the face of the person you were meeting for coffee.

Because this was Aliette. There was no doubt in Donna's mind about that.

She felt her shoulders tense. But not with fear. No, this was definitely a feeling of anticipation. She had beaten the Wood Queen before—sort of. Tricked her, giving herself and her friends enough time to escape the Elflands. Although Donna had soon realized that the Skriker was waiting for them out in the Ironwood— waiting to hunt them down like nothing more than meat.

The queen had planned that, of course.

What she hadn't planned on was that Donna

Underwood—a seventeen-year-old girl barely at the start of her training with the alchemists—would be able to defeat the Wood Monster.

As Aliette beckoned her closer, her red-tipped nails resembling claws, Donna wondered if this meeting had all been a terrible mistake. Perhaps she'd underestimated the queen's hatred of her, the ill-will she must still harbor against the human girl who had destroyed her favorite pet. And cost her the elixir that might have saved her kin.

Donna bit down on her fear and strode determinedly across the room, toward the wood-elf-disguised-as-a-human waiting in the shadows of the high-topped counter.

∽

Sitting at a table in Mildred's facing the Order's greatest enemy was one of her most surreal experiences so far. Donna shook her head. Why was she even surprised? Nothing ever seemed to be straightforward when it came to her life—maybe after this meeting, nothing would ever be the same again.

Paranoia caused her to wonder whether this might all be some kind of trick, or maybe a test. Perhaps the Order was watching her, waiting for her to screw up and betray them. Again.

She bit the inside of her cheek. She wouldn't let

herself think about those things—not when she was potentially holding her mother's life in her hands.

The Wood Queen stared at her, openly curious as she examined Donna as if studying an interesting new life form. *Which to a creature such as her,* Donna thought, *is exactly what I am.*

No, she told herself quickly. *I am her enemy, just as surely as she is mine. Don't ever forget that.*

The queen's glamour was both shocking and impressive. She had taken the form of a middle-aged, middle-class woman wearing a dark green suit. A full-length red woollen coat was thrown casually over the back of her chair. Her autumnal hair, glinting with russet highlights under the café's low-hanging lamps, touched her shoulders and curled slightly outward at the ends.

She looked like she was dressed to go to some kind of charity function.

Donna lifted her chin and met the bright green eyes of her enemy. "What do you want, then? Why go to all this trouble just to talk to me?"

"Ah, straight to the point, I see," the queen replied, in a disturbingly human voice. She sounded like a middle-aged opera singer, all rounded perfect vowels. "No manners, these humans . . ."

Donna almost laughed in her face. "Manners? What do you care about manners?" She lowered her voice, glancing around to make sure nobody could overhear. "You murdered my father, practically destroyed my mother, and kidnapped my best friend. I'm sorry, *Your Majesty*, but I don't think very much of your idea of etiquette."

The queen examined her finger nails. "Interesting, holding a human form again after all these years."

Donna gritted her teeth. Had Aliette even heard a word she'd said?

Sly leafy eyes met hers. They were surrounded with bright blue eye shadow, which made for a startling and slightly nauseating combination. "Donna Underwood, you whom we have known as Iron Witch . . ." she began. A scarlet-tipped finger gestured at Donna's gloves. "Since when have you cared so much about the magicians?"

"I've cared about the alchemists ever since you destroyed my family," Donna replied, careful to keep her slow fury burning beneath the surface. For now.

Aliette shrugged, a casual gesture surely calculated to arouse anger. "I destroyed nothing. Your ability to throw wild accusations has increased, child. I'm impressed."

"What are you talking about? Let's start with something you can't possibly deny: did you, or did you not, take Navin Sharma and hold him captive until I brought you the elixir."

At the mention of the elixir, the queen's expression darkened, but her voice remained level. "Oh, the human boy. Yes, I suppose that much is true."

Donna couldn't hold back a snort of disgusted laughter. It was either that or go crazy. Or maybe try to strangle Aliette right there in Mildred's, surrounded by a dozen witnesses.

"So if that part is true, what did I get wrong? Enlighten me."

Long, pale fingers pulled a silver cigarette case seemingly from thin air. The effortless show of magic made the hairs on the back of Donna's neck stand upright. She shivered as she watched the Wood Queen open the shiny case and pull out an unfiltered cigarette.

Just for a moment, Donna's arms began to tingle—that newly familiar sensation that seemed to be getting worse whenever she was faced with something particularly stressful. After Ivy had left this morning, it had taken her tattoos a full half-hour to stop moving.

Thankfully, this time, the moment passed and Donna breathed again. She gulped in the coffee-flavored air and gratefully allowed the lingering taste to awaken her. The pain in her chest was no less, but at least she could move her fingers without having to worry about the tattoos spiralling around her arms beneath her favorite black velvet gloves.

"You can't smoke in here," she snapped at Aliette, trying to regain control of the situation. She shook her head at how bizarre it was; what the hell did an elf queen need to smoke for?

"Oh, this little thing?" Aliette twirled the cigarette between her fingers, making it appear and disappear as it flashed in and out of view. Her nail polish shimmered like rubies.

"Stop that," Donna said, trying and failing to keep the irritation out of her voice.

"Stop what?" Aliette replied, opening her eyes wide and innocent.

Donna frowned, about to say something angry, then stopped. The queen wasn't kidding. Her "human" hands were empty.

"How did you . . . ?" Her voice trailing off, Donna figured it out. God, she was slow. If Aliette was powerful enough to hold a glamour this strong in the center of Ironbridge, then of course the cigarette case, the trick with the dancing cigarette . . . all of it was just part of the glamour. Fey magic. She hadn't been able to detect it because her whole body was practically vibrating with the queen's presence anyway. How could she possibly differentiate between what was real and what was merely created by the woman-thing sitting in front of her?

Taking a steadying breath, Donna knew what she had to do. It was going to hurt, but it'd be worth it if her plan worked. The iron in her hands and arms could affect fey magic, of that she was pretty certain. Maybe now was a good time to test that theory.

She slammed her right hand down over Aliette's, holding back just enough that the table didn't collapse. But she made sure the queen felt a good deal of her enhanced strength.

The woman's face hardly changed, but Donna detected the tightening of her lips and strain around her eyes. In fact, the more she looked, the more she could just make out the shimmer in the air around the queen. It was like that strange effect you can see over the horizon of a straight road on a hot summer's day.

Aliette hissed. "You little fool. If you break my glamour, how will you explain my presence here?"

Satisfaction seeped into Donna's bones like a healing balm. "I can't break your glamour, Your Majesty. I can only break your concentration—but it seems like that's pretty easy to do."

Okay, so it had taken a great deal of effort to detect that slight crack in the queen's armor, but she'd detected it nevertheless. She'd seen the shimmer of energy surrounding Aliette, seen how delicate the balance of her power truly was.

The Wood Queen was weak. Maybe even weaker than the alchemists suspected. Holding a full human glamour must be costing Aliette a crazy amount of juice; how was she doing it?

And that was when Donna's gaze fell on the purse strap looped over the Wood Queen's shoulder. The crack in Aliette's magic had opened wide enough to reveal the true nature of the purse.

Instead of looking at a leather strap, Donna found herself staring at a length of woven and knotted ivy and leaves forming a . . . belt. The Wood Queen's belt! She was wearing it as part of her glamour, disguising it as the shoulder strap of her human purse. *That's* how she was able to walk in the iron world and hold such an impressive glamour.

Donna's heart thumped hard enough to make her dizzy. She felt certain that the entire coffee shop could hear it, and for a moment it seemed as though the drumming of the Wood Queen's scarlet fingers on the tabletop matched the rhythm of her mounting excitement and horror.

Aliette met her gaze and, for a moment, Donna could see confusion clouding those wicked eyes.

"Give it to me!" Donna no longer cared if her voice carried. She was staring at the thing that could save her mother. She was absolutely certain of it. That belt held the key to her mother's sanity.

Aliette sneered. "Don't be silly. The belt is part of me—you cannot separate it from me, or me from it."

Donna licked her suddenly dry lips. "I could kill you," she said slowly. "I bet *that* would work."

She was surprised—and only a little shocked—to find that she meant it. Had death and violence become so commonplace to her? She wanted to regret her words, and the thoughts and feelings that lay behind them, but she'd be lying to herself if she said she was sorry.

Would she really try to murder another living being to save her mother? She was almost afraid to answer that question.

Luckily, she didn't have to. The Wood Queen was

tapping her fingers on the table again; it was like a nervous tick, and it made her seem even more disturbingly human. "You make empty threats, Donna Underwood. My death wouldn't serve you."

"Actually, Your *Majesty,* I think it would serve me pretty well."

Aliette smiled a particularly nasty smile and pulled the belt more tightly around her. "If you destroy me, then you destroy your mother."

Donna narrowed her eyes, trying to see through the queen's words as easily as she'd seen through her glamour. "You're lying."

"Don't be so quick to decide between truth and lies, child. You are not so good a judge as you seem to think."

"What does *that* mean?"

Aliette raised perfectly plucked brows. "Is it so hard to understand? I am not speaking in riddles."

"Says you," Donna muttered. She bit her lip and thought for a moment. "Okay then, let's try this. Will you answer a question for me?"

The queen's painted mouth quirked up at one corner. "Is that your question?"

Donna scowled. "No, of course not. But as a show of good faith, I want to know something."

"You may ask." Aliette arranged the sugar and cinnamon shakers into a neat line.

Taking a deep breath and plunging ahead before she could lose her nerve, Donna leaned forward. "Back in the Ironwood, and again just now, you kept trying to put doubts in my mind about the people in my life. About the Order. As though you know something I don't. I want to know what you're talking about—whether you're just playing with me, or whether there really is something I should know."

There, she'd said it. Her knees turned to liquid and she felt glad she was sitting down. Voicing her fears, especially to an enemy, was dangerous to the point of suicidal. Pandora's Box seemed to be a recurring theme in her life, and Donna wondered if she was ready to truly take the lid off and see all the evils that lurked inside.

But hadn't she already done that, just by being here?

The Wood Queen sat up straight and looked Donna in the eye. "Whether or not it is something you *should* know is another matter entirely, but I do not lie when I tell you that your precious magicians have kept important truths from you."

"But how do you even know that?"

The woman's painted brows rose in genuine surprise. "Because I have had dealings with the magicians for centuries. How else?"

Donna shivered, realizing how truly old the creature sitting before her was. It was sort of humbling.

She licked her lips, knowing that she wouldn't have the chance to ask questions in this way again—Aliette obviously wanted something from her, and Donna needed to use that to her advantage.

"You might have dealt with the Order for centuries, but their ranks changed over time. You act as though this is . . . personal. What aren't you telling me?"

"Perhaps their ranks have not changed so much as you think."

What? This was getting too weird, and Donna couldn't help but listen to the rising fear that urged, *go back while you still can.* But of course she pressed on. What else could she do?

The comforting sounds of cups clinking and milk being steamed brought her back to the room. She took a deep breath of the freshly ground coffee scent wafting over them from the nearby counter.

"Who exactly are you talking about? No more games. No more riddles."

Aliette's fake human eyes gleamed. "You persist in pretending that you don't know these things."

"But I *don't* know!" Donna glanced around nervously, aware that she'd practically shouted with frustration. She blew out a breath. "I really don't."

The queen shook her head, mockingly. "The Magus has you all well and truly in his thrall."

The Magus. Simon Gaunt. "You're saying that Simon has been around for . . . longer than it appears."

"Of course; since when is anything about the alchemists what it appears?" Aliette's tone was flint-hard. "The Archmaster's power weakens daily as his life trickles away, like the sand of human life does. Each grain a moment, a year. A life. The Magus continues and continues, never changing. Never dying."

Immortal. Simon was *immortal*. No wonder he was so furious about the loss of the elixir. He'd been using it for years. For centuries!

Donna frowned, leaning forward with interest despite her growing horror. "Why are you telling me this?"

Aliette's red-tipped hand gestured at nothing. "A token of my good will."

Donna snorted. "Right. You're a monster who feeds on the lives—the souls—of innocent humans. You've been doing it for centuries. Why should I believe anything you say to me?"

"Am I really so much worse than your precious alchemists? They deal in demon souls, I in human souls. We do what we must to survive—isn't that the way of all things, whichever world they live in?"

Donna's temples throbbed. "Demons? Now you're telling me that Simon is summoning *demons?*"

"Ah, if it were only as simple as mere summoning," Aliette said, a mysterious smile playing across her mouth.

"I don't believe you."

"Then you are even more naïve than I thought."

Donna's mind was whirling as fast as the tattoos across the backs of her hands. Her confusion, combined with the nauseating pain in her fingers, forced her to lean her head forward and focus on nothing more than getting through the next moment.

She took a slow breath, not wanting to see the almost feral interest on the queen's face. *Ask her something else—distract both yourself and her*, Donna thought. "Do demons even have souls?" she blurted out. It was the first thing that she could think of.

"Of course. All living things have a life force—a soul, for want of a better word. Your language is so limited . . ."

The desire to run rose up in her like a physical need. Some part of her begged her to do that very thing—right now: *push back your chair, stand up, and walk away.* Leave. Don't look back. Do not pass Go. Do not collect $200.

But she couldn't. Her shoulders slumped. She had to know the truth, and, no matter how much she wished things were different, she was pretty certain that Aliette knew something important. Something about her parents and about the alchemists, and about that terrible night in Ironwood Forest more than ten years ago.

Here goes nothing, Donna thought. "What happened to my parents; to Patrick and Rachel Underwood? You must have been there when my father died. What were we doing in the Ironwood in the first place?"

"You think it is so easy? That I will just solve your petty problems like . . . *that*." Aliette snapped her fingers right in front of Donna's face, making her jump.

"Why not?" She stuck out her chin and tried to look braver than she felt. "You know what happened; you must!"

The queen's face lit up with a horrible combination of triumph and cunning. "It is not *I* who has the answers that you seek, child. Your Maker can tell you everything you want to know."

Shaking her head with frustration, Donna felt like putting her gloved hands around the woman's throat. This was getting them nowhere fast, and Mom might not have much time. Xan had said the curse worked fast.

"Fine. Then what do you want from me?" she said. "Why did you even want to meet me in the first place—I don't believe you'd take the risk of exposure to the iron world just to drop mysterious hints and to screw with my head."

Aliette's glistening red lips spread into a gruesome smile. "Ah, so now we come to it." She tapped her fingers on the table.

"So? Just say it."

Tap tap.

Donna shifted in her seat and watched the queen's fingers tapping on the cracked table top. *Tap tap. Tap tap.*

She was about to explode when Aliette leaned forward.

"I want your power, little girl," she said, her voice dripping with a venom that left Donna breathless. "I want you to open the door to Faerie and send my kin back home."

"Home?" Donna repeated, feeling stupid.

"They are still dying. Two more, gone so quickly; I held them as their lives came to an end . . . as they slipped away into an eternally iron-sick existence. Wraiths, forever cursed to walk between realms." There was sadness—undeniable emotion—lingering beneath the queen's words. "You can help them; send them back home where we will no longer sicken and die. Open the door, send my people back to Faerie, and I'll return your mother's soul."

That was what this was all about?

"I don't know how to do that," Donna protested. "Opening the door to Faerie, I mean. You've made a mistake." Her heart sank as she thought of her mother's life slipping away.

"Really?" Green eyes glanced down at Donna's hands. "I wonder if you have discovered something else about your pretty markings, in recent days. They are changing, are they not?"

Shock was beginning to make Donna's head hurt. "How do you know about that?" There was no point in playing games—not with Mom's life literally hanging in the balance.

"How do you think I could send the changeling to you so easily? I felt the shift in your true power—I have been . . . waiting."

Shivering, Donna pressed back against the comfortingly *real* plastic chair. "You know what's happening to me?"

Aliette laughed; even in her human form, it carried

119

the sound of rustling leaves. "It is not something that 'happens' to you, girl. You are simply realizing the power that has always been there."

Donna shook her head, not sure what to say to that.

"You are the Iron Witch, are you not?"

None of this made sense, but if there was any hope for her mother, then she would grab it with both hands. No matter what the cost. And the alchemists had hardly proved themselves trustworthy. She had to make her own choices.

Clenching her fists in her lap, Donna locked eyes with the Wood Queen. "You're so sure that I can do what you need me to do?"

"Yes."

"But . . . I don't know how."

Aliette cocked her head in a disturbingly birdlike gesture. "Then find out, child. The Magus hides many secrets—I'm sure, if you give it some thought, you will uncover the information you'll need." Her expression turned unpleasant. "You are not without your resources, as we have already seen."

Donna ignored the jibe. She didn't doubt that Simon's laboratory held all kinds of esoteric knowledge, but a guide to her "true power," as the queen insisted on calling it? Opening doorways to other realms . . . was that even possible? If it was, she had to find out now—and quickly. Mom was running out of time, and Aliette's offer was tentative at best.

Donna knew better than to deal with this creature again, especially after the way things ended last time. But what else could she do?

Aliette gazed at her with those pitiless eyes. "Tick-tock."

And then she shifted her eyes downward, staring with undisguised delight at the elegant ivory watch that had just appeared on her bony, fake-human wrist. It was almost as though she'd never seen it before in her life—which she probably hadn't.

More magical tricks. *Tick-tock.*

"Stop that," Donna said, surprised at the strength in her voice. "If you thought I was capable of opening the gateway to Faerie—and if that's what the elves need in order to survive, to go home—why didn't you ask me that before? I mean, before you sent me for the elixir? We could have saved all this time . . ." *And I could have saved Mom from going through whatever she's suffering right now.*

The queen raised those ridiculously perfect brows again. "Back then, the elixir of life was the only solution I could see—I didn't know that your powers would emerge this late in your growth cycle."

Growth cycle? Donna let that go, but couldn't help finding the woman's choice of words interesting. "We don't know for sure that I even *have* these powers."

"There were signs that I have been looking for, and now I *am* certain." Aliette's tone allowed no room for argument.

"But why go to all the trouble of taking Navin, before? And Maker. You could have used my mother against me at any time you wanted."

The queen sneered, then flicked her wrist and a deck of playing cards appeared in her hand. She fanned them out with an impressive flourish. "Why play my strongest hand right away? Your mother was my insurance policy."

Biting back a scathing retort, Donna watched as her enemy made the cards dance between her crimson-tipped fingers.

Make your choice and then live with the consequences. That's what her mother had said, in the dream-that-was-not-a-dream.

Aliette snapped her fingers and the cards disappeared. She leaned forward and gripped Donna's gloved wrist. "If you agree to this, there will be no going back. Your mother cannot survive longer than two more nights."

Donna snatched her arm out of the queen's grasp. "But I still need to figure out this so-called ability of mine. That's not fair!"

"I seem to remember a similar conversation when we stood in the Elflands. Since when is life fair? What gives *you* the right to have life fall into place so perfectly?"

"I didn't mean that."

"It hardly matters what you mean. You're a child with too much power—power that you can't control." Aliette narrowed her venomous eyes. "But you will learn, and you will learn quickly."

"Or?" Donna made it a challenge.

"Or your mother will die; it is as simple as that. Once the curse has been set, it kills the human host within three nights."

Three nights. So the curse had been "cast" on Mom yesterday, which meant one night had already passed. Panic threatened to overwhelm her.

The queen placed her hands on the table, as though preparing to push back her chair and leave.

"Wait," Donna said. "If I agree, how does this work?"

"Tomorrow night, we will meet in the Ironwood and you will open the gateway so that my people can survive."

By then, the hearing would most likely be over—including the verdict. So maybe spending some more time at the Frost Estate wouldn't be such a bad thing after all . . . it could give her the opportunity to find a way past Aunt Paige and back into Simon's laboratory, where she could hopefully find out what she needed to know about opening the door to Faerie.

Donna met Aliette's unblinking gaze.

"Okay," she said. "Give me back my mom, and I'll do it. I'll help you."

Eight

Back at the Frost Estate, still shaking from her encounter with the Wood Queen, Donna knew she should head straight to the depressing Brown Room that Robert had taken her to yesterday. But she hesitated. She was early anyway, and she wanted to be alone to think. She'd always done her best thinking in Quentin's library—the Blue Room.

The alchemists were no doubt busy talking about her over their civilized lunch of sandwiches and gourmet coffee, so she only had to worry about running into the mansion's staff. Even if she *did* meet any of them while she was sneaking around, it was doubtful they'd care about what she was doing—it wasn't like they were employed as prison guards. There was a cook whom Donna knew she was unlikely to see, a housekeeper, and a couple of cleaning staff. Mrs. Lesniak, the housekeeper, had been with Quentin and Simon for as long as Donna could remember. She was a pleasant woman, though completely uninterested in children.

She made it to the Blue Room in a matter of minutes and breathed a sigh of relief. Pressing her ear to the door—and hearing nothing but the ticking of the grandfather clock that had caused so many problems two weeks ago—Donna slipped into the room. The door closed with a loud click, making her cringe as it echoed out into the corridor.

"Donna, how nice to see you," Quentin Frost's voice said from behind her.

Crap. She turned around slowly. Obviously, she wasn't the only one who wasn't hungry enough to spend time with the other alchemists.

Quentin was sitting in his favorite armchair with a large book on his lap. His silver hair glinted underneath the overhead lights, and his beard looked freshly trimmed. She realized that he was watching her, obviously still waiting for some kind of explanation.

"Archmaster," she began, wondering how she

was going to get out of this. "I just . . . um . . . needed a book."

The elderly man's eyebrows raised. "A legal volume, perhaps, to help you with something concerning the hearing?"

Donna's shoulders slumped. "I know. I'm sorry—I was just trying to delay the inevitable." Honesty was probably the best policy; at least, she hoped it was.

Quentin gestured at the couch placed at an angle near his armchair. "Won't you join me?"

Feeling nervous again, Donna sat on the very edge of the blue velvet and folded her gloved hands in front of her. She waited for Quentin to say whatever it was he was going to say. If he was about to tell her off for wandering around the estate when she was supposed to be on trial, there wasn't really much she could do about it. Except to feel grateful that it was just the two of them, perhaps; no Aunt Paige and no Simon.

Quentin placed his book on the rosewood coffee table, next to the elemental chess set that had always seemed so mysterious. Donna craned her neck to see what he'd been reading, and couldn't resist a smile when she saw that it was an ancient-looking copy of *The Count of Monte Cristo*. Typical Quentin reading material.

"I'm glad we ran into each other," he said. For a moment, Donna thought she saw a glimmer of the mischievous humor that the Archmaster occasionally displayed, but it was gone so quickly she couldn't be sure.

"It's nice to have an opportunity to talk to you without all the ceremony."

She wanted to agree, but thought it might be better to say nothing. She nodded carefully, wondering where he was going with this.

He smiled. "I knew you'd find your way here—I wanted to make sure it was me who caught you, not Simon or your aunt."

Donna's heart beat faster. She tried to sit still, but this was getting way more interesting than she'd thought it would be. "Why? Why wouldn't you let Simon have yet another excuse to call me insubordinate or a . . . a traitor?"

Quentin's face was serious, but she didn't think his expression was accusatory. "You're not a criminal, Donna. And I certainly don't believe you're a traitor."

Hope flickered to life inside her. "You don't?"

"Of course not. I know you love your aunt and care about the Order—as much as you can."

"What do you mean, 'as much as I can'?"

"You're seventeen years old—you're not even a legal adult yet. When you turn eighteen, you'll be expected to take up your parents' legacy and become an initiate. But . . ." His voice trailed off as he seemed to choose his words more carefully. "Don't you think I know how much you want to leave? And perhaps even go to a regular university? But of course, you know how difficult that would be. Times are changing out there in the world—don't think I'm not aware of that—but not so much here within the Order."

Donna's hope sputtered and died, but only because she could hear the unspoken subtext in his tone: he understood how she felt, but it wasn't likely she would ever get to choose her own life—her own path. Sure, he was being kind about it, but Quentin Frost was still the leader of the most powerful of the four alchemical Orders.

A dark thread of suspicion wove its way into her thoughts: *unless Quentin isn't really the leader.* Maybe in name, but now that she knew the truth about Simon Gaunt's power—his *immortality*—it was difficult to figure out the dynamics that she'd long taken for granted.

The old man watched her carefully as he rubbed an age-spotted hand across his beard. "Responsibility can be a heavy burden; I know that more than many people in this world. And yet...still...even with that weight on our shoulders, there are always choices."

Donna jerked upright in her seat. *Choices?* She immediately thought of her dream—and of the choice that she'd only just made. She wondered if Quentin could read the guilt on her face.

Anyway, when it came to the Order, surely she *didn't* have a choice in the direction of her life. Hadn't he just said that? Feeling confused, Donna wondered how best to approach this. She rarely got the chance to speak to the Archmaster alone; he was either in his small laboratory at the top of the house, or right here in the Blue Room reading, or in the quarters that he shared with Simon.

She bit her lip and wondered how much she could say to him. And then she just thought, *screw it.* What had happened to the Underwood spirit?

"Quentin, may I speak freely?" She couldn't help showing him respect; he was just about the only person within the Order that she *did* feel genuinely respectful toward.

He nodded, smiling slightly.

She leaned forward and tried to get her thoughts straight before speaking them aloud. Sometimes she rushed in and then had to backtrack; maybe she could do things differently this time. "I don't *really* have a choice in my future, do I? You know that better than I do."

"Since when have you lacked the power to make your own decisions?" His voice was firm, but still there was the echo of kindness in it.

"Aunt Paige has never made a secret of what is expected of me."

"Just because there are expectations of us doesn't mean we can't make our own choices." Quentin raised his brows and leaned forward in his chair. "Do you understand?"

Donna thought she was beginning to, but that didn't make this conversation any less . . . unexpected. "You're saying that I don't have to stay with the Order?"

"I'm saying that, even though all of us *want* you

to stay with the alchemists—even me, Donna, I won't pretend otherwise—you will still make your own choice in the end. We cannot keep you against your will."

She tried to focus on what Quentin was saying. "But if I have the freedom to choose, why has my aunt always told me that I *don't* have a choice? This doesn't make sense."

"Dear girl," Quentin replied, "you are far more intelligent than this. Don't you see what I'm saying? It is not up to me—or Paige or Simon or anyone else in the Order—to give you permission to make your own way in life. I think that's what you want to hear from me, but that permission is not mine to give. Once you're an adult, at least in the eyes of the law, you will be able to do whatever you think is right. That doesn't mean that the alchemists will agree with you, but perhaps that won't be something you think about."

"Of course I'll think about it!" Donna twisted her hands together, finally beginning to understand what the Archmaster was saying. It was a strange and disturbing conversation to have, but maybe it was one that she should have had with Aunt Paige a long time ago.

Quentin's smile was gentle, an old regret in his eyes. "You'll think about it—you may even feel guilty if you go against the future that we have mapped out for you—but that doesn't mean you absolutely can't defy the desires of the Order."

Donna slumped against the soft cushions and

wondered if she dared to do that: to defy the Order. She *did* understand what Quentin was saying, but that didn't make it any easier to contemplate following through on it. She had lived her whole life in the shadow of her parents' reputations. Patrick and Rachel Underwood were legendary in the history of the alchemists; she had even seen their names appear in a book of alchemical lore published several years ago. She'd found the volume among the many books lining the walls of the Blue Room and studied the sections that focused on recent history of the Order of the Dragon. It was clear that the Underwood name held very real significance—her father's ancestors were among the founding members of the Order.

Carrying on family tradition was important to the alchemists. It was maybe even the most important part of being born into a secret society—a society dedicated to finding and protecting the power of immortality while defending humanity from the fey throughout centuries of war. The war between the alchemists and the wood elves was a silent one—a *secret* one—but no less deadly for that.

Mulling over Quentin's words in her mind, Donna frowned. This could easily be the most significant conversation she'd ever had with him—she needed to make sure that she understood everything the Archmaster was really trying to tell her.

"Are you saying that I *should* follow my own path?" she asked.

He shrugged. "I can't tell you that, Donna, as much as you might wish it."

"But you're Archmaster. If anyone can give me that freedom it's you, right?"

"If I did that, child, I would be betraying everything I have devoted my life to."

Donna's stomach hurt. "But what makes me so important? I'm just one girl . . . surely the Order can go on without me. Surely you can let me go."

"It's not my place to do that." Quentin's face creased into familiar lines of thought. "My responsibilities are greater than you could ever imagine, and part of that responsibility is ensuring the survival of the Order. In an ideal world, you would be apprenticed to an alchemist and become a full initiate—a "moon sister", to use the ancient term—as soon as you graduate high school." He fixed her with his familiar bright eyes. "But, as you well know, we do not live in an ideal world."

Donna smiled as it dawned on her. He wasn't giving her permission to leave—he couldn't do that without going against his duty—but he was giving her permission to make her own decisions. That didn't mean things would be easier for her, because to leave the Order would mean a very real betrayal. At least, it would mean that to the alchemists, and certainly to her aunt and to people like Simon Gaunt. But if Quentin said she could choose, then perhaps that meant she could find the courage to do it; to go against everything she'd been brought up to believe her life would be.

The thought filled her with equal parts excitement and terror, but it gave her hope that there might be another path for her life.

"Of course," Quentin continued, and Donna immediately felt her heart sink, "we have invested more than just time and energy in your upbringing. Your tattoos—the magic that runs through your body, magic crafted by Maker as a result of his lifetime of work and experience—are the legacy that you will take forward with you on your journey through this life. What has been done cannot be undone."

Donna licked her lips and leaned toward the old alchemist once more. She knew he was telling her something important, but her mind was racing and it was difficult to think straight. "Legacy? Do you mean my strength?"

Quentin slowly shook his head. "Not just your physical strength. There is so much more that I could tell you, if it were . . . permitted."

"Whose permission do you need to tell me things, Quentin?" Donna was genuinely confused. "You can do anything you like."

Quentin released a sharp bark of laughter. "Ah, dear Donna, if only it were that simple." He chuckled again, shoulders shaking with the knowledge of something she didn't understand.

"Do you mean . . . Simon?" There, she'd said it. She'd asked him.

All trace of humor was wiped from Quentin's face; it was as though his laughter had never existed. "Simon is more powerful than you have been led to believe, that's certainly true. But I think you know that already."

And you're not answering my question, Donna thought, narrowing her eyes. Not really.

"But *you're* Archmaster, not Simon. No matter what he's capable of when it comes to the magic he can craft. Right?"

"Simon has more invested in the Order than you realize. I'm afraid I can't tell you more than that. But regardless"—Quentin leaned forward so that he could touch the back of Donna's gloved hand—"you don't have long to wait before you can make your own decisions. No matter what the consequences of those choices might be."

In other words, the shit will most definitely hit the fan if I try to leave the Order when I'm eighteen, Donna thought. She almost laughed, because Quentin wasn't really telling her anything she didn't know already. And yet, despite that, it had still been a strangely enlightening conversation.

"Anyway," Quentin said, withdrawing his hand and using the arms of the chair to push himself to his feet, "I should really get back to the others. Who knows *what* important matters they are debating over lunch." A wry smile crossed his face.

"Shouldn't you have been there all along?" Donna couldn't resist asking. "You know, *debating* with them?"

"They can do quite well without me for half an

hour," he replied, fixing her with a piercing look that Donna wasn't sure how to interpret. "The other Orders don't join us too often these days, so they probably got sidetracked into deciding on other matters before they even get to your . . . punishment."

Donna couldn't hold back a snort. "Nice to know they've got their priorities straight."

Quentin's mouth quirked behind his beard. "Of course, they're alchemists. Nothing is done without discussion and an agenda as long as my arm." He held up one of his arms, just to demonstrate quite how long that agenda might be.

"You've been hiding from them!" Donna accused, realizing it was true as soon as the words left her.

The Archmaster winked. "I have no idea what you mean."

Smiling now, she wondered if he would make her go with him.

As Quentin walked toward the door, he hesitated—a slowing of his step she almost missed, it was so brief—as he passed the beautifully carved grandfather clock against the wall. His hand brushed the front of the polished case, perhaps an unconscious gesture of affection. He took the final few steps to the door and stopped with his fingers resting on the brass handle.

"I trust you'll wait here until someone comes to collect you?" His back was to her, but Donna thought she saw his shoulders tighten.

"I will," she replied. Her eyes flickered to the grandfather clock. Aliette's words rang in her mind, as clearly as the chime of that clock when it struck the hour: *the Magus hides many secrets.*

Quentin turned around to face her again, almost as though he could read her thoughts. "There are enough books to keep you occupied in here," he said.

"Of course. You know how much I love it here."

Apparently satisfied, he opened the door and stopped in the doorway, turning to look at her once more. "Speaking of books," he said, "you might want to ask Paige about your mother's journal."

"Mom's . . . what?" Donna flushed, feeling her heart begin to race.

"Her journal," he repeated. "I know you've always kept one—you got that habit from her, you know."

She gripped her hands tightly together and forced herself to stay where she was. Why was he telling her this? And why now? "I didn't know that," she said, speaking slowly and trying to sound like she didn't have the urge to fly out of her seat and beg him to tell her everything he knew about Rachel Underwood.

"Yes," Quentin said, apparently unaware of the inner turmoil his words were causing. "Rachel filled pages and pages. I remember your aunt being particularly concerned about security, fearing your mother's diaries might be found one day."

Donna stared at Quentin as though she'd never seen

him before. *What the hell?* He was telling her something potentially huge here, right? But as she felt a spark of hope that something of her mother might have survived— something more than the shell of humanity left at the Institute, now in that hospital bed—the hope faded. Surely if Mom had kept journals, Aunt Paige would have disposed of them long ago.

Quentin stroked his beard and looked down at the floor, as though deep in thought. "You know, I remember Rachel was so worried that someone might read her journals, she took them to Maker and asked him to help her with a particularly powerful protective ward. I'm sure I'm not just imagining that." He crossed his arms and fixed Donna with his blue gaze. "But then again, I'm just an old man. My memory isn't what it used to be."

And before she could reply—before she could ask him anything else—he left the room and closed the door firmly behind him. Donna allowed herself to sink back against the squashy cushions of the couch. She tried not to let excitement carry her away.

Mom had kept a journal, just like her—and this journal might still exist, if Quentin was right. But if there really were diaries belonging to her mother, why hadn't Aunt Paige given them to her on her sixteenth birthday, when she'd given her Mom's other belongings? There was a trunk under Donna's bed, filled with her father's personal items and a few of Rachel's, too. But there had never been any journals. And Aunt Paige hadn't mentioned them—not even to tell her that maybe they were lost.

Donna suddenly had a strong mental image of her mother's red hair falling across her face as she leaned over a book, scribbling with an ornate fountain pen and filling the pages with looping handwriting that seemed at once familiar and strange.

But first she had to figure something out, somehow.

Donna let her gaze fall once more onto the grandfather clock that hid the secret entrance to Simon Gaunt's laboratory. Temptation was brewing dark and thick inside her, rather like the strong herbal tea Maker always gave her whenever she went to see him for check-ups on her tattoos.

This was her chance.

She wondered whether Simon had done something to protect the hidden catch that released the clock from the wall. She knew it would reveal a narrow doorway—a doorway that led to a long corridor under the grounds of the estate, all the way to the Magus' laboratory. Simon's lab contained ancient alchemical tools that she hadn't previously believed truly existed, despite her upbringing and education.

She stared at the grandfather clock and made a decision. Aliette had implied that answers might be found there . . . and, after all, hadn't Quentin said she could make her own choices?

He also said that I have to live with the consequences of those choices, she reminded herself firmly.

The words brought to mind those spoken by her mother in last night's dream—the dream that had seemed like more than a dream.

Donna knew that if she intended to uphold her bargain with the Wood Queen and save her mother, she needed to learn how to access abilities she wasn't even sure she possessed. "The Iron Witch"—that's what Aliette had called her. Was there *really* more to being an Iron Witch than magically forged tattoos that gave you super-human strength?

There was only one way to find out.

Nine

The corridor seemed to go on forever—and it was *cold*—but Donna reminded herself it wasn't like she hadn't been here before. The seemingly natural, mutlicolored gemstones that lined the damp stone walls shed enough light that she managed not to stumble as she headed for Simon's lab, growing more confident the closer she got.

She'd been prepared for the rotten egg-stink of sulphur this time, but that didn't make it any less unpleasant.

The door to the lab greeted her with its familiar, doom-laden plaque:

OUR WORK BEGINS
IN DARKNESS AND IN DEATH

She still couldn't understand why it had been so easy to open the clock and get all the way down the corridor. There was no way, after what had happened last time, that Simon wouldn't have added security. She hoped it was possible that he was so engrossed in the deliberations of the hearing that he simply hadn't noticed her tripping an invisible ward, although that was highly unlikely.

Frowning as she stepped into the laboratory, Donna looked nervously around. She scanned the shelves for signs of Simon's freaky alarm system, but she couldn't see the screaming bronze statue that had alerted the Magus of her and Xan's presence last time.

Slow Henry, the huge oven—or "athanor," as the alchemists called it—was puffing away to himself in the center of the room. There wasn't much about the ancient art of alchemy that was cute and fuzzy, but the giant furnace that served as the focal point of most alchemical experiments was given an affectionate nickname.

Donna shivered in the cool atmosphere and wrapped her arms around herself. She took a step back, toward the doorway, and hit something warm and solid—

"Hey, watch it!"

Spinning around, Donna came face to face with Navin.

"Oh my God, Nav!" She threw her arms around him in relief. "I thought someone had found me."

He held himself stiffly in her arms for a moment, before relaxing against her and resting his hands on her shoulders. "Someone *did* find you." He pushed her away so he could look at her, and his familiar grin brightened his whole face. "Me."

Donna wanted to cry with happiness. Not only was Navin here, not only was he hugging her back, but he was smiling at her—the first real smile she'd seen from him since the fallout after his rescue in the Ironwood. Here he was standing in front of her in his wonderfully familiar jacket, grinning from ear to ear.

In Simon's *lab*, of all places.

"Nav, what are you doing? How did you get down here?"

He looked mildly suprised. "I followed you, of course."

She hugged him again, checking that he was as real as he looked. She felt a rush of confidence with her friend at her side. *No more tears over Mom's condition*, Donna vowed; *no more dark thoughts about not having a mom.* She was going to save Rachel Underwood no matter what.

Pulling away, Donna suddenly noticed that Navin was looking at her like she was crazy.

"What?" she said, rather too defensively.

"Where were you just then, Don?" There was concern on his face now, a genuine concern born of the bond they shared. It wasn't the same sort of bond that she'd felt growing between herself and Xan, but it was no less important—and she'd certainly known Navin a lot longer than she'd known the mysterious Mr. Grayson . . .

"Sorry," Donna said, trying to focus on what was going on right here and now. *Simon's laboratory. Navin. Danger of discovery at any moment. Business as usual, really.* "I was just thinking about how cool it is to see you."

Navin ran a hand through his thick black hair and did the single-eyebrow-raise she'd grown so fond of. "Yeah? Well, most people don't stare off into space and drool when they're happy to see someone."

"Shut up, Sharma." Donna shoved him playfully, purposely doing it hard enough to make him stumble.

He grinned again. "I know you like attacking me—I can't blame you for not being able to restrain yourself. I am, after all, undeniably attractive—but could you go a little easy today? It's been a weird and screwed-up kind of weekend."

Donna was gasping with laughter at this point. "Are you asking me to be *gentle with you*?" She was hardly able to get the words out.

"Pretty much, yeah."

They looked at each other for a moment and then cracked up.

Donna tried to get herself back under control, reminding herself where they were. "Stop it, we have to be quiet. And what are you doing here, anyway?"

"I was looking for you. I gave Maker the slip and tried some of the public rooms—I saw the Blue Room on my way in today, which made me remember what you said about that grandfather clock."

Donna frowned. "I actually meant, what are you doing here at all? I thought your part in the hearing was over." She blushed, conscious of what he'd done for her. "Thank you, by the way. For testifying. When I saw you, I—"

"Was overcome by my total awesomeness?"

She rolled her eyes. "Something like that."

He bumped her shoulder with his, and that was all it took for her to feel that everything was right with the world. Despite the fact that it very clearly *wasn't*.

"So, you're here because . . . ?"

"Oh," he said. "I asked Maker if I could be here for the verdict. They don't know exactly when that will happen, so I get to stick around."

Donna almost cried with gratitude. "Really? You wanted to be here to support me?"

"Actually, I was kind of hoping to see you hauled off in handcuffs. Handcuffs are hot."

She didn't know whether to laugh or hit him. She decided to take the non-violent option, and it wasn't long before they were both giggling like little kids.

Then his expression turned serious again, his dark brown eyes offering the empathy she'd missed so much. "Hey, I'm sorry about your mom. How is she? I wanted to ask you yesterday, but I couldn't get anywhere near you. I tried to come see you, I really did."

"You did?" She tried not to look as dejected as she felt. "Nobody told me that."

Navin reached out and touched her cheek. "Of course I did. You really think I'd let a little bit of magic keep me away?"

Donna didn't know what to say to that. "Mom's in a coma," she blurted out. There would be no more secrets between them. "Xan says Mom's under an elf curse, which confirms what Maker suspected all along: that the Wood Queen must have a lock of Mom's hair. That's what the elves use to drain humans of their life force, but Xan says it's Aliette's way of keeping her people alive."

"Wait, slow down," Navin said. "Xan was at the hospital?"

"Yes, I needed him to tell me if there was fey magic involved with Mom's condition. With her sudden collapse, I mean."

Navin was nodding, but she couldn't help noticing the line that had appeared between his brows. "Right, of course. So, what can we do about it?"

And there it was: she'd only just vowed not to keep secrets from Navin, but now here she was, acting on the basis of a deal she'd struck with Aliette. A deal she hadn't told him about. *I'm not hiding it from him,* Donna told herself. *I'm protecting him—there's a difference.*

If the explanation felt hollow, she did her best to ignore the nagging doubts. She'd been so obsessed with finding a way to help Mom, she hadn't stopped to think about how Nav might feel about her spending time—by choice—with the Wood Queen. The same "woman" who had arranged his abduction and bargained with his life like it was nothing.

She swallowed her fear. Maybe she *could* try being honest with him without actually spilling her guts right there and then. "Will you trust me if I can't tell you everything right now?"

"Why can't you tell me?"

"I can," she said, quickly. "I will. When we're out of here—but we can't risk being found in Simon's lab."

Navin watched her face carefully as Donna's emotions swept across her features. He stepped forward and folded her into his arms again. Her head rested comfortably on his shoulder and she took in the familiar scent that she loved so much. The smell of his jacket; his hair gel; the faint aroma of Indian spices from his dad's cooking.

"I trust you, Underwood," he whispered into her hair.

"Thank you." Taking a deep breath, Donna pushed away from him and met his eyes. "I can do this. Tell me I can get through the next couple of days—please?"

He did the eyebrow thing again. "Of course you can.

And, whatever it is, you don't have to do it alone. You know that, right?"

She nodded, ever though she also knew that she wouldn't allow Navin to be hurt by the fey again. She'd rather have him hate her. "I know."

He looked around them at the seemingly random piles of alchemical paraphernalia, his eyes wide. It was as though he was finally noticing their surroundings, and Donna was relieved at his shift in focus.

"This place is different from Maker's." He made it a statement, but there was still the hint of a question behind the words.

"Maker is a different sort of alchemist. He didn't take the usual route—initiate, adept, alchemist, and then magus. He's descended from a mythological line of men and women who were talented with . . . making stuff." It was tough trying to explain something that she'd taken for granted all her life. "His magic comes from his ability to create almost anything from metal."

"Like your tattoos," Navin touched her arm to punctuate his words. "They're sort of alive, aren't they?"

"Sort of," she echoed, suddenly feeling uncomfortable having his attention back on her. "Come on, Simon's bound to be the one to find us."

"I think Simon's probably too wrapped up plotting your downfall to care," Navin said darkly, rolling his eyes. "Honestly, every time he opened his mouth yesterday I wanted to punch him."

Donna almost smiled at that. Nav didn't really believe in violence, but she appreciated the sentiment. "Welcome to my world."

He laughed. "What the hell has that guy got against you, anyway?"

"Oh, you mean apart from the fact that I lost his precious elixir?"

Navin's expression turned thoughtful as he leaned against the workbench behind him. "I know, but I don't think that's enough to explain the resentment he clearly has toward you. There's more to it than that."

Donna frowned. "It must have to do with my parents, but I don't know what it could be. Aunt Paige won't say a word against Simon, and I can hardly ask my mom."

Navin's face lit up. "Maybe not, but you might be able to find out from the journal that Quentin told you about."

"Maybe . . ." Donna's voice trailed off and she stared at him. "Wait a minute—how do you know about that? I only just found out myself!"

He smiled enigmatically. "You're not the only one with special powers."

Donna mock-glared at him, wishing she could do the eyebrow-raise trick. Now would be the perfect time.

Navin laughed, cutting her some slack. "I was listening outside the library door when Quentin was talking to you."

"You were? Didn't Quentin see you when he left?"

"I don't think so. But I kind of got the feeling he wouldn't care, even if he did."

Donna secretly agreed with him, especially the more she thought about her conversation with the Archmaster. Something about the way Quentin had looked at the clock before he left—and hadn't he *touched it*?—made her wonder if he'd been giving her another opportunity to look around in the lab. But that was crazy . . . wasn't it?

Then again, he *had* left her alone in the Blue Room, and he knew that Donna wasn't the sort of girl to just sit around waiting for the Order to summon her. She hated having to wait for things and, even more than that, she hated feeling powerless. It was a strange thing to feel when you had super-human strength, but there had been far too many times in her life when she'd been completely out of control and unable to make her own decisions.

Being able to punch a hole in a door didn't mean much when you had to follow orders all the time and your whole life was mapped out for you by people who thought they knew best.

She nodded in the direction of Simon Gaunt's main workbench, which was currently filled with jars of all shapes and sizes. The main feature was a long, narrow tube that wound around and around in half-circles, like a hollow glass snake.

"I think coming here again—to the lab—has helped me to confirm something, I suppose." Donna frowned, testing out the Wood Queen's claim by speaking it aloud. "About Simon and why the alchemists have hidden the truth about him. I was always brought up to believe he was just the secretary of the Order of the Dragon. It's an important role, but it's still an *administrative* role. Definitely nonmagical. Quentin's the Archmaster, so he should be the one with all the power, but I've seen his lab and it's nothing like this. It's more like . . . a hobby."

Navin frowned and looked at the equipment piled up on the bench. "So you think Simon's the one with the power."

"I know it," she said, not quite ready to admit to Nav that she'd had it confirmed by the Wood Queen. In person. "But it's weird. I mean, it doesn't make sense—why would Quentin go along with it? Why spend all these years pretending that Simon *isn't* a magus?"

"Maybe they only pretended for your benefit. It could be that the other alchemists know. Or, at least, the most important ones."

She bit her lip and thought for a moment. "That would make sense, except for the fact that Robert knows."

"Robert?"

"You know, the young alchemist wearing a lot of black. He was sitting with the representative from the Order of the Crow."

"Oh, right. Guyliner Guy."

Donna smiled. "That would be him. Robert's from

London, which is where the central power of the Order of the Crow is based. He's an adept, past the apprentice stage but he only just qualified. He's hardly someone that I'd expect to be aware of the really big secrets within the four Orders."

Navin was nodding, a serious look on his face. He said, "I think Guyliner Guy liked me."

Thinking this was a strange thing to be talking about at a time like this—even for Nav—Donna decided to humor him. Sort of. "Really? That's nice. Acceptance by the very people who call you a commoner and treat you like trash."

Surprise crossed Navin's face, no doubt at the venom in her tone. "No, I mean . . . I think he *liked* me." He slow-winked, and then grinned.

"I know, you already—" Donna stopped talking, finally getting it. "Oh! You mean he *liked* you."

"Definitely." He looked almost proud. "I'm attractive to both sexes, baby! I'm a metrosexual."

She snorted. "That is *so* not the right word." But she couldn't help smiling back at him. Shaking her head, she gave up on trying to get her friend to talk sense. In all honesty, she was just glad to have him back by her side—they were a team, and she hoped they always would be.

Navin, meanwhile, had crossed the laboratory and was rummaging through the paperwork on a cluttered workbench. "Maybe there's something here that will tell you more about Simon."

"There's bound to be lots of stuff that will tell me all kinds of things about him. The problem is, I don't really know what I'm looking for." *And it's not Simon I really want to find out about*, she thought guiltily. She needed to find evidence—information—anything to support what Aliette had told her about opening the door to Faerie. Only she hadn't actually told Nav about that. Yet.

He stretched up on tiptoe to a wooden shelf high above the bench and ran his hand along it.

Oh. Crap.

She had a sickening feeling of déjà vu.

Donna leapt toward Navin, cursing herself for letting him wander around and touch things without her sticking close by. It felt as if she was moving in slow motion; or maybe she was the one moving at regular speed and everything else around her had slowed down. Either way, it seemed to be taking forever for her to run from one side of the laboratory to the other.

She could see Navin reaching, trying to see what was on the shelf above his head. She felt her legs move and her arms reach out, even as she watched her friend's fingers touch the base of the bronze statue and move it to the very edge of the rough-hewn shelf.

The statue toppled and began to fall—

—and as it fell, it started screaming.

Ten

Donna had been here before, with Xan, but as the screaming bronze head tumbled toward Navin, she realized that the danger was even greater than being discovered: the lump of carved bronze was heavy enough to give Navin a concussion.

She reached him as the statue hit his outstretched arms—despite his shock, he'd managed to deflect the thing—and grabbed him. There was a clash of bodies as she tackled him to the ground and the statue landed beside them with a solid thump of metal on stone.

"Shit!" Navin gasped from his position sprawled on the cold floor, Donna on top of him. "Get off me, Underwood. You weigh a ton."

"Excuse *me*, I just saved your ass. Well, your head."

They both turned to look at the bronze carving. It was lying on its side on the stone floor beside them. It was staring right at them from hollow eyes. At least it had shut up when it hit the ground.

"Ugh. That thing is so creepy." Donna repressed a shudder.

Navin was busy climbing to his feet, reaching down to pull her with him. "I take it you've met before," he said dryly.

"Sort of." She dusted down her jeans and checked for damage. Apart from a faint throbbing coming from her hip, she was unhurt. "Are you okay?" It seemed Navin hadn't been so lucky; he was holding his left arm awkwardly.

"Smashed my elbow on the floor, but no permanent damage." He moved it gingerly, showing her that nothing was broken.

Donna gazed down at the statue. She remembered how they'd made it shut up before—Xan had stamped a heavily booted foot down on it, and that had seemed to do the trick.

Edging closer, she nudged it with the toe of her sneaker.

"Hey!" The voice sounded stretched thin somehow, like it was coming from somewhere far away. She remembered hearing it speak in answer to Simon's commands, and it creeped her out now just as much as it did back then. "Get your stinking feet off me," it said.

Navin's face drained of color. "Woah. Did that thing just say something?"

Donna raised her eybrows. "Why so surprised? You heard it scream on the way down."

He shook his head, gazing at the statue in horrified fascination. "I don't know. I guess I didn't really think the sound was coming from . . . it." He met her gaze, his eyes glittering wildly. "It's an 'it', right? It kind of looks like a *him*."

Donna shook her head. "I honestly have no idea what it is, but I suppose it does look like a man's face."

The statue had a hooked nose and a strong chin. Its head was carved with a strange hat—more like a skull-cap—that looked like it belonged in another century.

And this time, the horrible thing was actually *talking* to them. It was beyond freaky.

"What's the matter," the statue said. "Cat got your tongue?"

Its mouth didn't open when it spoke, but its strange voice was still coming from between the thin golden lips. Donna's stomach turned over when she realized that the only part of the bronze head that did move was its eyes.

She glared at it, refusing to be afraid of a lump of

metal. "I've just never heard a statue speak before." She felt vaguely ridiculous talking to a head on the floor, but this was the state of her life right now. She shouldn't really be surprised at the whole new level of crazy she'd just achieved. Perhaps it was something to be proud of, she thought, more than a little hysterically.

Navin crouched down next to the head. "Do you want me to put you back on the shelf?"

"Touch me and I'll scream for the Magus," it retorted. "Leave me right where I am, and he'll know his precious lab has been infiltrated."

Donna scowled. "Just pick it up, Nav."

"Oh, I like how it's *me* that has to touch it. You're the one wearing gloves . . ."

"And you just asked the damn thing if it wanted to go back on the shelf. What, were you volunteering *me* for the job?"

The statue cleared its throat. Or at least, Donna thought, if it *had* a throat that's what it sounded like it was doing. "If you would kindly stop talking about me as if I wasn't here and leave the laboratory, maybe I'll tell the Magus that I fell on my own."

Navin snorted. "Yeah, like I believe that."

"Believe what you want, young man," it said in an offended sort of tone. "I don't care one way or the other."

Donna sighed and bent down to grab the statue. She didn't give herself time to think; she just wanted the thing off the floor and back where it belonged. Even if it *was* going to tell Simon about his uninvited guests, there was something about the bronze head lying down there on its side that was sort of pathetic.

She scooped it up, ignoring the spluttered protests, and placed it on one of the shelves. She couldn't reach the top one, but managed to push it onto the wooden shelf below. Perhaps Simon wouldn't notice his magical alarm system had been disturbed.

Yeah, she could hope. Maybe she should brush the dust off the top shelf; there was bound to be a clean space where the head usually sat.

Just as she was wondering this, the statue fixed her with its sinister eyes. The dark and hollow spaces had deep-set, carved eyeballs with black pupils that flickered, almost as though they were projected onto the bronze by a camera set up opposite the shelf. She almost wanted to look over her shoulder, just to check—to see if this was some sort of elaborate trick—but she knew it was point-less. The eyes had moved while the head was lying on the floor, too, so there was no way it was anything other than what it seemed to be: a living bronze statue.

Of course, that didn't mean that was what it actually *was*, but that's certainly what it *seemed* like.

"Do you have a name?" Navin asked. He was looking less pale, much to Donna's relief.

"Of course I have a name. All spirits have names." There was no mistaking the offended tone of the statue's voice.

Donna couldn't keep the surprise out of her voice. "You're a spirit?"

"What did you think I was? A statue? A . . . *living statue*?" Spooky noises emitted from the bronze head, almost as though the stupid thing was laughing at her.

Donna scowled. "Well, you can hardly blame us. And last time we met, all you did was scream and bring Simon down here."

The statue sniffed. "That is my job. I'm the Magus' personal protection system for all his ridiculous experiments. Do you have any idea how demeaning my life has become? The only company I have—apart from Gaunt—is Slow Henry over there." The statue rolled its eyes. "And let me tell you, they don't call him Slow Henry for nothing."

Donna thought her brain might explode with the weirdness, but she tried to keep it together. "So, are you going to tell us your name?"

Navin's shoulder touched hers as he stepped nearer. Donna figured he was trying to protect her, and although she didn't exactly need his protection, she had to admit that it felt nice to have him close by.

The statue's eyes flicked between them, making a creepy clicking sound. "You may call me Newton."

"As in, Isaac Newton, the alchemist?" Donna almost laughed. "Please tell me you're being ironic."

"It's one of my best features," Newton replied. "Of course it's ironic, you stupid girl. I can't just give out my true name, because then Gaunt could trap me here forever. At least this way I still have a chance."

Nav rubbed a hand across his face. "And you're a spirit? What kind of spirit?"

Newton opened his eyes wide. "A *demon*. Oooh, scary!" If he could grin, Donna was sure that's what he'd be doing.

She also wondered when she'd started thinking of it as a "he."

Navin went quiet and just stared at her. The expression on his face clearly said, *Oh my God, what is going on, please tell me this is all a bad dream.*

Donna touched his arm in what she hoped was a reassuring gesture. She addressed the statue, trying to figure this out. "You're a demon? In a statue . . ." She didn't know much about the demons—apart from the fact that they existed. But they were in their own realm, she'd been told, just as the majority of the fey were safely locked away in Faerie. That's the way it worked. Humans in the Earth realm; the fey in Faerie; and demons in . . . Hell. There wasn't really a human name for the demons' true home, but sometimes Donna had seen it referred to in alchemical texts as the Otherworld—sort of a shamanic term, from what she understood, and many alchemists preferred that name to "Hell", which had too many Christian connotations.

Newton gave her an almost sympathetic look. "I realize this is difficult for your tiny human mind to comprehend, but this lump of ugly metal is merely a vessel. I'm a demon. Not a very important one, admittedly, but still . . . the Magus summoned me and trapped me here."

A wave of nausea washed over Donna, making her knees weak. Aliette's words shrieked in the back of her mind, but she tried to block them out. If it turned out that the Wood Queen was the only person actually telling her the truth about anything, she might start hyperventilating.

She shook her head. "No way! Even Simon, much as I can't stand him, wouldn't deal with demons." She was trying to convince herself as much as anyone else. *If it were only as simple as mere summoning*, Aliette had said.

Now it was Navin's turn to reassure her. His arm went around her shoulders as they stood talking to a bronze statue that claimed to be a trapped demon.

Newton's black eyes clicked. "If you want to deny the evidence of your own eyes, I wouldn't *dream* of getting in the way."

"But what does he want with you?"

"Power," the statue intoned. "What else is there?"

Donna was more than a little sick of finding herself stuck in the middle of complex power struggles. And it seemed the dynamic now involved three factions—until now, she'd believed the demons weren't contenders. Not *really*. Sure, they were the ones who'd set the Tithe that effectively kept all of the fey disenfranchised, but that wasn't exactly something that the alchemists worried about.

But Newton's presence here seemed to go a long way toward confirming the Wood Queen's sinister hints—which meant demons were part of the power games being played out in Ironbridge. *And who knows where else?*

Donna took a deep breath. She needed to concentrate—Newton could have information about opening the door to Faerie, or even about her own powers, if she could find a way to get it out of him. Out of it. *Whatever.*

Nav was glancing between the two of them, but for once seemed to lack something smart to say.

The statue's eyes drifted shut. "If that's all you got, you can leave me to catch forty winks. Don't slam the door on your way out, children."

"Wait," Donna said, stepping forward. "I have questions."

"Don't we all, dear," Newton mocked.

She let that go. "How long have you been here?"

Click. Eyes open again. "How long have *you* been here?" Newton asked.

Navin shifted behind her. "He's jerking you around, Don. We should just get the hell out while we still can."

"Nice," Newton said. "Get *you*, taking the mother country's name in vain."

Donna frowned at the bronze head. "Actually, I was being serious."

"So was I. How long I've been here is irrelevant. Get to the point."

Her stomach clenched. Newton was waiting for . . . something. She just needed to find the right question. She was sure of it. "The point? Okay, I'll get to the point. You listen to what goes on in here, right?"

If its face could sneer, that's exactly what it would be doing. "You call that getting to the point? I'll answer one question—*anything* to relieve the boredom, you understand—but I will only answer a good one."

Then it blinked twice. It was so creepy, but Donna resisted the visceral urge to retreat.

"Someone's coming," Newton added.

"What? Who?" Heart pounding, Donna looked behind her as though she half-expected to see Simon Gaunt standing right there, all smug and eager with his glasses steamed up.

"A crow. Flying toward you, little Underwood."

Navin's hand tightened on Donna's arm, and they looked at one another for a moment.

She grimaced. "He might mean Robert. They probably sent him to collect me from the Blue Room."

"Better get moving then, kids. Don't want to get caught out after curfew." The statue's voice had turned mocking again.

"Don, seriously . . ."

She waved him away. "Just another minute." She took another step forward, bringing her within inches of

Newton's cruel features. She gazed into the blank depths of those inhuman eyes. There was no time to think; no more time for anything but the question she was allowed to ask. She couldn't even worry about Navin hearing it.

Donna stripped off her left glove and held her hand in front of the statue's eyes. The magical silver wound lazily around her arm. This time, she didn't even notice that the tattoos had started moving.

"Apart from *these*," she said, clenching her fist to punctuate the words, "apart from these iron markings, what is it that makes me the Iron Witch?"

"Ah, a *good* question. At last." Newton sounded almost impressed.

Painfully aware of Nav's anxiety to leave, Donna did her best to tune him out. "Is it a question you're going to answer?"

"The answer you seek is already inside you."

Her heart sank like a stone. "What kind of Zen crap is that? Who do you think you are, *Yoda*?"

"I know what you want, and my answer stands: you have already activated your powers, girl. There's nothing more I can tell you."

Scowling, Donna turned away. "Come on, Nav. This is a waste of time."

He hesitated. "Should we just . . . leave it here like this? As Simon's slave? It's as trapped as we are."

"I can hardly fit him in my bag." Not that she would; that horrible thing had just played her for a fool.

Newton fluttered his eyelids. *Click, click.* "I promise to be very quiet."

"No," she said. "Absolutely no way."

And there *was* no way—she couldn't help a demon. Apart from it going against everything she'd been brought up to believe, demons couldn't be trusted. Everybody knew *that*. They lied. *It's a fact*, she reminded herself fiercely.

But then, so do alchemists, said a dark voice inside her as they ran from the room and headed back up the passageway. Behind her she heard that awful, grating voice offer one final message. She tried to close her ears to it, but the words were loud and clear—even above the sound of their pounding feet:

"There's a storm coming, little Underwood—can't you feel it?"

As her sneakers hit the hard-packed earth of the corridor's floor, another thought came to her, bright and clear and sharp as a blade: How had the statue—Newton, or whatever its real name was—managed to repeat almost the exact same words she'd heard her mother speak in a dream?

Eleven

Donna stared out of the car window at the little house she shared with her aunt. They'd moved here just over three years ago, and it was living here that had brought her and Navin together. On the one hand, she gave daily thanks for the serendipity that had led Paige Underwood to purchase the house next door to the Sharma family in an effort to blend in with ordinary people. On the other hand, it was hard to be thankful when all she'd managed to do was drag her best friend into a whole world of crazy.

From her spot in the back seat, Donna glanced in the rear-view mirror and caught Aunt Paige's relaxed expression. Navin was in the passenger seat—he'd called shotgun, much to her aunt's irritation and Donna's amusement.

They'd escaped from Simon's lab just in time, meeting Robert in the Blue Room the very moment Donna had clicked the grandfather clock back into place. The afternoon session that followed had been long and tense, and the alchemists still hadn't been able to reach a verdict —they wanted one more night to "sleep on it." Navin had been pleased that they would reconvene for a third day, because it meant he could get out of going to school on Monday.

She was glad Navin had been with her, down in the lab, when all her suspicions were confirmed. Yes, the Order of the Dragon had lied to her. Or at the very least, they'd twisted the truth and omitted facts, which led her to make wrong assumptions. *Very* wrong assumptions.

How could she have been so stupid? Donna wanted to kick her own ass for believing the party line she'd been fed for the past decade, but at the same time, she knew she had to start cutting herself some slack. Why *wouldn't* she have believed Aunt Paige all these years? This was her *family*. Shouldn't she be able to trust her?

Until very recently, Donna hadn't ever had a reason not to trust her aunt.

Back in the house, having said her goodbyes to Nav in the darkness that shadowed the sidewalk, Donna demanded that her phone be returned. She'd been without it ever since returning from the Ironwood, and she wanted to call Xan without worrying that Aunt Paige would listen on the extension.

Paige had actually tried to refuse. "How can I trust you with it?"

Trust. There was that word again. Donna resisted the urge to tell her aunt what she really thought, instead fixing her expression into one of calm acceptance. "I'm just processing everything, Aunt Paige. Give me a chance to prove to you that I can change."

Lying made her feel sick, but at least it got her phone back.

Not that it did much good—Xan wasn't answering his phone. He wasn't answering *either* of them; his cell went straight to voicemail, and his house phone just rang and rang.

Donna lay on her bed for a while, watching the glowing numbers on her digital alarm clock change. Her aunt had gone to bed, but there was no way Donna would be able to do the same. How could she possibly sleep? In a sudden rush of emo-drama, she wondered how she'd ever be able to sleep soundly again; too much had happened.

Too much needed to be fixed.

As her thoughts drifted back to her mother, Donna

remembered what Quentin had told her about Rachel keeping a journal. She pulled off her black gloves and stretched her fingers, trying not to look too closely at the silver spirals of iron branded into her pale flesh, and thought about her aunt. Paige was an organized woman, and most of her important documents were either locked in the family's safety deposit box at the bank, or kept in her study downstairs.

Donna knew that Aunt Paige had a steel box in the bottom drawer of her desk—she remembered seeing it a couple times and wondering about it. Once, when she'd been maybe eight or nine, she'd even asked what was in it. Paige had just said, "Treasure." Just the kind of thing you'd tell a curious little girl.

Biting her lip, Donna wondered if she dared to do what she was planning to do. Aunt Paige had no idea that she knew her mother's journal existed, so she would have had no real reason to hide them somewhere outside the house. In fact, if there was any kind of delicate information contained inside them, they were likely to be safer *here*, under magical protection.

Okay, she thought, making a decision and pushing down the inevitable guilt that rose up inside her. She was getting good at sneaking around. Maybe it was time to do a little more.

Donna had never entered the study when her aunt wasn't actually *in* it, and not because she was oh-so-respectful of Aunt Paige's privacy. Rather, it was because the room was protected by wards laid down and regularly boosted by alchemical incantation. Donna had learned this the hard way when she'd been much younger. It wasn't as though the wards, when tripped, actually hurt the person breaking in—it was more that the intruder became marked with indelible magical ink, kind of like the ink used by banks to protect large sums of money. Except the alchemical version was invisible to the human eye and didn't leave you splattered with bright, incriminating dye.

So, if she really *was* determined to do this—and she was—then Aunt Paige would know about it. She'd feel the ward break if she was awake, but perhaps her being asleep would buy Donna some time. Still, there would be no doubt about what had happened—Paige would be able to detect the evidence the minute she laid eyes on her.

Donna was surprised to find that she no longer cared. She wanted the truth: about the Order and about her parents. Maybe she would even find out what really happened that night in the Ironwood.

She stood outside the locked study door in the nighttime silence of the house, squeezing her hands into fists and gazing at the tattoos. As they wound their way from beneath her elbows to the tips of her slender finger, the iron markings flashed with their own inner light and power.

Just as she was beginning to wish she'd put her gloves

back on, that physical sensation hit her chest like a heavy blow. Donna stopped herself from crying out, then forced herself to wait out the discomfort. Once again, the feeling wasn't restricted to her hands and arms—the familiar pain she'd experienced occasionally over the years—but was something that radiated throughout her whole body. Something new.

When it was finally over, Donna effortlessly snapped open the locked door handle and stepped into Aunt Paige's office. She didn't allow herself to think about it. She'd spent way too long worrying about consequences, and not enough time taking action.

Things were about to change.

∞

Minutes later, Donna was sitting cross-legged on the floor of her aunt's study with the heavy metal box—sort of like a small trunk—in her lap.

She was surrounded by framed family photographs, faces from the past looking down on her from the walls and reminding her of her connection to something greater than herself. Family was so much . . . bigger than her current circumstances. That thread might be stretched tight, almost to breaking point, but it was still there, in the smiling eyes of Patrick and Rachel Underwood in happier times.

For a moment, she couldn't help feeling surprised

that Aunt Paige even kept them in here. But then, Patrick *had* been Paige's brother. Sometimes it was too easy to forget that.

Donna opened the lid and almost reverently lifted the soft emerald material that lay across the top of the contents. It was a huge swathe of cloth, made of the smoothest velvet she'd ever seen or felt. Her throat tightened as she wondered if this was something her mother had worn.

It was a long, old-fashioned dress, not something you could ever really wear in contemporary society—not unless you were going to a costume party, anyway—but it was still beautiful. Donna rubbed the material against her cheek and inhaled the scent of pine needles.

How strange, she thought, that it should smell of something so natural after all these years of being shut away in an iron trunk. She tried to remember her mother's scent, perhaps when Rachel had comforted her after a bad dream, but it was no good. Those memories were gone, and Donna was almost overcome with bitter-sharp sadness. The only scent she now associated with her mother was the acidic smell of disinfectant from the residential home.

And really, she didn't even have that—not with Mom hooked up to all that machinery in a stark white hospital room.

She couldn't help wondering what had possessed Aunt Paige to keep this remnant of the past. Maybe it had some special significance to her, or maybe she was more sentimental than Donna had thought.

Placing the silk-lined dress carefully to one side, she examined the rest of the contents. What she saw there brought any faith she might still have in her aunt crashing down. As something inside her crumbled, it was almost immediately replaced by a glowing shard of anger.

There was only one other item in the box.

With shaking hands, she grasped the leatherbound journal and stared at it for a full minute. She was afraid that if she moved, something would change and the journal would prove to be nothing more than illusion—like a fey glamour left behind to torture her with possibilities. Fool's gold.

A bitter laugh escaped her, and she swallowed the taste of betrayal.

Unwinding the thick cord binding the book, Donna opened the cover and gazed at the ornate frontispiece. She read words that she never thought she'd see, in handwriting she'd almost forgotten:

RACHEL UNDERWOOD'S JOURNAL:

In the event of my death or incapacity, please pass this book to my daughter, Donna. Thank you.

It was signed, simply, *Rachel*. The *R* was tall and curved, the kind of writing that was better suited to letter-writing from another century. She was surprised to feel warm tears fill her eyes. She hadn't seen her mother's handwriting for so long—she hadn't even been able to hold a coherent conversation with her for ten years. It felt like Rachel was somehow reaching out to her from the past.

Donna turned to the first page.

I am afraid.

Terrified . . . that's probably a better word for it, although even that doesn't come close to the constant state of dread I find myself in. Every day I wake with that suffocating black cloud pressing me into the bed. Every day, Patrick tells me I am making myself ill—that things within the Order aren't as bad as I fear.

But I know he's wrong.

The Order of the Dragon has become . . . sick. Rotten at its core. And what exactly is the core of our merry band of alchemists? More to the point, who is the core?

Not Quentin. Certainly not Paige—though she wishes it were otherwise.

No, the person destroying everything we've done is Simon Gaunt.

He's like a cancer, eating away at the heart of all that used to be good about the Order. The work we did once meant something—we protected people. Our ancestors built the iron bridge that stands guard at the entrance to the city. As the town grew up around the bridge, and expansion took humans way beyond the confines of the original boundaries, our role as protectors became more important than ever.

The wood elves waited in the Ironwood; waited for any slight slip that meant humans might fall through the cracks and enter the wrong part of the forest. They took their chances when they could.

But there's one important part of the current standoff that Simon seems intent on forgetting. Or, more likely, ignoring.

The wood elves stick to their territory. They are no longer as powerful as they once were. The iron world has all but stolen their ability to wear an elfskin strong enough to walk our streets undetected by people who know how to spot them.

People like us.

And yet Simon is intent on wiping them out. I've talked about this with Patrick time and time again. Yes, the dark elves are dangerous. Yes, they have hurt humans in the past, and many years ago they even killed alchemists in battle. I am not denying these truths.

But to destroy the Ironwood entirely, and to attempt to wipe the Elflands from the face of the earth—along with any other remaining fey—is surely nothing more than genocide.

Aren't we better than that?

I think Simon might be crazy, I really do. He will start another war, and it can't be permitted. It isn't right.

Even worse than all of this, though, is the chosen method, the weapon they have selected to aid them in the task of destruction. I have to protect Donna from Simon's plans for her. This isn't how things are supposed to be—she's just a child. There must be a way to get her to safety. I can't let them use my daughter as a weapon against any of the fey. Her abilities are so raw, so newly grown.

I heard Simon telling Quentin that Donna will be our "ticket to Faerie". I heard him, and I refuse to believe that I'm imagining things again. Now he talks not only of destroying the Elflands on the edge of our world, but of wanting to enter Faerie itself—and cause who knows what mischief.

And he intends to use my only child to do it.

Maker will know what to do—I must speak with him. But I have to find out for sure whether or not he's been compromised. If he has, then I don't know—

Twelve

"What do you think you're doing?"

Aunt Paige's voice was loud in the silent room, sounding like the sharp crack of an old tree branch breaking in the Ironwood.

Donna stood up quickly, ignoring the rush of blood to her head and clutching the journal to her chest. "I'm reading something you should have given me years ago."

Her mother's words echoed in her head: *war, genocide . . .*

Weapon.

She glared at her aunt. This was her mother's journal; that meant it belonged to *her*. Just the fact that it had been gathering dust in Aunt Paige's study was the worst kind of betrayal she could imagine. All of her fears—all the doubts that had been building in recent weeks—came crashing down on her.

The Wood Queen was right about so many things within the Order, no matter how sick it made Donna to admit it.

Her aunt's face flushed. "You would have gotten that on your eighteenth birthday."

"Says who?" Donna couldn't believe what she was hearing. "You're talking as though it's a bequest of some kind. Mom isn't dead, you know, much as you might wish she was."

Paige took a step back, all the color draining from her face in a single moment. "That's not true." Her voice shook. "That's a terrible thing to say."

Trying not to feel guilty, Donna lifted her chin in an unconscious gesture she'd inherited from her mother. "You might as well have her locked away in the attic so she can't shame the family and endanger whatever the hell your agenda is."

Her aunt was beginning to recover. "You're talking nonsense. Where have all these ideas come from? I can only assume it's that . . . creature filling your head with paranoid propaganda."

"*Creature*? Oh my God, what is *wrong* with you? Xan is a person! And he's not filling my head with anything, let alone 'propaganda.'" Her voice vibrated with barely repressed rage. "Xan doesn't have any contact with the fey—he's completely alone."

"That's what he told you, is it?"

"Don't you *dare* turn this into an attack on him. You're no better than the worst kind of racist!"

Aunt Paige folded her arms, gripping her elbows with white-knuckled hands. "That's ridiculous. If I were a racist, I wouldn't have been so happy that you found a good friend in Navin."

Donna snorted. "Oh, so I should be grateful that you decided it's okay for me to befriend a *commoner*."

"That's enough, young lady!"

"I'm just getting started." Donna sucked in a breath and prepared for battle. "Mom is lying in the hospital, in a *coma*, and nobody in the Order is doing anything to help her. I've been put on trial for saving Navin and Maker, and you've been hiding things from me for years."

"Hiding things?" Her aunt tossed dark hair out of her eyes. "What things have I hidden? You've always been a part of the Order—that's all we ever wanted for you. You're just too young to understand everything yet."

"How about the fact that my mother is under a curse?"

Paige hesitated for just a moment too long. "What

do you mean, a 'curse'? Has that boy been putting ideas in your head?"

"Stop doing that! Stop talking to me like I'm either seven years old or an idiot. This has nothing to do with Xan, and everything to do with the fact that you're hiding the truth. Mom is elf-cursed, so you might as well stop pretending you don't know that. I think you *want* her out of the way, and it suits you that she's getting worse."

"You have no evidence to support that," Paige replied stiffly.

Donna dug her shaking fingers into the journal's cover and waved it in her aunt's face. "What the hell do you call this, then?"

Aunt Paige's lips tightened momentarily and real anger flashed in her eyes. "The ravings of a mad woman."

"I knew it!" Taking a step back as though Paige had hit her, Donna knew things had gone too far. There was no going back now—maybe not ever—after a fight like this. "You've always hated her."

"Hated her?" Her aunt looked as though she might deny it, but then her shoulders straightened. "That's too strong a word, but I'll admit we never got along."

"You always pretended that you did, though; at least, while I was growing up. After the attack, I mean."

"Donna, it's more complicated than that . . ." Paige's voice trailed off. She was beginning to look as though she regretted opening up quite as much as she had.

"So explain it to me." Maybe she was actually going to learn something useful. Something *true*. "We have all night."

Her aunt's eyes slid away. "I have to go out. That's why I got up and found you here—in my study."

"Yes, looking at *my* things."

"Stop being childish. They belong to Rachel, and as you so rightly pointed out, your mother is still alive. Which doesn't make them yours yet."

Donna shook her head. "The diary says I'm to get it if she's 'incapacitated,' not just in the event of her death. She wrote that herself, and you ignored it."

Aunt Paige had no answer for that, so Donna continued on the offensive. It felt good to get some of this stuff *out there*.

"And where are you going this late at night, anyway?"

"I can't tell you that, darling." Paige's voice had softened again, but it sounded hollow to Donna now. Seeing the growing anger on her niece's face, Paige hastily added, "I *can* tell you that it has something to do with your mother. Quentin might have found a way to help her."

Donna almost laughed at that, feeling white-hot anger gather in her chest and welcoming it. "That's complete crap! Give me some fucking credit."

Her aunt's eyes widened; she'd probably never heard Donna curse before, but she did her best to hide her discomfort. "You're upset, that's understandable."

"Upset? I'm pissed off!" Donna yelled. "Aunt Paige, why can't you just tell me what you're hiding? Why are you putting me through this?"

"*Me*?" Paige's voice rose. "Young lady, you're out of line. Who was it who broke into Simon's lab and stole the most precious artifact we own? The result of centuries of study, the last remaining drops of the elixir, with no more forthcoming until the Order of the Crow rediscovers the Philosopher's Stone."

"I couldn't let them die!" Donna screamed, trying to get through to the woman even while she knew that screaming wouldn't achieve much with her super-logical aunt.

"You should have come to me. I still don't understand why you didn't do that in the first place . . ."

Feeling miserable, Donna pushed a handful of hair away from her burning face. "Because I didn't trust you. I mean, I didn't trust the *Order*," she added hastily, seeing the expression on Paige's face darken. "And, quite honestly, I'm beginning to realize that I might be onto something."

"There's a lot you don't know, I won't deny it; but we would have told you when the time was right."

"But who gets to decide that? The 'right time' for you might be too late for *me*. In fact, it already is. Far too late."

Her aunt leaned against the wall, shoulders slumped. "Your mother didn't want you to have the journal until you were older."

Donna tucked the precious book under one arm and took a step back. She felt unbearably hot—as though she was coming down with something. "More lies. Why wouldn't Mom want me to have it? And how could she have told you that, anyway? She lost her mind thanks to your precious Order. You're doing it again, Aunt Paige. Stop lying to me."

Two bright spots of color appeared on her aunt's normally smooth cheeks. "You go too far, Donna. I am *not* lying, and I certainly don't have to justify my actions to you."

"If you're not lying to me, Aunt Paige, then you must be lying to yourself."

"Don't patronize me. You forget yourself."

Donna raised her chin, feeling the anger that she'd held in for so long begin to expand throughout her whole body. "No, I think I'm finally beginning to remember myself."

Her aunt turned away, confusion and anger warring with something else in her expression—something that Donna couldn't quite name. "That's enough. You're still a minor and you are under my care whether you like it or not. Go to your room and perhaps we can talk about this in the morning. When you're more composed."

Donna gritted her teeth and tried to remember to breathe. "I'm sick of being composed. I want to know what you're hiding about my parents, and why Mom was so afraid of the Order."

Her aunt reached toward her, blazing eyes focused on the journal in Donna's arms.

Shocked that Aunt Paige looked as though she might be trying to snatch the book from her, Donna backpedalled, stumbling as she hit the heavy oak desk.

"Give it to me. Your mother wasn't well, even before the attack. You can't take everything in that diary as the truth you're so desperate for." Her voice cracked. "Trust me, please. You don't want to read the ravings of a mad woman."

"I can't believe you're saying that again," Donna whispered, trying to figure out if she was more angry than scared right now. She hoped so. Anger might be the only way through this nightmare. "Mom was driven mad by the Wood Queen. You know that's true, even if nobody can prove it. Quentin said as much to me when I was younger. He told me about the elflocks, and that they—"

Aunt Paige was shaking her head as she cut in. "It's not true, Donna. We tried to protect you from finding out about Rachel, about how sick she really was even before that night."

The ground seemed to tilt beneath her, and for a horrible moment Donna really thought she might collapse. "That's a lie!"

Eagerly, Paige pressed her advantage, taking another step toward her. "Why is it so hard to believe? Your mother was always . . . sensitive." Her lip curled, but the expression of distaste was fleeting, disappearing almost as quickly as it had appeared. "Especially with the way things were between her and Patrick."

"What? What do you mean?" Blood pounded in her ears, making it difficult for Donna to hear what her aunt was saying.

"I didn't want you to find out this way . . ." Aunt Paige's voice trailed off and, for a moment, the expression of regret looked genuine. "Your father wasn't the man you thought he was."

"You'd say anything right now," Donna replied, slowly circling backward around the desk, trying to keep the journal out of her aunt's reach. The door looked depressingly far away, so her only exit was the window behind her. She swallowed, wondering if she could throw it open and escape before Paige could grab her.

Squeezing her free hand into a fist, Donna felt so tempted to hit something it almost made her dizzy. Her eyes suddenly focused on her aunt's full length mirror, the one she used to check her appearance before holding meetings in her study.

Donna gasped at what she saw reflected there.

Her face was the color of the whitest paper, and her normally soft gray eyes—eyes that she'd inherited from her mother—were black. Donna had never seen herself looking quite so fierce. She almost didn't recognize the girl standing in front of her, and as she gazed at her reflection, the urge to smash . . . to destroy . . . hit her so hard she felt sick.

She had always been curious about what people meant when they said dramatic things like, "she finally snapped". She wondered if it really was like a rubber band snapping in two, releasing a furious storm all over whomever was unfortunate enough to be in the path of the onslaught.

But she didn't need to be curious anymore, because right then, Donna broke. All the confusion and doubt and fear, the loss and the anger, built to a crescendo inside her and . . . *snapped*.

As the dam collapsed, a tidal wave of power flooded through her.

"Donna, calm down!" Aunt Paige's voice was anything but calm, although Donna could only just make it out above the roaring in her ears. It was like listening to the ocean in a shell, only a thousand times louder.

All she could see was a bright glow of power that spread across her vision, seeming to fill the room with a light so bright that she thought her retinas might forever be scarred. Instinctively, she lifted her free hand to cover her face—to shield herself from the neverending white light that threatened to blind her—until she realized, with a bizarre sense of serenity, that the light couldn't hurt her because it wasn't coming from the outside. It was coming from *within her*. Her hands and arms were lit up like Christmas decorations, the glow so intense it made her eyes water.

More precisely, the light was radiating from the silver and iron tattoos that she could feel swirling around her wrists and arms, making her fingers tingle and her whole body vibrate with a power she didn't know she possessed. This wasn't merely the sort of power that made you physically strong enough to punch a school locker and crumple the metal like paper, or to snap a door handle with the flick of your wrist. It was more than that.

This was *real* power. It was more savage and yet more subtle, even though none of that made sense as it flashed through her adrenalized brain.

With her mother's journal still pressed under one arm, Donna allowed herself to look—really look, no matter how much it scared her—at what was going on with her arms and hands.

The tattoos *were* moving: shimmering and churning like silver waves against her barely visible skin, making patterns that she'd never seen before. It didn't hurt, not any more. In fact, it was beginning to feel undeniably good.

Donna smiled.

Her first and only coherent thought was, *Escape.*

Her second was, *Xan.*

And that was when the ground tilted beneath her feet and the world disappeared.

Thirteen

Donna found herself standing just outside the front door of Xan's house, at the foot of the stone steps, trying to figure out how the hell she'd gotten there.

Her next thought—one that came directly out of years of secrecy and that the alchemists would probably be proud of—was *Oh my God, did anyone see me?*

Xan's street was shrouded in early winter darkness, and the tall iron lamp on the sidewalk was flickering as though the bulb was ready to give out at any moment.

The cold air froze her burning cheeks, and Donna was glad for it.

She didn't know exactly what it was she'd done, but she was pretty certain it wouldn't have looked normal to anyone innocently walking by. Still clutching her mother's journal tightly, she tried to remember what happened.

Did *she* do this? It certainly hadn't been her aunt—Aunt Paige was an alchemist, sure, but real alchemy was more science than magic. It wasn't like you could cast a spell with instantaneous results. There was a crapload of research and experimentation in alchemy, then complicated ritual, followed by intent and focus. Those were the four stages of alchemical "magic," which were hardly consistent with most people's wrongheaded perceptions of the ancient art.

Donna's legs trembled and the bones in her hands and arms ached worse than they had in years. She bit her lip to keep from throwing up; the sudden wave of nausea took her by surprise. This remote travel had to be something to do with her new power, the abilities the Wood Queen had insisted she possessed. Power that her mother had hinted at in the pages of her journal.

As that thought hit her, Donna gratefully pressed the book to her chest, crossing her arms around it and hanging on as though it could protect her. *From the truth?*

She slowly became aware of a car driving up alongside her, but was unable to move—to hide. *To do something.*

With a burst of relief, she realized who it must be. Even in the dark, she could see that the car was a sturdy-looking Volvo with a badly faded crimson paint job. Even bent over and breathing hard, she could make out the familiar dents and rust spots.

And then Xan was there, a frown on his face that turned to surprise as soon as he figured out who was standing outside his house, looking like she was going to puke all over the steps. The timing of his arrival home was perfect, though she couldn't help wishing that her earlier calls hadn't gone unanswered.

She'd needed him tonight.

Donna watched as Xan's expression switched to concern. She knew what she must look like; how wild and panicked she seemed.

"Donna, what is it? Was it the trial? I'm sorry I didn't get your calls earlier, I—"

But he stopped talking when he really looked at her, standing shell-shocked under the flickering streetlight in the early hours of the morning.

She wanted to tell him. She wanted to tell him everything, to share the burden of all the awful things that had passed between her and Aunt Paige. And how could she even begin to explain how she'd gotten here? One minute in her aunt's study, the next . . . halfway across town. But the words wouldn't come. It was like something had frozen her, right there on Xan's doorstep. She looked down, suddenly conscious of the fact that she wasn't wearing a coat and that her tattoos were on display. No gloves.

She was so cold.

Xan rested his warm hand on her shoulder, drawing her into the house and closing the door behind them. His green eyes flashed brighter-than-human in the gloom of the hallway.

Donna wondered if her legs would hold her much longer. She wanted to lie down and sleep, maybe hide under a warm blanket and not come out for a very long time. Maybe not ever. She was horribly aware of the fact that she must look half-crazed, but she couldn't seem to move or speak. She realized that she was in shock, but knowing it and doing something about it were two entirely different things.

So she stood and shivered, with her arms a barrier across her stomach and her tattoos aching worse than ever.

Xan touched her cheek and she flinched.

He immediately pulled back, worry leaving a crease between his eyes that made him look much older. "You have to talk to me. I can't help if you don't tell me what happened. How did you get here? Did you take a cab? How long have you been standing outside, waiting? You must be freezing . . ."

Donna licked her lips and tried to speak. She felt like the heroine in a fairy-tale, struck dumb by magic and only able to regain her voice if she passed some kind of wicked test.

"It's all lies, Xan," she said. She was surprised to hear her voice so loud in the hallway. "All of it. My life, my parents . . ."

She shook her head, unable to go on. She could only gaze into Xan's eyes and hope he might be able to take away her pain. She felt like a coward, but right now that's what she wanted—someone else to carry the burden of truths she had finally begun to uncover. Being strong could only take you so far—she knew that now. Inner strength wasn't an infinite resource, and she felt worn down and stretched way too thin. An image of her mother's face as she lay in her hospital bed flashed into her mind, and Donna wondered if that was how she herself looked right now.

Except without the white streak, thank God.

Swallowing a hysterical laugh, Donna allowed Xan to lead her into the living room.

చం

"I don't want to talk, Xan," she said, hearing her voice as though it came from somewhere very far away. It reminded her, for a horrible moment, of the bronze statue's breathy voice. "I'm sick of talking."

As she said the words, she knew it was true. Talking at the hearing. Talking to Navin. Talking to her aunt.

It was all just *noise* and she'd had enough.

"Okay." There was no hesitation from him. "Whatever you need."

She didn't even want to *think*—especially not about how she'd gotten to Xan's in the first place. It was like she'd been so angry with Aunt Paige, so devastated and stripped bare, that something had loosened, deep inside, and then she's sort of . . . teleported. If this really had something to do with the abilities Aliette said she could tap into, she was seriously confused. What the hell did teleportation have to do with opening the door to Faerie? Nothing made sense.

Donna reached for Xan, conscious of how the flickering firelight caused her tattoos to glimmer and flash.

He pulled her into his arms and stroked her hair. He murmured nonsense in her ear and pressed her hard against the warmth of his body.

She waited for a moment, letting him offer much-needed comfort and basking in the intense heat that poured off him, reminding her again that he was *other*. If he were fully human, there was no way he would be that warm—not unless he was running a fever.

She lifted her head, knowing exactly what she was doing. She wanted to forget. Her whole being cried out for oblivion, but she'd never been someone who turned to drinking or drugs. She'd been taught too much about self-control over the years, due to the need to control her strength. Super-human strength on alcohol wasn't a pretty prospect.

Donna was sick of control. She wanted to let go—just this once—and be truly free.

So she kissed Xan, knowing that he wouldn't kiss *her* unless she made the first move. Not at a time like this; not when she was clearly devastated, even though he didn't understand why. He was too much of a good guy to take advantage of her pain and confusion. But luckily for her, she thought with a wicked grin that seemed to come from nowhere, he wasn't *too* good.

There was no hesitation from him. Xan moved warm hands to her face, his long fingers trailing fire as he explored her mouth with his.

They had only really kissed (not just the kisses for greeting or saying goodbye) once before. The night after they'd told each other their stories in Mildred's café, they'd shared a real kiss just outside Ironbridge Common. It had been new and exciting and filled with promise. But this . . . *this* was so much more.

Donna felt something open in her chest, like a bud unfurling in the face of the sun. She felt herself slowly coming alive under Xan's touch. Even though she still didn't understand how she'd suddenly traveled from her house to Xan's, or how it was linked to saving Mom, right now she didn't care.

Then Xan pulled away, and Donna grumbled at the loss of his warmth. He held her at arm's length, and she couldn't help being pleased to see how much he was struggling to control his breathing.

And she could relate—the guy knew how to *kiss*. She tried not to think about all the other things he undoubtedly knew how to do, or all the other girls he might have done them with. He was way more experienced than she was, and she was worried that would show.

"Donna, wait, we shouldn't—"

She cut him off by pulling free of his grip and placing the unmarked palms of her hands on either side of his face. "Shhh. I don't want to talk. I already told you that."

"Tell me what happened."

She shook her head. "Kiss me again."

Xan frowned, but she could tell he was torn. "I don't want you to do something you'll regret. You're upset . . ." His voice faded as she traced the fine lines of his cheekbones and stroked his caramel-colored hair back from his forehead.

"I'll be more upset if you don't shut up and kiss me." Donna could hardly believe what she was saying; it was like a different person was emerging from a dark cocoon. She'd been buttoned up so tight for so long, and it was incredibly liberating to be wild.

If only for one night.

Xan pulled her hands from his face and held them tightly. His golden flesh looked darker than ever against her pale skin and silver tattoos.

Donna couldn't help wondering if touching the iron hurt him at all—it had, once, the first time he'd touched her. But if he felt any discomfort she certainly couldn't detect it in his face, and his grip never faltered as he pulled her hands down to his chest and then wrapped them around his back.

"Xan," she whispered, pressing close and trying not to think about what she was doing, "make it go away, please. I don't even want to think."

His eyes drank her in as he stroked her tousled hair back from her hot face and examined her, as if looking for something that might be written on her skin.

Then he parted her lips gently with his, kissing her even more deeply than before.

Donna's mind went deliciously blank. She'd even stopped worrying about whether she was doing it right—she just followed his lead and let him guide her as the movement of his mouth against hers turned her stomach to hot liquid. Her knees trembled, and this time she knew it wasn't anger or fear or a need for comfort that made her hold onto him for support.

He pulled back, and she was about to protest when she realized he'd only done it so he could lift her into his arms. He cradled her against him and carried her upstairs. It was quite a change to allow someone *else* to be the strong one. It felt unbelievably good, and Donna never wanted it to end.

Xan kicked open the door of his bedroom and laid her on his bed, stumbling a little and throwing a black T-shirt and a crumpled towel onto the floor. He lay down beside her, his hip pressed against hers. Her body ached and she reached for him again.

He locked eyes with her. "There's no rush, okay?"

Donna ignored him and kissed him again, her stomach fluttering as he said her name against her mouth. Xan rolled onto his back and pulled her on top of him. Her hair tumbled around his face, but they didn't break lip contact and she gasped as his hands kneaded her lower back and pressed her against him.

And then he pushed her away, making her gasp, but before she could complain he gripped the hem of her shirt and pulled it up and over her head in one fluid movement. Everything went dark for a moment until Donna emerged from the material, her arms above her head, one hand still tangled in the shirt, her cheeks flushed. She didn't dare meet his eyes as a wave of shyness threatened to make her want to shrink back—all her so-called wildness and bravery trembling on the brink of something she couldn't put into words.

But it was a fleeting sensation. Xan grabbed her and flipped them again; this time he was on top, leaning his elbows on either side of her, supporting his weight as he began kissing her again. It was as if he could kiss her forever and it would be enough for him. There was a feeling of desperation in the intensity of his lips on hers, as though he was worried he might lose her if he broke contact for even a moment.

Donna thought she might explode from the heat building between them, but that didn't stop her from pressing even harder against him.

Xan suddenly stopped his exploration of her mouth, sitting back on his heels to look at her, and she stared up at him with wide eyes. He was so beautiful; it didn't seem fair that someone so gorgeous should have been through so much pain. She tried to push those thoughts aside— there was no place for them here, in this moment. It was like they'd entered a secret oasis away from all the horror of both their lives.

Xan's eyes never left hers and a slight smile tugged at the corner of his mouth.

Donna took a shuddering breath, feeling her heart beating crazily. "What?"

He shook his head, the hint of a smile spreading into something more real. His teeth flashed in the near-darkness. "Just thinking how unbelievably beautiful you look."

Her cheeks burned. "Stop it."

"No, I mean it." He grinned, quickly tugging off his own shirt and tossing it behind him.

Swallowing, Donna gazed at his chest and wondered if she was drooling. She couldn't tear her eyes from the almost ethereal glow of his skin.

Xan trailed warm fingers across her stomach and she tried not to worry about whether her tummy was sticking out too much. *Should I suck it in?*

He splayed a large, warm hand across her ribs with a strangely determined expression on his face, and his finger-tips brushed the edge of her bra. Of course, she thought with disgust, she just *had* to be wearing her oldest underwear today. It had been the first thing she'd grabbed this morning while dressing to meet the Wood Queen.

Was that really only this morning? She didn't want to think about it—not now, with Xan.

Donna wasn't sure what to do with herself. Just lie there? She desperately wanted to touch Xan, and yet her limbs felt impossibly heavy. She could quite easily stay there with his hands on her, unmoving and unthinking for the next few hours.

His voice was husky, "Come here."

Donna wanted to argue: *But I'm so comfy*. Still, who was she to argue? She took a deep breath against the sudden trembling in the pit of her stomach and wriggled into a sitting position beneath him.

"Look at me," Xan said.

"I am," she replied, still gazing at his chest.

"At my *face*, Donna." There was laughter in his voice, and that was all it took to break the unbearable tension she'd been feeling.

Swallowing a nervous giggle, she forced herself to meet his eyes. His pupils were huge; they'd almost swallowed the stunning green that marked him as something other than human.

"I want you so much," he said. There was no false seduction in his voice; all she could hear was the naked vulnerability that occasionally sneaked through when he was with her. "But we should wait."

Wait? What did he mean, *wait*? "But I'm ready now," she heard herself saying, her voice almost a whisper. "Xan—"

She stopped talking as he put his hands on her waist and shifted them both so that she was sitting on his lap, her legs wrapped around his hips. If this was his idea of cooling things off, she needed to have a serious talk with him.

"This isn't right," he continued, earnestly. "I don't want to take advantage of you, not when you're so upset. It's not the way I imagined it."

Fighting the slowly rising tide of disappointment and trying to focus on the positive, Donna touched his cheek. "You've imagined this?"

He laughed, golden cheeks flushing. "Of course I have. Shit, Donna. I may be a gentleman, but when it comes down to it, I'm still just a guy."

Warm laughter bubbled inside her chest, and the feeling of joy was so unfamiliar—so *shocking*—that for a moment Donna didn't even recognize it. She blinked back tears and threw her arms around him, squeezing Xan as tight as she dared and wishing that she could just stay here with him and never leave. She didn't want to think about the alchemists and the demons, or the Wood Queen, or even her mother. Not right now. Everybody she knew except Navin played games with her, made life-changing decisions *for* her, and it made her sick. It seemed as though all the people in her life spent their time manoeuvring various pieces around a giant chess board (like the games of alchemical chess that she'd watched Quentin and Simon playing, back when she was a child), and she herself was one of those pieces— nothing more than a bargaining chip or an expendable infantryman sent kicking and screaming to die for a cause she didn't even believe in.

Donna looked into Xan's eyes and saw her determined reflection gazing back. No, she wouldn't be the Order's weapon. Not for anything—or any*one*. Her mother's fears for her would *not* be realized. She was a person, not a thing, and only she had the right to decide how she would live her life.

Feeling the comfort of certainty slip into place, Donna took a deep breath and pressed her lips against Xan's. Here was something else she had the right to decide—who she wanted to be with, and when she was ready to take that step. She might only have known Xan for a few weeks, but she wanted to enjoy the fleeting moments of safety while she could.

Alexander Grayson might be many things, but he had never pushed her around or forced her to do anything that made her miserable. Sure, he had the whole other-wordly-guy-with-a-past thing down pretty well, but "mystery" did not automatically equal "dishonesty."

As that thought crossed her mind, Xan pulled away for a moment and smiled at her, understanding smoothing away the worried expression he'd been wearing ever since telling her that they should wait. Maybe he felt the shift in her, from emotional-wreck-seeking-comfort to someone who actually knew what she was doing and was making a choice based on love.

Love? Donna caught her breath as Xan gently pushed her back down against the pillows and stroked her face with fingertips that made her tingle all over. Did she love him? It wasn't as though *he'd* professed true love to her, although she knew he cared. Could she really feel something like that so soon?

She didn't know, but whatever this was—whatever this might one day be—the delicious sensations racing through her body, reminding her that she was alive, left her in no doubt that it was absolutely *right*.

But as Xan leaned down to kiss her again, that sense of rightness suddenly transformed into a gut-wrenching pain.

She doubled over gasping, holding her arms around herself as though she might be able to hold the pain still, keep it quiet so that it couldn't do any damage. It felt alive inside her. Donna didn't know how she knew that for sure, but the thought arose, unbidden, with cool certainty.

Xan's eyes were filled with shock and concern. "What's happening? Did I hurt you?" He grabbed her shoulders, frantic. "Is it me?"

You? she wanted to say, but the words wouldn't come out. How could it be anything to do with him?

She remembered that he didn't know about what had happened to her tonight, about the power that had brought her to his door when she'd simply thought of the place she'd most wanted to be. Maybe he thought she was having some kind of freaky reaction to making out with a half-fey guy, but she couldn't reassure him because there was no breath left in her body.

There was only light.

It was a different sort of light than the warm glow that had filled Xan at her mother's bedside. It was the same light she'd experienced in Aunt Paige's study—her tattoos became flashing silver beacons and moved across her arms so fast that her fingers went numb.

Xan was kneeling on the bed in front of her, clearly unsure whether or not he should touch her again. "Donna, your eyes!"

She reached out to him, half-blinding them both with the radiance from her hands. "It's okay—"

She didn't get to finish; she couldn't reassure him before she left him. There was no time. She barely had the presence of mind to grab Xan's discarded shirt before the power took her.

The earth moved—and not in the way she'd been hoping for—and her mind coalesced into a sharp point of need. Where did she *need* to be?

There was a moment of clarity, and then nothing.

Fourteen

This time Donna landed on her hands and knees, already heaving but having nothing in her stomach to bring up. She was relieved they hadn't gotten around to eating anything yet.

She was half-dressed (barely even that) and somewhere in the middle of Ironbridge Common—with no money, no cell phone, and no idea of how the hell she was going to get back to Xan's.

Crap.

And it was freezing.

Donna sighed with relief when she felt the material of Xan's black shirt clutched in her left hand. *Thank you, thank you,* she repeated to herself, not really sure who she was thanking but saying it anyway. Just in case.

She tried to stand up, but her head and stomach had something unpleasant to say about that. Whatever was happening to her, she had to see Maker—and fast. Except, of course, Maker seemed to be good at his own sort of disappearing act lately. She looked down at her tattoos, which were spinning crazily around her hands and arms, and she desperately wondered how she could hide them. She must look like she was holding two spitting, silver fireworks.

God, this was not going to be easy to explain to a late passerby, or, worse, one of the Common's night rangers.

The air was middle-of-the-night cold, and Donna pulled on the shirt while wishing her feet weren't bare. At least she still had her jeans on. She didn't even feel embarrassed, noticing that, so maybe she was finally getting over her stupid shyness about this kind of stuff. And making out with Xan hardly seemed important in the face of her current situation.

She managed to pull herself upright, taking deep breaths as she slowly took in her surroundings. She knew Ironbridge Common so well, surely it wouldn't be too difficult to figure out her exact location within it.

Because life can't possibly screw with me any more . . . right?

She was relieved to see the faint glow of what must be the stylized street lamps that lined the main paths through the center of the Common. If she could see them from here, at least that meant she wasn't too far from the most familiar, well-lit paths. Clenching her toes against the cold, damp grass, she began picking her way through the gloom.

She was almost to the nearest lamp when her foot hit something sharp. She cursed, hoping it was just a stone or something relatively harmless, but by the way her heel stung, she suspected she'd just stepped on glass.

Wincing, she tried to hop while keeping the lamp in view. She was going to have to reach the street somehow, find a cab, and get herself out of here.

And hope she didn't get mugged, or worse.

Just as she had that particularly cheerful thought, she saw movement ahead of her. Half-expecting Ivy to appear—it wasn't like things could get much worse—she tensed but kept going. There was someone waiting on the main path; someone tall was watching her approach.

She heard a familiar voice that almost made her break down there and then. "Donna!"

Xan burst into a run and within seconds was by her side, sweeping her into a bone-crushing hug and not letting go even when Donna gasped a protest. She could hardly breathe, but right at that moment she really didn't care.

"What happened?" He sounded frantic; it must have been terrifying for him to have her just . . . disappear like that. Literally in front of him. How would *she* have felt if things had happened the other way around? She would have thought some kind of dark magic had taken him away from her. She would have thought she'd lost him.

Donna shuddered and burrowed deeper into his embrace. She didn't want to think about losing Xan—not ever.

Finally, he pushed her away but still kept a death-grip on her upper arms. She wondered if she'd have bruises, tomorrow, but didn't have the heart to tell him he was hurting her.

Xan was actually trembling. She could feel it all the way through his body as he held her. "Donna . . ." His voice was raw, almost as though he'd been shouting and had exhausted it. "You have to tell me what the *fuck* is going on. Tell me you're okay, please . . ."

She couldn't hold back a sigh of relief when he finally released her, but she resisted the temptation to rub her arms. She didn't want to make him feel bad. "I'm okay, really. See?" She tried to stand up straight, but the pain in her right heel was pretty agonizing now.

He frowned. "You're hurt."

How did he know that? "It's just a scratch. I think I cut myself on a stone or something."

"Here," he said, ignoring her protests. "Sit down, let me see."

Xan led her to a nearby bench—one directly beneath one of the brightest lamps in the Common's central meeting point—and pressed her down onto it. He shrugged out of his coat and wrapped it around her shoulders, and Donna gratefully poked her arms through the way-too-big sleeves.

She would really rather be getting back to the house, but Xan wasn't going to budge until he'd seen where she'd been hurt.

"How did you find me?" It was uncanny, the way he'd reached her so quickly—especially considering the way she'd exited his bedroom.

For a moment, she thought Xan was going to avoid the question, but thankfully he met her eyes and nodded. It was as though he was confirming something to himself, or gathering the courage to tell the truth. "I haven't been entirely honest with you about some things, Donna," he said. He dropped his gaze and stopped, struggling to find the words. "I mean, it's nothing really bad—I promise—but there are things I can do that I've been hiding."

She tried to smile, despite how cold she was out here. "That seems to be going around."

His lips twitched, but his expression was bleak. "It's not that I don't trust you; I'm just so used to keeping my abilities hidden. And I swear I've been telling the truth about how limited they are . . ."

Donna touched his cheek. "But they're not quite so limited as you first let on? It's okay, I sort of figured that out. It's why I called you to the hospital to see my mom, you know. And then you started glowing."

This time he did smile, and it was like the sun chasing away black clouds. "Yeah, I can see how that might have made you wonder."

"And it's not like I haven't got some new things to tell you," she continued, thinking of Aliette with something like terror.

"That can wait," he said. "Let me see where you're hurt, then we'll get home."

But as soon as he reached for her foot, Donna saw the shimmer of something *other* appear, as though reality itself was twisting into something new. The disturbance was right in front of her; she could see the air ripple just beyond the curve of Xan's back.

He stopped moving, the warmth of his hand a pleasant tickle against her cold ankle. His eyes went wide and his face was rigid with a tension she didn't under-stand. He turned around slowly, and she could no longer see the expression on his face.

Ivy had returned.

Xan released her ankle and stood up with a jerk, totally unlike his usually fluid grace.

The fey girl approached, an almost-human expression

on her moon-stained face. If Donna had to describe it, she'd say it looked as if Ivy had seen a ghost.

Xan just stood there, staring. She still couldn't see his face, but his shoulders were tense under his gray sweater, and his back was completely rigid.

Sure, Ivy was sort of strange, but it wasn't like Xan was unfamiliar with strange.

"Xan," Donna said, wondering what was wrong with him. "This is—"

"Ivy," he breathed, his voice barely more than a whisper.

Donna looked from one to the other. "Wait, you know each other?"

Ivy's normally childlike expression was nowhere to be seen, replaced with an unknowable pain in the depths of her leaf-green eyes. "Alexander . . ."

Xan must have remembered how to move because he closed the distance between them instantly, standing within touching distance of her. "Ivy, you died—they told me you were dead! I looked for you, but I actually started to believe you'd really gone."

She shook her head, joy beginning to light up her whole face. "It wasn't a true death."

He frowned, nowhere near ready to believe. Donna sensed anger simmering beneath the surface of tentative hope. "What the hell does that mean?" Xan asked. "And if you weren't really dead, why didn't you tell me?" For a moment, Donna thought he'd been about to embrace the strange-looking being, but now he withdrew into himself, pain clouding his eyes. "I mourned you for almost a year."

Ivy hung her head, scattering leaves as she shuffled her feet. "I am sorry, Alexander. I couldn't tell you I was still alive. You must believe me—it was for your protection."

Xan shook his head, angry now. "Protection? You lied to me in the worst possible way. What was so bad that you couldn't have gotten word to me, sent me some kind of message?"

Donna gritted her teeth and tried not to think about what Ivy might have been to Xan. Then her exhausted mind made a connection and she realized that Ivy must have been the "mentor" that Xan had briefly told her about—the person who had taught him about his fey heritage when he was all alone with his confused dreams and memories—and who he had believed to be dead. Perhaps Ivy had also been his . . . what? His girlfriend?

Her heart felt like it weighed a ton.

Then Donna immediately felt like a total bitch for being so selfish; she was better than this. *Wasn't she?* Swallowing the painful tightness from her throat, she tentatively touched Xan's elbow. "What's going on?"

He didn't look at her. "That's what I want to know." He was still glaring at Ivy. "I'm waiting to find out why the only friend I ever had faked her death and lied to me for the last year."

The girl bounced with agitation, shedding leaves wildly as she tried to reach out to him. "No, it wasn't like that—"

Xan knocked her hand away. "Don't touch me."

"Alexander, please," she wailed. Her strange face was so expressive, and she made such a picture of perfect misery that Donna couldn't help feeling a pang of sympathy.

Xan's face went savage, his normally golden skin bleaching paler than Donna had ever seen it. His eyes spat green fire. "Forget it, Ivy. Seriously, don't come near me ever again."

The more angry he become, the more this strange creature scattered leaves and lost the human cast to her features. Beneath the glamour, Ivy's face looked sort of pointed and fox-like. She was pretty, but in an ethereal way that left no doubt as to her faery blood.

He glanced at Donna, and she saw the glint of unshed tears in his eyes. It made her feel a little better, to know that this uncharacteristic fury was hiding a deeper pain. "And leave Donna alone, too," he added. "If you screw with her I'll fucking kill you myself."

He spun away from them both, stalking to the edge of the pathway. When he reached the bench he gripped it with white-knuckled hands, bending as though trying to catch his breath after an exhausting run.

Donna stood frozen, feeling useless and horribly confused. She should go to him. She should go to Xan and comfort him, but her legs wouldn't move. What was wrong with her?

Ivy stood crying silently, silvery tears making bright tracks down her thin cheeks. "Donna Underwood," she whispered. "I only came to see if you had made progress on the queen's task before tomorrow night. I did not know you were friends with Alexander. Please, talk to him for me. Tell him I didn't have a choice. I—"

"Oh, just shut up." Donna was furious, but she knew her anger was more about her confusion than anything. She knew she'd feel terrible, later, for lashing out at the nearest target—Ivy—just because it was way too easy. But right now? Right now it felt pretty damn good. "Leave us alone." She slowly backed away, unable to tear her gaze from the girl's horrified expression.

Xan's voice shook her free of the sense of unreality that seemed to have taken hold of her. "Are you coming with me or not, Donna?"

Turning away from the now sobbing girl, Donna ran toward Xan. *Of course she was going with him.* What did he think—that she would leave him, too?

As they headed out of the Common, Xan with his head bowed and his hands stuffed into his jeans pockets, Donna fought the urge to take his arm.

Whatever had just happened, she couldn't stop the feeling of dread that was rising up from the pit of her stomach. Tonight, everything had changed between them—for the better, she'd believed just an hour ago. And now?

Now, that lingering thread of happiness had already turned to ash . . . just waiting to be blown away on the freezing winter breeze that cut her cheeks and made her eyes fill with tears.

And so it begins.

Today Donna proved, beyond all doubt, that she was born with the power that most alchemists would die trying to obtain.

It is her seventh birthday this weekend.

What are we going to do? Patrick has told me to wait—to trust that we can work something out with Quentin that will mean she'll live as normal a life as possible within the Order—but I don't trust Simon. That man isn't what Quentin believes him to be, I'm sure of it.

Either that, or our Archmaster knows something that we don't—and yet still doesn't believe it's something to be feared.

I grew up believing in Quentin Frost, but now he seems to stand in Simon's shadow. And Simon Gaunt's shadow is a dark and twisted place. If I'm certain of anything these days, it's that.

Patrick thinks I'm being over-emotional— letting my feelings take over, which I find too easy to do—but I know I'm right. Last week, when we were visiting the estate, the look that Simon gave Donna when he thought I wasn't watching . . . my skin crawls just thinking about it now.

It was the sort of look that would make an outsider feel uncomfortable to witness. But I am certain that the expression of . . . lust . . . in his hateful eyes was all about the power he thinks Donna might possess. She is nothing but a resource. Perhaps even a weapon.

Power is the only thing that matters to men like Simon Gaunt, especially power that is held by others. And a child like Donna is seen as an easy target to someone like him.

He will never, ever, use my daughter. I'll make sure of that, even if I can't convince Patrick that I'm right to fear the Order.

Fifteen

Simon called the room to order in his most pompous voice, causing Navin to catch her eye and smirk. Trying not to giggle, Donna was glad of the distraction. She was also incredibly relieved that he was allowed to attend the verdict. It was nice to have someone in the room who was genuinely on her side.

The moment of truth had finally arrived, and she knew she should be paying more attention, but she was exhausted after last night. Xan had fixed up her foot pretty well, and then driven her home at her insistence. As tempted as she'd been to stay out all night, perhaps to punish Aunt Paige, Donna had thought better of it.

Okay, if she were honest, she didn't really feel like staying with Xan after the revelation that he and Ivy knew each other. Clearly they'd been involved in some way beyond a mentor-student relationship, but really, she wasn't jealous. It wasn't that.

Not exactly. It had more to do with the fact that here they were, yet again, with something major that Xan hadn't told her about. Donna didn't think he had a duty to inform her of every past female friend or girlfriend, but considering his close connection with Ivy—and how he'd suffered after he thought she'd died—Donna did wonder that it hadn't rated more than a brief mention. She wasn't sure if he and Ivy had actually been *together*, but that wasn't the point.

At least, that's what she told herself.

It wasn't like she didn't have more important things to worry about right now. Apart from dealing with whatever the verdict was, she needed to find a way to use her weird new teleporting powers to open the door to Faerie. These two things really didn't seem related, but she only had the rest of the day to figure out how she was going to uphold her part of the bargain with Aliette—it was either that, or lose her mother forever.

Quentin nodded at Simon as he slowly stood up and faced the cramped room, the small space filled to bursting with the representatives from all four Orders. Simon rocked gently on the edge of his seat, almost as if he was preparing himself to jump up and object loudly if he didn't agree with the verdict.

Though, of course, he would already know what that verdict was. Donna's heart pounded as she tried to get Robert to look at her, wondering if she'd imagined the brief moment of camaraderie they'd shared in the Brown Room that first day. The young alchemist was busy shuffling through papers, however, and she watched curiously as he handed a few sheets to Miranda Backhouse. They didn't seem particularly engaged in the proceedings, but before Donna could try to figure out what they were doing, Quentin's voice made her sit up and listen, all her attention now focused on his lined face.

"The Order of the Dragon speaks for all the alchemists gathered in this room. Are you in agreement?"

A murmur of agreement passed from alchemist to alchemist, each representative nodding in response to the familiar words of ritual.

Quentin cleared his throat, keeping his gaze straight ahead. His expression was impossible to read. "As Archmaster of the Dragon alchemists, and as the duly appointed spokesperson of all gathered here today, it is my duty to give voice to the verdict reached by the representatives from the Orders of the Dragon, Crow, Lion, and Rose."

She sighed as Quentin listed her "crimes" against the

Order once more for the record. Donna tapped her foot and wished to be anywhere but here, wondering if her bizarre new abilities might choose this moment to whisk her off to some other place. No matter how scary and painful it was, even that might be preferable to *this*.

"It is the decision of this hearing that the pre-initiate, Donna Underwood, will be apprenticed to the Order of the Crow as soon as she has graduated from high school."

Donna couldn't stop herself; her legs propelled her to her feet even before her brain had fully engaged with what she was doing. "What? You're sending me to *London*?"

Her knees felt weak and her head had that horrible pins-and-needles feeling that meant she might be about to faint. Black dots swam before her eyes and she made a grab for the back of her chair to steady herself.

"Sit down, Donna," Aunt Paige said, her voice firm but not unkind.

Donna had the urge to give her aunt the finger, to scream at her and tell her that she didn't have to listen to her anymore. Not after the fight they'd had . . . the one that neither of them had mentioned. Yet.

She took a deep breath and looked desperately at Quentin. "But—"

Simon glared at her. "Show respect for the Archmaster and sit, young lady!"

Feeling sick, Donna wordlessly slid back into her seat. She hated doing anything that Simon told her to do, but she honestly thought she might fall over if she didn't sit down again. There'd be time to ask questions later— time to find out what the hell her aunt had agreed to on her behalf. But, *oh my God*, she thought, her mind racing with too many things at once. London? What were they doing? What about Xan?

And what about Nav? She looked up and found herself gazing into her best friend's brown eyes—eyes filled with growing shock and anger that mirrored her own. With an effort she dragged her gaze away and tried to focus on the rest of Quentin's words.

"Specifically, Donna will be apprenticed as an initiate, under the supervision of Miranda Backhouse, for a period of one year—to begin with. Miranda is in need of a new apprentice since the graduation to full adept of her previous charge, Robert Lee."

At this, Donna looked across the room to where the lanky young alchemist sat slouched next to Miranda.

"Donna will aid in the creation of a new Philosopher's Stone, so that the Order of the Crow can work on creating a fresh sample of the elixir." Quentin paused and met her shocked gaze. "This has been decreed and voted upon unanimously, and is deemed fair in light of the loss of our most precious commodity."

Her throat tightened and, although she was horrified at the thought of being effectively exiled, Donna also couldn't help wondering if this was . . . right. Maybe she *should* be the one to help create a new elixir. She had, after all, thrown away the last precious drops held by the Order of the Dragon. Okay, so she hadn't exactly known at the time that it had been the last remnants of the priceless elixir, but that wasn't the point. She'd been willing to risk everything that the alchemists had worked for centuries to protect, both from the population at large (in order to stop wars being fought between humans over the potential for immortality) and from the fey (who were becoming more interested in what little power the alchemists still held).

Quentin leaned heavily on the dragon-carved lectern. "Miranda Backhouse would like to say a few words."

The petite woman rose from her seat and began speaking, formal words filled with that quiet strength and power that Donna had noticed the first day of the hearing. She listened as Miranda outlined the program of study that would be devised for the newest initiate admitted to the ranks of the Order of the Crow.

Donna let herself imagine really going through with her sentence . . . which would mean traveling to London and working with this woman. Learning from her. Embracing the destiny that belonged to an Underwood born into the alchemists, and finally learning their true secrets. Because, in truth, she really didn't know more than a tiny percentage of all there was to discover about the possibilities for alchemy. She now understood the potential for corruption and lies—that much had become clear from her mom's journal—but surely it wasn't like that everywhere. Maybe the Order of the Crow was different, even honorable. Perhaps she could fulfil her parents' ideals in London, far away from Simon and the crumbling remains of the Order of the Dragon.

"And finally, I would like to extend an official and cordial welcome to Donna Underwood." Miranda turned to face her. "Although you will be joining us under difficult circumstances initially, we hope you'll learn to enjoy your time in London. I have much to teach you, and, if I'm honest, I am particularly excited to have the unexpected opportunity to work with such an intelligent young woman."

She stopped for a moment and smiled, a genuine expression that lit up her face. "It has been a long time since a moon sister was admitted to the Order of the Crow, and we in England have a long affinity with the more powerful of the female alchemists from previous centuries."

Donna found herself responding to this woman, trying to picture herself in a country so rich in the history of alchemy. If she could just find a way to open the door to Faerie and free her mother from the Wood Queen's power, maybe she really could get a fresh start.

But there was no way she could think about London now, not with so much at stake. Perhaps later . . .

Swallowing a wave of sadness, Donna noticed that Miranda was still looking directly at her.

"Donna, do you have anything to say?"

"Um . . ." She licked her lips as she felt all eyes in

the room come to rest on her. Sweat broke out on her forehead; she hated being the center of attention. "I don't think so."

Quentin raised his eyebrows. "Come now, Donna. I know this is a potentially uncomfortable situation, but it's also an opportunity. Surely you have something to say about the future we would like to see you embrace."

He made it sound like she had a choice, but Donna knew it was just Quentin being courteous—despite what he'd hinted at in the Blue Room yesterday. Sure, he'd said that ultimately Donna could choose her own destiny, but that didn't mean the Order would make it *easy* for her; in fact, they were making it as hard as possible, and would probably continue to do so for the rest of her life. And if she did manage to save Mom, could she then run off to England and leave her mother here with the Order of the Dragon? What would Mom really want for her?

Donna had never felt so alone.

Miranda had moved to stand directly in front of her, but oddly, Donna hadn't even noticed her move. She shook herself and looked up into the pleasant, softly lined face of this woman who could become someone important to her in the future—if she went along with the hearing's verdict and allowed the alchemists to send her away.

Exile. The word echoed loud and ugly in her mind.

Miranda Backhouse extended a hand and raised thin blonde brows at her, a half-smile curving her mouth into something inviting. "Will you join us in London, Donna?"

There it was again: the illusion of choice. It made Donna want to say something nasty and childish, but she found it difficult to be so ungracious in the face of Miranda's apparent friendliness and open acceptance of an apprentice who could turn out to be a troublemaker.

She took Miranda's hand and stood. The older woman kept her gloved hand in her own and had to look up, now, to meet Donna's eyes.

"Are you really giving me a choice?" Donna asked, pitching her voice so that everyone in the room would hear her. She was relieved that it didn't shake too much, despite the nervous jolt of adrenaline that shot through her.

Miranda's calm gaze didn't leave hers, though she did release her hand. "The choice is in whether you will embrace the opportunity for redemption that we offer."

Donna frowned, her heart beating faster as anger blossomed in her gut. "So there *is* no choice. Not really." She made it a statement.

Simon rose from his seat beside Quentin's. "The representative from the Order of the Crow asked you a question, Underwood. Do her the courtesy of a reply. You can whine about it later."

Quentin's eyes flashed a warning at his partner and Donna was surprised to see Simon sit back down, fuming quietly to himself. She filed that morsel away for future consideration; she really couldn't figure out Quentin and Simon's dynamic.

Swallowing, she did her best to ignore Simon's unfriendly gaze burning into her and instead turning to her aunt. "Did you agree to this?"

Aunt Paige tucked her dark hair behind her ears and pursed her lips. Her eyes flickered briefly to Quentin, but then met Donna's. "I abstained from the vote."

So Aunt Paige hadn't sold her out after all. Donna knew she should care more about that, but right now she found it hard to care about anything where her aunt was concerned. Not after last night.

She licked her lips and met Miranda's eyes. "All I can say, if you want me to be truthful, is that I'll think about it. I understand that I don't really have a choice, but at the same time . . ." Here she glanced at Quentin. "At the same time, I could choose to leave the Order entirely."

A murmur of unrest flowed among the gathered alchemists.

"I'm not saying that's what I'll do," she said, speaking fast. "I'm just saying that this is a lot to take in, and if you really expect me to 'embrace my destiny' and move to another country—even if it's only for a year—I need time to come to terms with it."

There, she thought. That sounded reasonable, and she wasn't committing herself either way.

Simon gave her a nasty smile. "Well, you might want to come to terms with it quickly—you'll be fast-tracked through graduation and begin your studies in England next month."

January! And what did he mean, "fast-tracked" through graduation? Could they even do that? Her shoulders slumped. Of course they could; they were alchemists, and they had money and power. Influence. She only had to take finals at her old high school anyway, and she had no doubt that those could be taken any time the Order chose.

And yet, as she watched understanding grow in Navin's dark eyes, mirroring her own uncertainty, she realized that she had barely a month left to make some of the most important decisions of her life. Decisions that could hardly be taken without her mother's advice and guidance—*if* Donna could get her back.

Time was running out. Just a few hours left to save her mom's soul, and despite the threat of exile hanging over her, she couldn't think about anything else right now. The only way to change things, as Donna had learned over the last few weeks, was to take matters into her own hands and *make* something happen.

Starting now.

Sixteen

Donna wasn't exactly proud of what she was doing, not to mention how undignified it was. Hanging around suspiciously in an ancient-looking bathroom at the Frost Estate, preparing to tear the metal grille from the tiny window, was far from where she imagined she'd end up today. But she'd picked this bathroom for her escape from the mansion specifically because it was in one of the oldest wings—it wasn't likely that anyone would be using it.

There was no way she could stay here a moment longer, despite the fact that she was supposed to be waiting for Aunt Paige to finish up some business with Quentin. Simon had insisted Donna wait in one of the guest bedrooms, well out of the way.

Anyone would think they don't trust me, she thought with a grim smile. If her aunt really believed that she was just going to wait around like a dutiful alchemist-in-training, she was in for a surprise.

Hadn't Aunt Paige figured it out? Last night really had changed everything between them. Their fight wasn't just a typical family argument, the ones that blow over the next day so that things can go back to normal. Nothing could ever go back to normal now, not as far as Donna was concerned.

"Crap," she muttered, almost slipping on the cracked plastic toilet seat. Nervously, she shot a quick glance over the top of the stall and was relieved to see that the bathroom was still empty.

She crouched on her precarious perch and grabbed the window ledge with both hands. Pushing her fingers through the wire bars of the grille, she pulled with as much strength as she dared. The teeth-rattling scraping made her cringe, but she kept pulling and easily removed the now-twisted metal from the frame. Screws popped and fell to the tile floor with a loud tinkling sound, and she wondered if it was realistic to think that nobody could hear the racket she was making. Stealth wasn't exactly her strong suit; but it would have been nice if she could have exercised a *little* of it, just this once.

She laid the mangled steel grate on top of the dusty toilet tank, careful to avoid the flush mechanism, and unconsciously brushed her gloved hands against her jeans.

The window opened inward, which she'd been careful to check before even attempting this, but the sun was high in the clear blue sky and it wouldn't be difficult for a casual passerby to notice a seventeen year old girl climbing out of a second-floor window round the west side of the estate.

Donna looked down. The drop didn't look too big, and it wasn't like she hadn't climbed out of windows before. *Yeah, because I'm such a daredevil*, she thought, pressing her lips together as a blast of icy wind hit her face. She scrambled to a crouch on the outside window ledge. Her back was bent so low she could feel the belt on her jeans digging into her stomach and, despite the cold, she wished she wasn't wearing her long gray winter coat.

Nevertheless, she had to get out of here, and all the regular exits were being watched—either by actual people or by remote viewing (the magical kind). If she could just get back to Xan's house, she could finally tell him about the Wood Queen's demands and see if he could help her figure out how to use her new abilities to do what Aliette wanted. Donna wasn't going to let Xan come *with* her to the Ironwood, not this time. She wasn't about to put a friend in danger again—not after what happened a few weeks ago with the elixir.

Research assistance and moral support, however, were things she was willing to ask him for.

Looking down again, she was relieved to see that the narrow path circling the house was empty. She took a deep breath as she sat on the window ledge, then grabbed the frame and slid down until the only things holding her entire weight were her magically enhanced hands. Her legs dangled out into space.

Donna gritted her teeth to keep from crying out in pain. She might be super strong, but that strength was only in her forearms and hands. Her shoulders? Not so much. Swinging from a scarily rotten window frame was all well and good in theory, but it felt as if her arms were about to be pulled out of their sockets.

She could probably jump down easily enough—it wasn't that far, really—but thinking about doing something and actually doing it were entirely different.

Why did it always seem so much more straightforward in movies?

Her shoulders were burning and her feet scrabbled for purchase against the wall. If anyone walked by now, it was all over. Finished. The alchemists would throw away the key. She didn't give herself any more time to think—she had to get to Xan, and to do that she had to let go.

She forced her fingers to open just as the window

frame started to splinter under her weight, and fell to the winter-hard ground like a stone.

❧

The afternoon was bright and clear, the air cold enough to freeze her breath. Donna blew out and watched the white mist slowly drift away. Just as she reached the end of Xan's street, filled with its impressive-looking townhouses, she felt that horribly familiar prickle at the back of her neck. Her intuition seemed to be getting sharper every day, and she wondered if it had something to do with her strange new ability to . . . teleport, or whatever the hell it was she was doing.

She glanced over her shoulder, and her heart lifted when she saw a young, dark-haired figure. Had Navin followed her from the Frost Estate?

But the tall figure striding after her wasn't Nav at all.

It was Robert Lee.

"Wait a sec, Donna, would you?"

He half ran to catch up to her, and she reluctantly slowed her pace. They stopped at the crosswalk in silence for an uncomfortable moment.

Donna didn't want the young alchemist to follow her to Xan's house, which meant she needed to lead him somewhere else. Which would waste precious time. Irritated, she shoved her hands into her pockets and glared up at him. "What?"

A grin spread across Robert's angular face, his lip ring glinting against his pale mouth. "That's all you have to say to me, after I oh-so-kindly didn't give you away to your aunt?"

"What do you mean?"

"I saw you making your daring escape from the mansion, all impressive and superhero-style."

Donna's stomach clenched and she half-expected to see more of the alchemists following Robert.

"Oh relax, I didn't tell them," he said airily. "You owe me."

She didn't know what to say to that. *What could he possibly have to gain from letting her off the hook?* "What do you want?" she asked, her voice filled with suspicion.

"You don't give your trust easily, do you?"

Way to state the obvious. Donna simply raised her eyebrows.

Robert shrugged. "So, are we just going to stand and admire the traffic all day—fascinating as that is, of course—or are we going somewhere? I could come with you."

Could he *be* any more annoying? "I have to meet . . . someone. Whatever you have to do with your oh-so-exciting life, have fun. I'll see you later. And don't worry, I'll tell my aunt that you successfully shadowed me."

She headed across the street, thankful that the cross-walk light had conveniently started counting down right at that moment. Perhaps Robert would get the message and leave her alone.

"You have some big cars over here, you know that?" he said conversationally, keeping pace with her easily as they hit the sidewalk on the other side.

Donna kept walking. There was no way she was going to tell him who she was meeting, but at the same time it was pretty obvious that Robert wasn't going anywhere. She sighed, making a wide circle back toward the Common.

Robert glanced at her. "Are you going to visit the hot boyfriend I've been hearing about?"

Donna's jaw clenched. "You think I need a guy to protect me?"

"No," he replied, his voice surprisingly reasonable. "I just thought you'd want to spend as much time as possible with him before getting shipped off to my side of the Atlantic."

She refused to let him bait her.

Robert seemed unfazed by her silence. "Seriously, is your boyfriend really a halfling?"

"Don't call him that." Donna kept walking, increasing her pace even as she knew she didn't have a hope of losing him.

"What, 'your boyfriend'?" Robert's grin was wicked, making him look sort of devilish. "Oh, you mean the 'halfling' thing. *Please*. Don't get all offended on me."

Shooting a glare his way, she turned into a side street,

hoping he'd lose interest if she took the long way around. "I'm not offended," she replied. "I just think you're being rude about someone you don't even know."

Robert shrugged easily. "Don't get your knickers in a twist. I'm the last person to throw stones."

His British accent sounded more posh when he was teasing, and Donna had the feeling that he was laughing at her in more ways than she understood. "I have no idea what you're talking about. Why don't you just run along back to Miranda?"

Robert spun around, walking backwards in front of her, so she had no choice but to slow down and look at him. He clutched at his heart and staggered dramatically. "You wound me with your scorn, madam! And how dare you not let me enjoy the massive chip on my shoulder."

She almost laughed, but stopped herself just in time. He was pretty funny—sometimes—when he wasn't being intensely annoying. In any case, he seemed to be thoroughly enjoying himself.

"It could have been much worse for me, of course," he added. "I was almost apprenticed to the Order of the *Rose*."

Rolling her eyes, Donna was relieved to see they were almost at the Common. Maybe she could finally lose him there.

Yeah, she could hope.

Robert seemed to be on a roll. "Can you imagine

how well that would've gone down? The oh-so-cultured Order of the Rose, saddled with the illegitimate, half-Chinese, gay son of one of the most notorious alchemists in recent history?"

Donna tried to hide her interest, but she couldn't help herself. "Really? Which alchemist?"

"I bare my soul to you—a complete stranger—in a transparent effort to gain your trust, and all you care about is who the notorious parent is? What about my race? My sexuality? My—"

"Questionable mental health?" she cut in smartly, feeling quite pleased to have actually shut him up for a moment.

"Are you saying I'm mad? Considering that you just climbed out a window, one could make the argument that there's only one crazy person here."

Donna stopped walking when they reached the edge of Ironbridge Common and glared at him. "Just when I decide you might be okay, you ruin it all by speaking."

"Sorry," he replied, his shoulders shaking with barely repressed laughter. "You're just too easy."

She crossed her arms. "Like you'd care about that."

"Ah, so the lady does have a sense of humor. I approve."

Sighing loudly, Donna waited for him to tell her why he was being such a pain in the ass.

"Look," Robert said. "You're probably wondering

why I bothered to follow you, if I'm not intending to turn you in."

"The thought *had* crossed my mind."

"I think I just wanted to make sure you're okay."

She smiled nastily. "Because you care *so much* about how I am? Why, Mr. Lee, I'm touched."

He nodded his approval. "You're mastering the fine art of sarcasm already. Wonderful. We'll soon have you baking scones and drinking tea with milk and two sugars, don't you worry." His expression shifted to something more sly. "You'll make an excellent apprentice for Miranda."

That was all it took for any good feelings that might have been building toward Robert to melt away. She felt like punching him, and had to remind herself that she really didn't know this guy at all—and he wasn't Navin, no matter how much he made her laugh.

They'd reached one of the many areas of the Common where trees were planted on both sides of the path, and Donna took a deep breath of cold air. Her companion had fallen silent—thankfully— and although she was tempted to just enjoy the reprieve, she also had questions that perhaps he'd be able to answer. As they emerged from the canopy of leaves, the bright winter sun emerged from behind a white cloud and Robert's cobalt-blue highlights stood out in stark contrast to the regular inky blackness of his hair.

He indicated a bench. "Will you sit with me for a minute?"

He actually wanted to talk? "I really have to be somewhere," Donna said stubbornly. "And I'm going there *alone*."

"Five minutes." His expression was sincere, and for the first time she saw that he looked tired. Not that she knew him or anything, but the dark circles under his eyes were unmistakeable.

"Well . . ."

"Please?"

It was the "please" that did it. "Okay, five minutes."

Maybe Robert really was okay, and maybe he wasn't; but it didn't matter either way, because she didn't intend to become friends with someone so closely tied to the alchemists.

He tucked his long hair behind his ears. "Listen, I know we don't know each other and you have absolutely no reason to trust me, but working with Miranda wouldn't be such a terrible fate—"

Her shoulders tightened and she had to resist the temptation to leap to her feet. "*That's* what you want to talk about? You really are just here to give me the sales pitch on the Order of the Crow? Classy."

He flushed. "No, it's not like that!"

"But that's exactly what it sounds like."

Robert leaned toward her, capturing her gaze with an intensity that surprised her. "I just think you might do better away from Ironbridge. *Far* away."

"And you know what's best for me, all of a sudden? We only just met."

"It's not so much about what's *best* for you, rather than what might be . . . worse for you."

She stood up, straightening her coat and fiddling with her gloves. "You're not making any sense. If you can't just spit it out and stop with the cryptic shit, forget it. Time's up."

A sudden wind moved like cold fingers through her hair and Donna spun to look behind them. Perhaps she'd been right all along about being followed, and it hadn't been Robert she sensed before.

Frowning, she carefully examined the groups of people walking through Ironbridge Common, wondering if any of them were wood elves wearing a glamour. It made sense that Aliette might have her monitored. Perhaps the queen wanted to ensure Donna kept her end of their bargain, although it did seem strange that she'd risk expending more of her power when she could just send Ivy to tail her.

Thinking of the strange fey girl filled Donna with a confusing mixture of curiosity and envy. She immediately gritted her teeth against jealousy. She would *not* get hung up on who Xan might have been with before her. That was ridiculous, and not at all like the kind of person she believed herself to be.

But you've never fallen for anyone before, argued a

plaintive voice inside her traitorous heart.

Robert touched her shoulder, making her jump. "What's wrong? You look like you've seen a ghost."

A ghost? She smiled, knowing the expression came out wrong even as her lips curved. "Not exactly." She tasted bitterness on her tongue and swallowed it away.

She would *not* be that person.

"I'm fine," she added, shaking herself free of both the dark mood and the lingering suspicion about being followed.

"Donna, I'm sorry I offended you earlier," Robert said quickly. "If you're annoyed with me about what I called your boyfriend—"

She cut him off. "Forget it." *Like you care, anyway.*

Robert's angular features twisted in what looked like genuine concern. "I wish you'd listen to me."

"But you're not *telling* me anything."

"Come to London. I'm not saying that because they told me to—I swear that's true. Just . . . think about it."

Donna shook her head. "Like I have a choice."

"Yeah, you do. You're more powerful than you think."

She looked at him, narrowing her eyes and trying to figure out just what the hell he knew. "I have to go."

"Think about it." All humor was gone, wiped out like he hadn't recently been laughing and joking about gorgeous half-fey boyfriends. "You can't trust the Order of the Dragon."

Tell me something I don't know, Donna thought. But all she said was, "I really have to go."

She turned and ran through the Common, all the way back the way they'd come. Back toward Xan's.

This time, Robert didn't follow her.

Seventeen

Donna tugged her steaming mug of coffee closer and watched Xan—who was shirtless—working in the open-plan kitchen. The dining room, where she was sitting at a huge oak table, was separated from the kitchen only by a low partition made of artistically arranged stone. Xan was turned away from her, and she could see the scars where his wings used to be standing out against the tanned skin of his back. His shoulders were wide and his waist narrow; he was ridiculously perfectly formed.

It was only those thick, rope-like scars that marred his beauty. At least, they would in the eyes of most people. Donna's lips twisted into a bitter smile as she glanced down at the silver tattoos covering her arms and the backs of her hands. She knew a little something about pain and scars.

She looked up and found Xan watching her, casually sexy in a pair of low-slung jeans and bare feet. He was holding a bag of bread in one hand.

"How many slices?"

The smell of eggs made her mouth water. "Four."

He did the single eyebrow-raise she'd always envied in Nav. "I like a woman with a healthy appetite."

She blushed, suddenly feeling self-conscious around him. This morning's verdict, along with her escape from the mansion and her conversation with Robert, had left her reeling. But now that she was back here with Xan, everything they'd shared last night came back in a rush. Of course, there was still the tiny matter of Ivy and what the changeling girl's past relationship with him might have been, but she could keep that worry in the background.

It wasn't like she didn't have more important things to stress about. For a start, she had to decide which bombshell to drop on Xan first. The fact that she was being sent to London? Or the whole deal-with-Aliette thing? *Ah, decisions . . .*

Normally, it would be pretty tough to concentrate

when faced with a shirtless Alexander Grayson, but right now the only thing on Donna's mind was saving Mom's life. Xan had proven that he knew a few things about faerie doors, and she needed to hear any ideas he might have about sending the wood elves home. And after everything he'd suffered at the hands of the wood elves, he deserved to know what she was planning.

She could only hope that he would understand her motives—that he would still help her.

Xan turned back to the gleaming, modern stove and reduced the heat on everything. Tossing the bread back onto the wide expanse of marble-topped counter, he padded over to the table and stood next to her chair, gazing down at her with warmth in his viridian-bright eyes.

"You're quiet," he said.

She smiled. "Maybe I'm just shy."

"You don't have to be shy around me, Donna." He extended both hands and smiled at her in return.

Donna clambered awkwardly out of the chair and let herself be drawn into the warm circle of his arms. Her head barely came to his shoulder. She breathed deeply of his pine scent, rubbing her cheek against his golden skin as he held her tightly against him.

She rested her hands on his lower back and looked up into his eyes. "Let's not talk about me for a minute." She gave him a cheeky grin that made her feel more confident. "Are *you* okay?"

"Best I've felt in years. In fact, I can't think of a better way to spend my birthday."

There was laughter in his voice and she pulled back to see if he was joking. "What? It's really your birthday?"

He lifted one shoulder in what she took to be a vaguely self-conscious shrug. "It really is."

That made him twenty. *Twenty!* Aunt Paige would kill her if she knew she'd almost spent the night with a twenty-year-old guy. Not that she cared what her aunt thought about anything—not anymore.

"Happy Birthday to me," whispered Xan, his breath hot and inviting against her face as he bent his head to hers.

Donna shivered with anticipation, but before she let his lips touch hers she put both hands on his chest and pushed him away. "Hold it right there, Mr. Grayson." She mock-glared at him. "Why didn't you tell me it was your birthday?"

He tried to grab her hands, but she sidestepped him and crossed her arms. "Seriously, I wish you'd told me."

His shoulders slumped and the teasing expression drained away. "I never celebrate my birthday. It's been a long time since I had anything to celebrate." His voice was flat, giving nothing away.

Donna bit her lip and watched him for a moment, almost able to breathe in his sorrow. "What about your parents? I mean, before they got divorced and your mom went back to England. They must have done things with you to, you know . . . celebrate and stuff."

Xan shoved his hands into the pockets of his jeans, pushing them even further down his hips. He watched her through the too-long bangs that she always had the urge to cut. "Yeah, but only when I was a kid. I haven't had a real birthday . . . thing . . . for the last four years."

"Oh." Donna found it hard to imagine not being fussed over for her birthday. Despite the sadness and loss in her own life, Aunt Paige had always made her feel special on her birthday.

He shrugged and turned back to the kitchen. His voice was muffled as he clattered the pan with the probably dried-out eggs onto a ceramic tile next to the stove. "This is the first time in a long while I've felt like there was some hope for the future, you know?"

Pain tightened Donna's chest. She wished she could forget all the panic and drama in her life—put it on hold just for one more day—and give Xan the best birthday he'd ever had. But she didn't have time. Mom didn't have time.

"Xan—"

There was a loud banging at the front door before she could continue, and she almost let loose a scream of surprise. *What an idiot*, she thought with disgust. She was so on edge it was ridiculous, jumping out of her skin at the first loud noise.

Xan was already heading for the hallway. "It's probably just some mail for Dad," he called back over his shoulder. "Stay in here though, just in case."

In case what? she thought, idly tracing lines in the sugar she'd spilled. She was trying not to think too much about Aliette and their agreeement, but she knew that she couldn't keep it from Xan for much longer.

He kicked the dining room door shut behind him and Donna was left in sudden solitude. The sound of the humming refrigerator was the only thing to break the silence as she waited for Xan to get rid of whoever was outside. Tapping her fingers against the smooth wooden table, she found herself more able to look at her tattoos without wincing. Either this was a total coincidence, or it was some kind of weird side effect of her new teleporting super power.

The door opened and Xan walked back in, his face shadowed with what looked like barely repressed annoyance. Donna pushed back her chair, eyes widening as soon as she saw why Xan looked so uncomfortable.

Navin Sharma walked into the room, his ever-present biker jacket in place and his hair untidy from the sharp wind outside.

His hands were pushed deep into the pockets of his jacket, and the tension in his shoulders was probably only visible to someone who knew him as well as she did.

"Hey, Don," he said, his voice steady and his dark brown eyes focused only on her. "What's up?"

જી

Now this, Donna thought, was what could only be described as uncomfortable.

The three of them had moved to the spacious living room, Donna and Navin sitting at opposite ends of the long couch and Xan slouched in an armchair, his long legs stretched out in front of him and his bare feet golden against the impractical white carpet. He had refused to put on a shirt and just sat there belligerently, looking all masculine and dangerous, a coiled anger sizzling below the surface of his deceptively calm exterior.

The testosterone in the air had almost singed her eyelashes as she'd given Navin an awkward hug and then curled up in the furthest corner of the couch. *And what had gotten into Xan?* Sighing, Donna wondered if she should take the bull by the horns and tell them *both* about her bargain with Aliette. Tell them at the same time and then make a run for it, perhaps? See how angry they got, and no doubt listen to them try to make decisions for her about what she should and shouldn't do.

Yeah, that seemed like the perfect plan.

It wasn't that they wouldn't understand her need to save Mom's life, of course, but that wouldn't keep them from worrying about her safety—not to mention the fact that, once again, she was dealing with the very beings who had tortured Xan in his childhood and kidnapped Nav just weeks ago.

Donna pulled down the cuffs of her sweater and smiled nervously at her best friend.

"I was worried about you," Navin said, refusing to even glance in Xan's direction. "Your aunt has come over to my house twice already, asking about you—since you just disappeared from the Estate."

Of course she has, Donna thought savagely. She wants to tell me more lies. Anything to keep me within the ranks of her precious alchemists.

Clearly wondering about her silence, Navin continued. "Dad and Nisha are getting suspicious—especially since I cut classes today to be at the verdict."

"You were at the Frost Estate?" Xan's voice was harsh and accusing.

To his credit, Navin didn't wilt under those twin emerald laser beams. "Sure. *Someone* had to be there for Don."

Oh great, Donna thought, cringing internally. *Thanks for that, Nav.*

Xan continued to glare. "Of course. Because they're far more likely to let the commoner trash in before they'll let the halfling trash cross their sacred threshold."

Navin ignored that and turned his attention back to Donna. "So you're okay?"

"I'm fine."

He glanced at the shirtless Xan and raised an eyebrow. "Yeah, I can see that."

Flushing, Donna scowled at him. "How did you know I'd be here, anyway?"

He just looked at her with an expression on his face that said, *Duh*.

Flustered, she bit her lip and wished that both guys would make more of an effort with each other—this was the third time they'd met, and she was especially surprised at Xan; he wasn't exactly helping the situation. He could be a little nicer to her best friend. There was an unpleasant, self-satisfied sort of expression on his face that was really starting to piss her off.

Men. Seriously, why did she even bother?

Donna forced herself to take a deep breath. *Calm*, she told herself. *Stay calm*. She couldn't risk doing that bizarro disappearing trick at the moment—too much needed to be done. She'd already figured out that extreme emotion seemed to trigger the teleporting.

Xan stood up. "So, I have to get going."

She stared at him. "You do?"

"Yeah, sorry. I forgot about something . . . somewhere I need to be."

But I have important things to tell you! Donna tried to communicate this with her eyes and her non-existent telepathy, but he wasn't even looking at her. He'd gone all shifty, and she didn't want to call him on it in front of Navin.

Which is exactly what he'd counted on. That much was obvious.

Watching as Xan gathered his things and shrugged into his long coat, she wondered where the hell he could be going in such a hurry. What could be so urgent that he'd leave her when she'd just been exiled and still had to rescue her mother? Not that he knew any of that, but he *did* know she had something she needed to talk to him about.

Donna swallowed, trying a different approach. "I thought we were going to do something for your birthday."

"I'd love to," he said. "Tonight would be great, if that's okay with you."

"Sure," she replied, trying to keep her tone as casual as his. Tonight she'd be in the Ironwood trying to open a door to another world, but she couldn't say that now—not when she didn't understand why he would just disappear on her like this. Was Xan angry about Nav being here? And did that really offer the guy she'd almost slept with last night an excuse for bailing *right now*?

Interesting that they'd met *Ivy* last night.

Donna was beginning to feel glad they'd gotten inter- rupted by her crazy new ability before things could go too far between them; she didn't want to rush into some- thing with Xan if it turned out that all her instincts about him were wrong. She sincerely hoped she was right about him, of course, but she wasn't so blinded by her growing feelings that she couldn't be more careful.

He was already at the door. "I'll call you later."

And then he was gone.

Mom needs me, she told herself fiercely. Nothing—and

nobody—was going to get in the way of that. Not her aunt and the rest of the alchemists, not a changeling girl called Ivy, and certainly not Xan's erratic behavior.

But first, she was going to tell Navin everything—no matter what it cost.

Eighteen

So, Donna thought, feeling vaguely sick. *That went well, all things considered.*

Navin's face was tight with barely repressed hurt and anger. She touched his arm and couldn't help feeling the sting of rejection when he shook her hand off, despite knowing that she deserved it.

She had relayed the story of her meeting with the Wood Queen, and now they were heading to Maker's workshop. Donna was desperate for answers, and she knew the old alchemist would have returned to his warehouse after the verdict. Maker never hung out with the other members of the Order, not if he could help it. She'd invited Navin to come along in the hopes that it would help convince him that she really *did* want to share the truth with him.

So far, things hadn't exactly gone well.

A muscle flickered in the smooth cinnamon skin of Navin's jaw. "What were you even doing with her? I can't believe you'd go for *coffee* with that . . . creature."

Panic tightened Donna's throat. *Here we go again*, she thought. Her connection with Navin blanced on a knife-edge. The very reason she'd lied to him about her life for three years—or at least, hidden the truth from him—was to protect him from potential danger and to preserve the blessed normality of their friendship.

She took a deep breath and tried to think calming thoughts. "Nav, I had to see her. It wasn't like we were hanging out—she didn't really give me a choice."

His dark eyes glittered. "There are always choices, Don."

"Okay, fine." Anger flashed through her, and that felt better than fear or outright panic. At the same time, she wondered whether she might do her brand new tele-porting trick if she got too angry.

Everything was a mess, and getting more screwed up with each passing moment.

She blew out a breath and unclenched her hands. "You're right, I *did* have a choice."

Navin stopped walking and raised his dark brows, looking at her closely for the first time since they'd left Xan's house. "Can we rewind just so I can hear that again? You're actually admitting I'm *right* about something? This is a huge moment in the history of our friendship, Underwood. I may need to make a note for posterity. I may even—"

"Shut up." She rolled her eyes, weak-kneed with relief that he was teasing her. "You're not right about much, but you are this time. I did choose to see Aliette, and I'm sorry you feel betrayed by that." She rushed on before he could say anything else. "But I might actually have a way to save my mom—how could I let that opportunity go?"

He nodded, his expression more relaxed but still serious. "I know, you already told me that. I guess you couldn't."

"You don't sound convinced . . ."

"She tried to kill me. She had a knife at my throat. She sent her pet aliens to abduct me then threw me in a pit in the forest. I thought she'd leave me there to starve—to rot, and nobody would ever know where I was. My dad . . . Nisha . . ."

His voice was almost too quiet to hear, but she detected the anguish in it.

"I'm sorry, Nav. So very sorry." She felt tears in her eyes and looked down at the sidewalk. "I've betrayed you."

"You haven't betrayed me. No need to get dramatic." He nudged her with his shoulder as he sat down on the graffiti-marked bench. There was only one other person waiting for the bus that went to the industrial park hiding Maker's workshop.

"It feels like that."

Navin touched her arm. "Seriously, I appreciate you telling me."

She tried to smile at him, but she knew the expression didn't reach her eyes. "Are you sure you're okay?"

"I'm getting there, Don. It's a lot to process, but I'm trying—that's the best I can promise for now." He stretched his legs out and slouched down further against the seat. "Are *you* okay?"

That was just like Navin, checking on *her* at a time like this.

"Sure. Just tired."

"And—?"

"And a little scared, I guess." She looked at him again, seeing the understanding on his face. "Okay, *a lot* scared."

Navin nodded solemnly. "Well, I'm not ashamed to admit that I'm absolutely terrified. Does that make me less manly in your eyes?"

She burst out laughing, relief flooding her whole body. "You'll always be manly to me," she replied through gasps of laughter.

And that was all it took, just that moment of typical

Sharma humor to break the ice and bring them back to something approaching normality. Donna felt about a hundred pounds of weight lift from her very stressed shoulders. But she still needed to find a safe place for him to wait after talking to Maker; she couldn't risk him interacting with the Wood Queen again.

"Me, Navin. You, Jane," he declared, beating his chest.

Worried that he might start doing a Tarzan war-cry right here on the street, Donna hit Navin on the arm (carefully) to shut him up. "Keep it down, Sharma," she said, though without much conviction.

"I'm not a Red Shirt, Don."

"What?" It wasn't often he surprised her.

He ducked his head. "I said I'm not a Red Shirt. You know, like in classic *Trek*."

She didn't know whether to laugh or cry. "Your alleged retro sense of cool is fast becoming Geek Central, buddy."

"Like I care about that," he muttered. "I just . . . look, I know I'm a liability, and I hate that. Okay?"

"No you're not! How can you even say that?"

"It's true, and we both know it. I don't have super-human strength, and I can't walk through doors that don't even exist." He held up a hand to stop her protest. "No, let me finish. I have to say this. I don't have fey magic or alchemical magic or any of that cool stuff. I hate the thought of being nothing but cannon fodder.

You know what I'm talking about—I've made you watch enough *Star Trek* episodes."

"That's true," she replied, trying not to look like she found Captain Kirk hopeless rather than hot.

"I don't want to be the one who's always at risk on a mission, you know?" One corner of his mouth lifted in a tiny smile. "Especially when faced with green-skinned aliens."

"They're not aliens, and none of this matters anyway, because you're not coming with me to the Ironwood. Just to Maker's, okay?"

She hadn't known this was how Navin felt, but it explained a lot about why he kept his distance after they got back from the Elflands. Maybe it had more to do with how he thought about his role in her life, rather than because of the trauma she'd imagined he'd suffered at the hands of the dark elves.

"And it's not like you'll need me on future missions, anyway. Not now that you've got Xan as your new co-pilot."

"Do you see Xan anywhere here right now?" Donna's voice came out more sharply than she'd intended.

"True. He disappeared pretty fast, didn't he?" Navin leaned toward her with a conspiratorial wink. "I think he's scared of me."

Donna smiled but said nothing.

"So, what else aren't you telling me?"

The smile dropped from her face. "Um . . ."

"I know you, Underwood. You forget how well, what with your new boyfriend being on the scene all tall and floppy-haired."

She really didn't want to think about Xan any more. "Something else *has* been going on that I should probably tell you about."

He nodded. "With the Shirtless Wonder?"

"No, I mean with me! With these." She held out her arms.

"Oh." A strange expression crossed his face. "Okay, spill. You got a new tattoo somewhere . . . *interesting*?"

She bumped his shoulder with hers and saw the bus approaching. "You wish. I'll tell you about it on the bus—move it, Sharma."

As they stood and waited for the doors to hiss open and take them to Maker's workshop-disguised-as-a-warehouse, Donna wondered how many more discoveries she could take. It had been the longest few days of her life, and even now it wasn't over.

Not even close.

∽

Maker opened the door and squinted up at them from his wheelchair. "Well, don't just stand there. The two of you had better come in."

They looked at each other for a moment, and Navin let out an audible breath. "Now or never, right?"

Donna smiled. "Right."

"Carpe Diem!"

She was glad that Maker had already gone back inside. "You're on a roll with the clichés today, aren't you?"

Navin shrugged. "In for a penny, in for a pound. Who knows what the heck we're going to find out in here. Might as well throw in a few clichés for good luck. You always know where you are with a good cliché."

Shaking her head, Donna followed Maker into the workshop.

They soon found themselves perched on high-backed chairs pulled up to the central workbench. The surface of the desk was usually covered in all sorts of crazy-looking paraphernalia, but for once it seemed relatively empty. There was a large sketchbook and pieces of graphite, but not much else that Maker appeared to be working on. This was a nuts-and-bolts, get-your-hands-dirty, *practical* workshop. There was so much scrap metal piled up against the walls that Donna half expected to see an ancient car, its bodywork in need of a paint job and its engine stripped.

She jiggled her neck from side to side, trying to release knots of tension that were a near-permanent feature. She briefly wondered if it might be possible for her neck to seize up entirely. She glanced across at Navin and realized he'd been watching her as she tried to get comfortable. He flashed her an encouraging smile.

Maker rolled out of the little corridor off the main room, sitting upright in the sleek wheelchair that looked like it belonged in a science fiction movie and carrying a tray of mugs on his lap. It was just like the old alchemist to refuse to have any sort of discussion without refreshments. Maker had always said that a hot drink could solve most problems—Donna had heard that many times throughout the endless months of her rehabilitation—but she was pretty certain even Maker's famous herbal tea had met its match today.

The clatter of metallic wings jolted her out of her thoughts, and Navin's sharp intake of breath reminded her that there was more to Maker's workshop than just the old man himself. The converted warehouse was cavernous; deep shadows danced across the ceiling, making it difficult to see in the flickering candlelight. But you couldn't really miss the clockwork birds that flapped around their heads and swooped back up toward the high ceiling, noisily circling the rafters. They made a *clack-clack-squawk* sound, over and over again. She knew they spent most of their time up there in the darkness, but had no idea if they really had a . . . *consciousness*. She'd never thought to ask, and it was only now that Donna realized how strange that was. Out of character, really, for someone like her, who cared deeply about living things.

Perhaps she'd never really seen the birds as truly living. That was pretty short-sighted, and she felt ashamed of herself. It was as though the strange creatures were a reminder of the many incongruities in her life, and she'd purposely—probably unconsciously—closed her mind to the realities.

Watching them swoop low again, Donna suddenly thought how much Xan would like to see them. Once this was all over, she really should bring him here. She might be feeling let down by him today, but that didn't mean she would stop helping him in his quest to regain his wings.

She tugged off her coat and laid it on the corner of Maker's workbench, pushing aside an old sweater that had been lying in a crumpled heap.

Wait a minute.

Donna recognized that sweater. And, to be honest, even if she hadn't recognized it, she would have no doubt about its owner due to the musky pine scent that lingered in the air. It seemed like she didn't need to bring Xan to Maker's workshop after all.

He had already been here.

Maker's intelligent blue eyes followed her gaze and his lips thinned.

Donna raised her brows, challenging him to lie to her. "That doesn't look like your usual style," she said, nodding at the sweater.

The old alchemist placed the tray in front of her. "Could you pour please, Donna?"

He isn't even going to answer me? Fine. She could deal with Xan later; there were other things to figure out first.

But at least she was getting a clearer picture of where he'd been running off to lately.

Secrets, always secrets.

Pushing down another blast of anxiety, she poured herbal tea for the three of them and focused on what she'd come here for in the first place: finding out the truth about her tattoos and also, perhaps, something about her "abilities." Abilities beyond anything she could truly understand, powers that the Wood Queen wanted to use for her own purposes.

There were only hours left before the day would be over. Newton had told her that everything she needed to know was already inside her, but she didn't find that entirely helpful. She wished there was something like an *Iron Witch User's Manual* with a handy step-by-step guide to opening magical doors. That thought almost made her laugh out loud, and she pressed her lips shut to stop what would probably be a hysterical sound from escaping.

Surely Maker held the final piece to the puzzle—he had *made* her, after all.

Surely he could give the key to opening the door to Faerie.

One of the clockwork birds came down from the rafters and clattered to a noisy landing on the edge of Maker's workbench. Its eyes dilated with eerie realism, although it appeared to be entirely made of mismatched scraps of metal. It cocked its head to one side and watched as Donna sipped her tea. The bird's wicked-looking claws clicked impatiently and it made a metallic sort of *chirrup*. So weird. And sort of awesome, too.

She had a thousand questions, but she only had time to ask a handful. She took a deep breath and began.

Maker looked distinctly uncomfortable, but once Donna told him about teleporting from Xan's house to the Common, he'd had no choice but to listen. He probably already knew about the earlier disappearing incident, when she'd exploded with fury at Aunt Paige—surely Paige would have told him.

No wonder Maker hadn't looked surprised to see her on his doorstep.

"I've been reading Mom's journal, and it seems I was born with some kind of magical power—something I don't even remember," Donna said, watching him. "But other things have been happening lately too . . . and it all seems connected to *these*." She held up her arms. "Did you do something to me? I mean, when you fixed my injuries with the tattoos, did they have a side effect?" She tried to keep the impatience out of her voice, but it was tough when she glanced out of the window and saw how dark it was getting.

"I don't make mistakes," Maker snapped.

Her face heated. "I didn't mean that. I'm sorry if I offended you . . ."

Navin shifted beside her, but for once kept his mouth shut.

Maker waved away her apology. "No matter. If you had offended me, you'd know about it young lady."

Donna leaned forward, begging him for the truth with her eyes. "So, you healed me . . . but you also did something else. What was it?"

He fiddled with the cuff of his thick flannel shirt. "The markings healed your injuries, yes . . . but they also bound you."

"Bound me? Bound me how?"

"They bind your power, child."

Donna frowned. "But . . . don't the tattoos *give* me power? They make me stronger."

"Physically, yes. But without them, your true abilities would be so much stronger. Your potential has been deeply compromised."

She felt anger threatening to surface, but pushed it down. She had to know everything. "So, what about this thing that's been happening to me, the—I don't even know what to call it—the teleportation?"

Maker shook his head. "That is not your power."

"But that's what happened."

"The traveling is a side effect, just as your strength is a side effect of the iron tattoos I forged for you. I wanted you to have *some* protection."

Donna tried to take this in. Okay, so Maker had given her strength in order to . . . help her? Maybe that was true, but she still didn't understand about the teleporting she could now do so dramatically. There was far more going on here and she was afraid that something would happen to stop her from learning it all. She *needed* to know it, if she was to have any hope of saving her mother.

"So," she continued, trying to put all the pieces together, "what *is* this power of mine?"

Maker rubbed a hand across his eyes, looking as exhausted as she felt. "You can open doors between realms."

Donna stared at him. No wonder the Wood Queen wanted to use her.

"What you're experiencing right now," Maker continued, "are the effects of having the binding I placed on you, ten years ago, broken. You're . . . jumping between dimensions, for want of a better explanation. But for some reason, you're only actually managing to move within our world, from one location to another."

Navin leaned forward. "What broke the binding you placed on her, sir?"

"I suspect it was killing the Skriker that did it."

Donna's chest contracted. There it was again, the reminder of what she'd done in the Ironwood. Defeating the Wood Monster had been the culmination of ten years of silence and nightmares—silence from the Order about what had really happened to her parents and herself a decade ago, and nightmares of the worst sort that plagued her childhood. When she'd rescued Maker and Navin from Aliette just two weeks ago, fighting and killing the

Skriker in order to escape the forest, she had come full circle.

Donna took a shaky breath. "What were we even doing in the Ironwood that night, Maker?"

Real confusion filled his blue eyes. "The Queen took us. You came for Navin—and for me."

"No, I mean before that. When I was seven."

He bowed his head, and for a long moment Donna didn't think he would answer her. But then he looked up and nodded slowly.

"Your parents were trying to smuggle you away from Ironbridge—away from the alchemists—without the Order finding out. Rachel had gotten it into her head that you were in danger." His gnarled hands trembled and he placed them carefully in his lap. "She wasn't wrong."

Warm tears ran down Donna's face. Finally, after all these years of not knowing, the truth.

"Don . . ." Navin put his hand on her shoulder, warm and steadying, just like him.

But still, her heart beat wildly. "The Order found out their plans?"

The old alchemist nodded. He looked like he'd aged another twenty years in the space of five minutes.

"How?" Her voice was hard.

"Patrick confided in Paige . . ."

"She betrayed her own *brother*." Donna wiped away her tears. Duty over blood; why was she even surprised?

Silence rested heavily between the three of them,

the only sound in the workshop the clattering of metal wings.

Maker continued, his voice gruff as if filled with an indefinable emotion. "The Order of the Dragon tried to intercept them, of course, so your father led everyone into the Ironwood." He took a deep breath and looked up into the rafters. "Things got very bad after that."

Oh God, Dad. Her eyes burned. "I can never go back to them, Maker."

"You have to."

"I mean it. *Never.*"

His eyes were filled with a wisdom born of pain and too many years to count. "You have to, child. For your mother's sake."

"Why would you do this to me?" Donna stared at her gloved hands, then back at Maker. Her voice was barely a whisper. "Why?"

He sounded as old and exhausted as she'd ever heard him. "I did what I was asked to do. In some ways, that request saved your life. If we hadn't bound your abilities, you might not have survived—it was too much for such a young girl."

She waved away his attempt to make his actions seem like less of a betrayal. "Who told you to do it?"

Maker rubbed a wrinkled hand across his eyes. "Who do you think?"

Donna felt her heart grow heavy with certainty, the familiar resentment already building. "Simon."

Maker looked surprised. "No, not him."

"Then who?"

"It was your aunt who came to me with the request."

It was your aunt who came to me . . . The words rang inside Donna's head, bouncing around so that she couldn't make sense of them. She watched Maker's lips move, tried to understand what it was he was saying to her, but nothing seemed to be working right.

Aunt Paige? Even after everything she'd read in Mom's journal—and everything that Maker had just told her—she still found it hard to believe that the woman who'd brought her up for the last ten years could truly be such a stranger.

The rushing sound in her ears increased, causing the ground to tilt beneath her feet. Donna realized that she must have stood up, but she didn't remember doing it. She felt as though everything was happening to someone else and she wasn't even here. Her body was present, but her mind was elsewhere—perhaps floating up among the rafters, alongside the clockwork birds as they clattered and squawked.

Forcing herself to focus, she could just about see Navin's shocked face through the halo of light that was growing around her. *No*, she thought. *Not again—not now.*

Her friend's lips were moving, but she couldn't make out what he was trying to say. It didn't matter, anyway. There was only one place she needed to be, only way to bring Mom back.

The queen had told her, *Tomorrow night, we will meet in the Ironwood and you will open the gateway.*

So be it. Her decision had been made for her, perhaps even as far back as her seventh birthday when her supposedly impossible powers had first manifested—only to be magically bound by the alchemists.

Reality shifted, and Donna fell.

Oh, dear God, I never imagined I would pray ever again . . . but I'm doing it now. Patrick, my good-hearted, trusting husband, told his sister about Donna's abilities. Paige knows everything.

And now we are truly lost.

Paige Underwood isn't the sort of woman you reveal this kind of power to. She's ambitious in the worst possible way. Oh, she hides it. She does very well playing moon sister to Quentin, doing her duty and taking a low-salary job in local government in order to get closer to the decision-makers of Ironbridge City Council. She is very, very clever. And she's not afraid of hard work.

These things make her dangerous, but of course . . . she is Patrick's blood, and although I know he agrees with me, he won't admit it openly. At least, he won't go against her—not in public.

But to tell her. To share with her the terror I've been feeling, the dreams about Donna being taken from me. I don't know if I can forgive him, no matter how good his intentions. Why did he have to tell her quite so much?

Nothing will ever be the same again, and I've known that ever since Donna manifested the abilities that caused grown men to turn pale and look at each other as though we had a monster in our midst. Expressions of horror that soon turned to greed—a resource to be exploited is something the power-hungry Order will never give up on.

They make me sick.

My daughter was born different, yes . . . but that doesn't make her any less human. In fact, I think what Patrick and I are discovering about Donna makes her more than human. I believe she has a tiny piece of the prima materia inside her—first matter, sacred to alchemists, and one of the building blocks of reality itself. I don't know how or why; those things would need to be investigated, and I refuse to let her become a lab experiment. She is a person—the most important person in my life, and therefore to be protected.

She's still my little girl, no matter how different she might be, and I won't let them take her from me. I'll die before that happens.

But the terrifying thing is Simon. That sly bastard knows that I'll protect my daughter with my life.

Just as they want to use Donna as the ultimate weapon against our enemies, so she—my own daughter—is such a weapon against me. How can I act against Simon when Donna's life could be at risk?

I can't let them use her to further their plans. Once her power is fully manifest, it could be developed in all kinds of terrible ways. How easy it would be to enter the Elflands without the need of finding the Old Paths—perhaps even to enter Faerie itself. I heard Simon saying it to Quentin, just last night. They were arguing, and the word on Simon Gaunt's lips made my blood run cold:

Invasion.

Nineteen

The early evening sky was already a blank slate of gray cloud as Donna headed into the Ironwood once more. Her only companion was a changeling girl who, at one time, was somehow important to Xan.

Ivy looked more fey than ever, almost as if she had given up on all previous efforts to look human.

Donna raised her eyebrows as Ivy's hair flashed from brown to green to orange before settling into a warm, autumnal sort of red. "Wow, I wish I could do that with *my* hair."

Ivy's normally pale green cheeks flushed. "I'm not doing it—it's just my glamour not working properly."

Donna snorted. "It's broken?"

Looking increasingly uncomfortable, the fey girl skipped ahead. "I'm just not very good at holding it."

Ivy was such a strange creature, but she seemed mostly harmless. Donna wanted to find out more about how she'd gotten caught up in Aliette's games, but she felt too anxious right now to ask. She couldn't afford to get involved in the changeling's problems—she already had more than enough of her own.

The moment Donna had arrived on the outskirts of the Ironwood, Ivy had appeared from nowhere, seeming almost desperate to hurry their progress toward wherever the queen was waiting for them. The girl had hopped from foot to foot while Donna tried to focus on not throwing up; the re-entry, after each journey-between-locations, seemed to be getting worse, and she wondered if there was something Maker could do to help her control it.

As they walked deeper into the forest, Donna thought about how furious Xan had been when they'd first run into Ivy on the Common. Which of course made her worry about other Xan-related things—*what was he up to right now?* Seriously, maybe this was all too much for their budding relationship to survive. She'd seen his sweater in

Maker's workshop—they'd clearly been working on plans for his wings. Why wouldn't Xan share that with her? And what else had he been keeping from her? Donna's confusion was turning to anger as each moment passed, but she had to focus on the task ahead and try not to think about Xan. Now wasn't the time to get caught up in her own personal drama.

Now was the time to open the door to Faerie. She had been born with the power to send the wood elves home, freeing the remains of Ironwood Forest from their influence forever. And freeing the alchemists from the need to tear down the remaining trees and stand constantly watchful, in case the elves returned to their child-stealing ways.

Fear sat like a stone in Donna's stomach, but she tried to remember that she was doing a *good* thing— something that nobody else in the Order was capable of. Surely this was a course of action that could only bring positive rewards for the alchemists. Maybe they would even reconsider their decision to send her away.

Donna swallowed past the tightness in her throat. She knew it was unlikely that the alchemists would change their minds about her, especially if Simon Gaunt had anything to do with it.

And ironically, if she *did* manage to send Aliette and her people home—and the queen returned the elflock at the root of her mother's cursed psyche—she would get her mom back just as she was about to move thousands of miles away. Unless, of course . . . maybe Mom could get custody back. In theory, Donna might only have to wait long enough for her mother to cut through the Order's red tape, and the objections they were bound to voice, before she could come back home.

She followed Ivy deeper into the forest.

❧

Donna looked around the clearing, wondering, far too late, if this was all some kind of elaborate trap. She was out here, in the middle of freaking nowhere, following a changeling girl who was under orders from the Wood Queen. It was dangerous and, if she were honest with herself, pretty stupid.

But what else was new?

Winter branches like long arms with jagged fingers reached for her as they stepped off the path and into the circle of trees.

"Here?" Donna asked.

"Her Majesty should be here," Ivy replied, looking scared.

Then the Wood Queen appeared from a tunnel of leafless trees, flanked by two dark elves. The creatures scuttled along, bent low to the ground, their twig-like hands almost touching the ground. They looked even less human than they had just weeks ago, and Donna couldn't help but be shocked by their appearance.

Was this what Aliette meant when she said that her people were dying? It was as though they were becoming fully transformed into creatures of the earth. They barely held a humanoid shape, and their eyes were empty black sockets.

The Wood Queen, now that her elegant elfskin was no longer in place, looked mostly the way Donna remembered. She was tall and straight, with nut-brown skin; her face was a roughly hewn wood carving. Her clothing rustled and crackled, for it was made purely of the forest, and her twiggy fingers pushed moss-like hair behind her shoulders in a strangely human gesture.

Her lipless mouth smiled wickedly at Ivy, who seemed almost forgotten as she cowered at the edge of the clearing. "Child of the fey, you may leave us. Your debt is paid."

Ivy's huge eyes widened. "Your Majesty, am I truly free?"

"You are. Walk not in the Elflands again, and you will remain that way. Do you understand?"

Donna watched this exchange with interest. She was surprised to feel a huge burst of relief on Ivy's behalf—it must be amazing to be set free of enforced servitude.

The girl bobbed a bizarrely old-fashioned curtsey and then, with a final terrified glance at Donna, ran away faster than the human eye could follow.

Aliette used leafy fingers to detach a thick lock of dull red hair from her belt.

"As agreed, here is what I took from the alchemist called Rachel Underwood."

Donna's fingers closed over the grisly artifact. She couldn't repress a shiver, even though it was her own mother's hair. "Just like that?"

The queen's face twisted into what could only be described as a smile. Wood splintered around her mouth. "It was our bargain. *We* do not go back on our word, Iron Witch."

There wasn't really much Donna could say to that, given what she'd done with the elixir.

She swallowed. "What should I do with it? How do I get my mother back?"

"Burn it and scatter the ashes over running water, two nights from now when the sky is dark and the moon is new."

"That's it?"

"It is as I tell you. I will break the curse tonight, but Rachel Underwood shall not awaken until the new moon, when you release *that*."

Donna tucked the elflock safely into her jeans pocket. She felt excitement beginning to grow, but she refused to allow it to cloud her mind. This was so very far from over—she still had to uphold her part of the bargain, and she had a horrible feeling things weren't going to be as easy as Aliette and Newton would have her believe.

She wished that Navin were here.

Her mind immediately flashed on an image of Xan,

remembering how they'd faced down the dark elves together the last time she was in the Ironwood. Shaking her head with frustration, Donna gritted her teeth against a sudden wave of sadness. She was alone this time, and that was just fine. She'd been alone before, and had no doubt that she would be again—if she even survived this night.

Donna listened carefully as the Wood Queen told her exactly where the doorway to Faerie was located. She still had to figure out how to use the power that apparently existed inside her—to access it and open a door to another realm when she barely understood what was happening in the first place. But if she failed, Mom would die, and that was something that Donna couldn't allow.

Failure simply wasn't an option.

She gritted her teeth, pulled off her gloves, and faced the expanse of dark trees. The night sky above seemed to press down on her—reminding her of the lucid dream in which she'd heard her mother's voice—but she shook off her remaining doubts and focused on the depth of her feelings.

No more thought, just pure emotion. That's what seemed to trigger her power, after all. Why not use it, consciously, in an effort to do what was necessary? Love for her mother; fear of losing her; hatred toward Simon; anger at the way Aunt Paige had betrayed her; love and laughter with Navin; even her uncertain passion for Xan.

All of these things, together, filled her entire self—body, heart, and mind.

Donna was no longer aware of her surroundings; she was only vaguely aware of the shattering brightness that burst from her hands. Something like a gossamer-fine thread tugged in the depths of her being. She stretched out her arms, threw back her head, and envisioned a mystical gateway opening like a gaping mouth between the twisted winter trees.

Her iron tattoos wound around and around her arms in increasingly crazed patterns. Silver light surrounded her, reflecting off the living markings on the backs of her hands.

The last thing she remembered was the sound of Alitte's cruel laughter and the triumphant shrieks of the gathered wood elves.

Twenty

When Donna came to, she was lying on the cold ground looking straight up at the starless night sky.

Starless? She sat up quickly, feeling sick and spent, trying to remember what she was doing here. And where "here" actually was.

She shook her head and rubbed her face, realizing that her hands were bare. Shivering, she looked around the shadowed ground but couldn't see her gloves anywhere.

And then she remembered: Ironwood Forest. The Wood Queen. The door to Faerie. The gateway that she had succeeded in opening—at least, she *thought* she had succeeded. At least partially. She remembered the golden light before her eyes, but then the thread of power—the sliver of first matter, *prima materia*, inside her soul—had seemed to catch on something and everything had stopped.

Scrambling to her feet, ignoring the screaming resistance in every muscle, she was faced with nothing but the empty clearing and a radiant space between trees that held the shape of a huge rectangular blur. A door?

The door?

She had done it! And was still doing it, in fact—Donna could feel the thread tighten again, between herself and the gateway that was slowly opening.

A tall humanoid form stood in the glowing doorway, behind a bright veil, looking around as if surveying a strange new world. It seemed as if the silhouetted figure was watching her. Long hands touched the wall of light, pressing against it like they could push their way through, but the pulsing radiance remained intact. Donna thought it looked sort of creepy, and so unreal—it was almost like watching one of those puppet shows through a sheet.

Whoever—or whatever—was standing there, it couldn't get out. Not yet, anyway.

The power tugged at her stomach, as it had before, but this time was different; this time she had more control over it. Perhaps *consciously* using her new ability, and for its true purpose, had given her more understanding and control. Donna didn't think she'd be opening any more ephemeral doors anytime soon, but she at least felt more confident that she wouldn't accidently transport herself again.

She was feeling increasingly nervous. This was taking longer than she'd thought it would, and she was horribly aware of the fact that Navin knew about her bargain with Aliette. Would he tell Maker? She had left them under such . . . unusual circumstances . . . that there really wasn't any doubt that the Order would be in hot pursuit.

She tried to push those fearful thoughts away; her mental grip on the door that was slowly but surely opening was so tight, she was afraid to break the intense concentration. The Wood Queen had disappeared, but Donna had no doubt she was somewhere close by, ensuring that her Iron Witch followed through completely on the terms of their bargain. Perhaps Aliette was gathering her people so that they could return home as soon as possible.

Donna focused *inward*, trying to pinpoint the bright spot of power within her chest. If she had to describe what she was doing, the closest she could come was that it felt like molding clay on a potter's wheel—taking a shard of first matter and somehow shaping it into something new.

Sudden movement, all around, brought her back to

the cold darkness of the clearing. Her grip on the glowing thread faltered, and—just like that—her tattoos stopped moving. She fell to her knees on a pile of dirt and rotten leaves. The door was still there, pulsing with power.

She tried to catch her breath, but her whole body felt frozen and her chest hurt. She recognized Aunt Paige's voice and her heart sank.

This wasn't good; it really couldn't get any worse. If the alchemists arrived now, things could fall apart. Perhaps the door would close if she hadn't gotten it fully open before being interrupted . . . she didn't understand how these powers of hers worked yet.

Aunt Paige had gotten here way sooner than she'd expected. It should have taken longer for Maker to rally the troops.

Just then, Aliette and two more of her dark elves—accompanying her like twisted, vine-covered body-guards —appeared on a pathway on the far side of the clearing. The alchemists were filing into the clearing as well, staying close to the furthest edge, their faces eerily lit by the glow of the open door to Faerie.

Maker was there, and Donna was surprised that he could possibly have managed the journey without his chair. He was walking, carrying his stick and leaning heavily on the arm of a tall, skinny young man at his side.

Donna felt strangely glad to see Robert, although she wondered why he was still helping the Order of the

Dragon, especially after how he'd tried to warn her about it. Maybe Miranda had told him to stay close? When they'd talked on Ironbridge Common, Robert had made it sound almost like the Order of the Crow was monitoring its American counterparts.

She didn't know what it meant, but his face was serious when their eyes met.

Quentin, Simon, and her aunt completed the group. They were all carrying flashlights, and Donna desperately searched the trees for any sign of Navin.

He wasn't there, and for that she was intensely glad. The tension in her stomach eased back a couple of notches—her best friend was safe. Maker would have insisted that he stay behind, and there was no way Simon would have permitted a "commoner" to join them, anyway.

Donna couldn't help a slight smile. Nav would have argued up a storm, but he wouldn't have stood a chance against the Order of the Dragon. For once, she was glad of the control they felt entitled to exert over everybody around them—whether human, alchemist, or fey.

Before anybody could break the eerie silence, the steady light in the door between the trees flashed bright red—blood red—and the clearing was filled with the sound of an otherworldly screeching that seemed to come from everywhere and nowhere. The noise was different from the cry of the Skriker, though it still made all the hairs on the back of Donna's neck stand up.

Aunt Paige's bloodless lips pulled back in a wordless

snarl. There was a spot of lipstick on one of her teeth, savage and crimson like blood.

"What have you done, you stupid girl?"

Donna pushed herself to her feet, wondering if she had the strength to stand. She felt wrung out like an old cloth. Her throat was parched and her legs trembled. "I'm just sending them home—I saved Mom!"

"And damned the rest of us," her aunt retorted.

"What are you talking about?" Donna's voice seemed too loud as the nerve-shattering noise stopped. "Maker, tell her!"

But Maker wouldn't meet her eyes.

The Wood Queen stood to one side of the door, watching the scene unfold with a strange expression on her face. She showed no sign of fear, despite being effectively surrounded by her enemies.

Simon was crouched beside Quentin, who seemed to have fallen to the ground when the screeching started. The Magus was solicitous as usual, but his face was a mask of horror—an expression that Donna wasn't used to seeing on the odious man's face.

She stepped toward the Archmaster. "Quentin, what happened?"

Simon blocked her path. "Don't touch him," he hissed.

Donna felt her heart go cold. She knew there'd been every chance that Aliette would trick her in some way, yet she'd still gone ahead with their bargain. She didn't understand what was so terrible, but she knew everybody else believed it was pretty bad.

"What?!" Donna glared around at the gathered alchemists. She searched out Robert, looking for some kind of reassurance. "All I did was open the door to Faerie—they can go home now. No more wood elves."

She tried to push down the rising wave of panic that clawed at her throat. "It's a good thing—right?"

Aunt Paige's eyes were pinched with barely repressed fury, but at least she seemed to have regained some measure of control. "Faerie can only be opened one way, you little fool. From the *inside*."

"I . . . I don't understand . . ." But Donna was beginning to. Her feelings of anxiety and uncertainty were slowly morphing into black-winged horror.

Robert was nodding. "I'm sorry, Donna. Faerie really can only be opened one way—and it's not from *our* side of reality."

"Then . . ." She stumbled over a fallen branch as she backed up a step, not looking where she was going. "What have I opened?"

Aliette's face split into a wicked expression of triumph, her lipless mouth slashing her cheeks almost in half.

But before Donna could direct her questions at the manically grinning queen, the figure in the doorway moved. She had to scrunch up her eyes against the bright glare that burst out of the door, bathing the entire clearing with an unforgiving white heat.

A tall figure stepped out of the radiance and into the clearing.

He was . . . beautiful. Stunning, in an inhuman way that went beyond anything she ever could have imagined. Xan was handsome, sure, but this was something else entirely. There was an intoxicating quality to this being's presence, something that went beyond the mere beauty of his physical perfection. Whoever this newcomer was, his aura was filled with a power so charismatic that he had his audience reeled in before he even opened his mouth.

He was tall and slim, with silver hair that brushed the shoulders of his perfectly cut black jacket. His face looked as though it had been chiselled out of the finest marble, and his eyes looked like two pieces of gleaming onyx.

And he was looking right at her.

"Greetings, human." His voice was low-pitched, almost melodious in its lilting rhythms. "You may call me Demian. The Otherworld is grateful to you for the gift of freedom."

Donna's legs gave way, and she fell to her knees once more on the carpet of dead leaves. Whether it was the shock of his words and the creeping sense of horror taking its toll, or whether it was physical exhaustion from opening the door, she couldn't say. Maybe it was even the painful weight of Demian's *presence*. Whatever it was that had caused her sudden weakness, she hated herself for it, even as she tried to drag herself back to her feet.

"Let me help you," the stranger said, courteous in the manner of someone who belonged to another time and place. He reached toward her, and she found herself allowing him to grasp her bare hand in a cool grip that spoke of hidden strength.

Pulling her upright with no effort at all, the man called Demian spoke again. "Donna Underwood, you have fulfilled a task we did not expect of one such as you. We thank you, truly. We are in your debt."

He kept hold of her hand, seemingly fascinated with the spiralling patterns across her skin.

"We?" Donna found her voice and took comfort in the fact that it didn't shake. She tugged her hand free, pleased that her strength clearly surprised this newcomer. "Who are you talking about?"

She already knew, in that dark place of terror she was trying to stuff down in order to stop from screaming.

What have I done? The words echoed around her head, as though in an empty chamber. She tried to meet this stranger's eyes as she waited for the response that would seal her fate—and seal the fate of too many people to count. If she really had made such a terrible mistake, she should, at the very least, suffer the consequences. The pain in her heart whispered of the price she might truly pay later on, but for now, she simply attempted to remain upright in the face of the most beautiful evil she had ever seen.

Demian's face broke into a smile that broke her heart

with its perfection. His black eyes glittered with the weight of centuries.

"It is the demons who offer you their gratitude. We are free after almost two centuries of imprisonment at the hands of the alchemists—and it is all thanks to you."

Twenty-one

Donna remembered to breathe just as all Hell—quite literally—broke loose.

Simon was trying to drag Quentin from the clearing, while Robert guided Maker to another gap in the trees. Aunt Paige seemed frozen, watching the demon speaking to her niece by the glowing doorway.

A door that was, even now, beginning to fill with more silhouettes.

Demons.

How many of them there might be, Donna couldn't say, but the portal to the Otherworld was at least partially open, and she only knew that they had to get out of here—all of them. Even her aunt. Much as Donna wanted to hate her, she couldn't let Aunt Paige just *stand* there.

Demian turned his attention to the wall of light holding his people back, and Donna took what could be her one opportunity.

She ran the other way. "Aunt Paige, *run!*" When the woman didn't move, Donna grabbed her by the shoulders and shook her. "I said, get out of here—now!"

Giving her a shove toward the path that Simon had just taken, she headed back for Maker and Robert.

"Donna," the young alchemist said, "it seems you really know how to get the party started."

She gasped with shocked laughter, knowing she was close to breakdown. "Yeah, I'm a party girl. You got that right." She reached for Maker's arm. "Let's get him out of here."

Robert nodded, and they half-carried the old man from the clearing.

As they made it onto the main part of the pathway, Donna realized that she hadn't seen the Wood Queen leave.

Closing her eyes briefly, she swallowed down a wave of bitterness. Maybe Aliette considered them "even" now. Was this all about *revenge*, for destroying the elixir and double-crossing her the last time? Would the queen really bring about Hell on earth as payback? There had to be more to this—freeing the demons must somehow benefit the wood elves. The puzzle wasn't complete, but Donna hardly had time to worry about filling in the missing pieces now.

When Aunt Paige met them on the branch-scattered path and took Maker from them, putting her arm around the alchemist's shoulders and guiding him over the rough terrain, Donna really began to think they might be okay. At least, the others could escape—that's what counted.

She turned to Robert and smiled, looking for a sign of encouragement from him as they watched her aunt lead Maker to safety.

His face was serious again, but at least he was still standing beside her.

Donna touched his arm. "Is Navin safe?"

A half-smile twitched at the corner of his mouth. "They had to more or less lock him up in Maker's workshop to get him to stay put."

Relief flooded her, but then adrenalin immediately returned. She glanced nervously back at the clearing that held a doorway to Hell. "Listen, we don't have much time. I need to go back there."

"I'm sorry, I must have misheard you, what with the bloody apocalypse almost upon us. Did you just say you have to go *back*?"

Donna pressed her lips together and simply nodded.

"Are you quite mad?" Robert asked. "You can't possibly—"

"I'm sick of being told what I can and can't do. Robert, I opened that door, so I figure I'm the only one who has any chance of closing it."

He was shaking his head, a determined expression stamped across his face. "It's too late for that. We should get out while we still can."

"You're not listening to me!" Donna hadn't meant to shout, but well . . . there it was. She was furious. Not with Robert, and not even with the Wood Queen. Not really. She was disgusted with *herself*. "I have to make this right."

The sky above them flashed to life, as though some ancient god had switched on a long-forgotten light switch. Bolts of pure energy snaked through the inky blackness, jagged and bright against the cold night. Donna ducked, instinct taking over, even though the impossible lightning was miles away.

Robert grabbed her wrists, holding the tattoos as though they were nothing. "Donna, trust me when I tell you this: you won't be able to close that door again. The legends say it took a dozen alchemists to secure it, two hundred years ago. Breaking a lock, even a magical one, is far easier than fixing it—do you understand?"

She did. She understood what he was telling her, but she had to try. *Dammit*, she was responsible for releasing a species potentially far more powerful than the wood elves.

The ground shuddered beneath their feet, bucking and rippling so hard that Donna would have stumbled if Robert hadn't had a tight hold on her. A sound like thunder smashed through her whole being, and for a moment she let herself consider getting out of this place.

But only for a moment.

She twisted her arms from the young alchemist's grasp, not even bothering to apologize when he cried out in pain.

"Bloody hell, woman! What did you have to do that for? I think you broke my fingers."

Ignoring him, she turned and ran back toward the clearing—to the door that would unleash an army of demons at any moment. She heard Robert crashing through the undergrowth in pursuit.

Which was when two shadows slipped from between the trees and blocked the path ahead of them.

"Move!" Robert yelled, pushing her into a large patch of prickly bushes.

"Hey, watch where you're—"

But Donna didn't get to finish whatever she was going to shout at him. Her eyes widened in shock as she saw the two shadowy figures move toward Robert with inhuman speed. From her position half-collapsed in the undergrowth, she watched in growing horror as the figures made a grab for him. They were moving so fast it was difficult to see what they truly looked like, especially in the near-darkness, but she was beginning to realize that they were under some kind of glamour. Only it wasn't a glamour she'd ever seen before—not like an elfskin, used by the dark elves, and not even like the shimmer of disguise she'd detected on Ivy when they'd first met.

As one of the shadows easily wrestled Robert to the ground, the other turned its impassive attention on her.

Donna didn't intend to be prey. Not tonight. She clambered out of the brambles, her coat catching on thorns that seemed to be trying to drag her back down again. Angrily, she ripped off the coat, throwing the shredded pieces behind her and squeezing her hands into silver fists.

Whatever these creatures were, they obviously belonged in the Otherworld.

The shadow man's eyes were cold blank spaces, and its whole presence made her shiver. It glided toward her the moment she set foot back on the scattered dirt and stones of the path. In the sudden brightness of an other-worldly lightning bolt, she could see the skid marks her sneakers had made when Robert pushed her out of harm's way.

The creature was nothing more than a silhouette. Quite literally—it was like a man's tall, thin shadow had stepped off a wall at noon and decided to attack two pass-ersby. Only Donna knew this was no chance encounter.

It slid closer and raised an arm.

She threw herself to the side, rolling on the ground

and gasping with pain when her shoulder made contact with something sharp. For a moment she thought she'd cut herself—again—but soon realized that the burning pain in her shoulder was getting worse. The shadow man had hold of her, and was dragging her to her feet. Her feet scrabbled impotently against the earth, desperately trying to get away from this silent monster, but it was stronger than anything she'd ever come up against before.

Even the Skriker.

With the image of the fey hellhound flashing through her screaming mind, Donna gritted her teeth and put both her hands around her attacker's wrist. She squeezed as hard as she could, trying not to think about the human-shaped arm and how real it felt, but instead imagining she was cracking a very large nut.

It released her, although it didn't make a sound. Donna could only hope she'd hurt it as she tumbled to the ground and rolled immediately back to her feet.

Without letting herself stop to think—to be afraid—she swung at it with her right fist, gasping with shock as her hand went right through it and her momentum carried her forward—

—and right *through* her attacker. For a moment she was encased in cold and dark, her bones grinding and aching as she passed through the blackness and fell out the other side, skidding to a halt and whirling back to face the creature. Nausea reared its ugly head in her belly, but she clamped her teeth together and held up her fists again, vowing that if they got out of this, she was going to learn how to fight correctly.

Robert had somehow gotten himself free of the other monster and was running in her direction. "Donna, we need to get the shadows into a circle!"

"A circle?"

She felt young and inexperienced, hating it but knowing she didn't have the tools to deal with whatever these things were. "Shadows," Robert had called them, and she wondered if that was their true name or whether it was just something he'd come up with there and then. Her hand had just gone straight through the creature that grabbed her—which didn't even make sense. How could something be solid enough to take hold of her arm, but then be like a ghost when she punched it with her other hand? If they could change their density at will, her enhanced strength was effectively useless—perhaps she'd gotten lucky when she'd managed to free herself before. It was as if the shadow had adapted to her abilities and could use her strength against her.

"What are they?" she managed to gasp, even as she kicked out at her assailant and stumbled when her leg sliced through its shadowy body.

Robert was there beside her, digging in one of the many pockets of his jacket. He drew out what looked like a small black pouch, but before she could say for sure, she was lifted high above the ground by seemingly invisible hands and thrown across the pathway.

Donna hit a tree trunk on the way back down, and she bit back a cry of pain. She would *not* give that thing the satisfaction. If it even felt emotions like satisfaction. She was having a hard time thinking of the creatures as anything other than thoroughly inhuman—almost alien. And it had just grabbed her again, which meant it had turned solid enough to do that. Perhaps that meant she could get in a good strike of her own before it went all . . . shadowy again.

She groaned from her current position, lying flat out beneath a skeletal tree. Maybe getting up was going to be a lot harder than she'd anticipated. Her ribs ached and she felt sick.

The shadow man stood over her, just . . . watching.

Robert dodged around it and reached down to scoop her, one-handed, off the ground. "Get behind me, Donna."

Oh, God . . . those words. *Get behind me, Donna!* She felt sick as a dark and twisted memory of her father almost overwhelmed her.

Wanting to argue with Robert, but knowing she was way out of her league—at least until she knew more about the shadows—Donna did as she was told. Whatever he was doing, she didn't want to get in the way of that. He was so serious and in control; there was a lot more to Robert than she had initially given him credit for.

But then again, he was a fully-trained alchemical adept, even if he *was* from the Order of the Crow; she'd been brought up to believe that it was only the Order of the Dragon who still actively practiced any form of magic.

Robert tossed a handful of what looked like salt at the advancing creature.

This sort of looked like magic to her.

He spared her a glance. "They're demon shadows. Not true demons, but close enough, in terms of anything we have experience with. Sort of like a first wave of attack, I suppose."

Demons . . . Donna swallowed against a feeling of sheer terror as the full weight of what was happening came crashing down on her. A vivid image of the bronze statue in Simon's lab flashed through her strained mind; Newton had claimed to be a trapped demon.

And now here, the very next night, she was coming face-to-face with more demons. Or demon shadows, as Robert called them.

"How do you know this?" She grabbed Robert's arm and pulled him toward her as the second creature—the one that had tackled him to the ground earlier—recovered from whatever he'd done to it. Maybe he'd used the salt on it; it seemed to make them shrink back temporarily. Like slugs, she thought with disgust.

Both shadows stood perfectly still, watching and waiting for them to make a move. It was creepy, as though the creatures had begun to mirror their actions, tracking them like the prey she so desperately *didn't* want to be.

Robert pulled out another pouch.

"How much stuff are you carrying, anyway?" she asked, pushing down her fear and trying to focus on getting out of this in one piece. "Who the hell do you think you are, Batman?"

Robert actually flashed a grin. "Close. Try James Bond, darling."

She choked on a strained laugh. "Yeah, because you're *totally* like James Bond."

"I'm more 007 than caped crusader, I'll have you know." He sounded genuinely offended. "Suave, well-dressed, skilled in the arts of multiple types of combat, and highly attractive to both men *and* women . . ."

The demon shadows moved in tandem, as if controlled by the same mind. Closing the short distance between themselves and their targets, they reached out with misshapen, inkblot fingers.

Robert grabbed Donna's hand and ran, pulling her behind him so fast that her feet dragged along the ground.

"Wait, stop!" She slammed on the brakes and used her strength to resist him. She didn't want to hurt him again—no matter how annoying he'd been in the past—but she still needed to get back to the clearing. Robert was taking her away from the doorway.

She tugged hard on his arm, feeling him trying to drag her toward a group of trees on the far side of the pathway. Feeling only vaguely guilty, she squeezed his hand tightly in hers until he cried out in pain.

"Stop *doing* that! Whose side are you on?" He shook his hand free and rubbed his fingers gingerly, giving her a murderous look.

Donna glanced over her shoulder and shivered as the shadow men did their creepy gliding thing toward them. *Didn't these things ever give up?*

She fixed him with what she hoped was a sincere expression. "I'm sorry, but we can't just run. I won't leave those things here—not if they're a threat to people." Maybe if she appealed to his heroic sensibilities, she could get him to help her fight them—and then return to close the gate to the Otherworld.

Fear cramped her stomach as she thought of facing Demian again, but she wouldn't let that stop her.

Robert shook his head quickly. "Do you see other people around? The only ones in any danger are you and me."

"I told you before, I don't want you to protect me."

"And I don't want you getting in my way," he shot back. He had the pouch in his hand again. "Stand still." He scattered salt around her in a circle, bending over to reach the ground while trying to keep an eye on the shadows.

"Why are you doing that?"

He didn't reply, but she was pretty sure the muttering under his breath wasn't complimentary toward her. For one moment she'd actually thought it might be some kind of alchemical incantation, but then she heard the words "idiot" and "useless".

Oo-kay. Not a spell, then.

"Originally, I was going to trap them in a circle—we can't destroy them. The best we can hope for is to hold them for a while." Although his voice was matter-of-fact, she could detect a faint thread of worry running through it. He was working faster now, scattering salt wildly around both Donna and himself.

"Why aren't they moving?" The creepy things were now just standing there, swaying. Like giant, man-shaped rattlesnakes.

"Waiting for us to run—they're hunters. The movement gives them something to track." He stood up, breathing heavily from all the bending and salt-scattering. "Okay, that should do it."

"Do wha—?"

"Lux!" he shouted.

Brilliant light blasted into an uneven circle around them.

Donna stared at it in wonder—although it was bright, she could still look at it without having to squint.

"I thought you said you were going to put *them* in the circle," she said, feeling trapped and nervous.

"Change of plan. We'll be safe here until they get bored."

"What if they don't get bored?"

Robert glanced down at her. "You're a regular little ray of sunshine, aren't you?"

Donna rolled her eyes, trying to hide how truly terrified she was. "But now we're stuck here. That doesn't seem like such a smart plan to me."

"Where there are two shadows, there will be more, trust me. Did you think this was it?"

"No, of course not. But I don't like being trapped here—I need to do something."

He looked down at her, his dark eyes fierce. "So far, all you've managed to do is get yourself tossed around. This is safer."

Although she appreciated the fact that he didn't mention how it had been *her* who'd let them out in the first place, she still wished she could try closing the Otherworld door. Despite Robert's dire warnings about how it had taken lots of alchemists and some serious mojo to do it before, surely she couldn't leave the Ironwood without at least making an attempt.

She sighed. "They're not going anywhere, Robert."

But the shadow men did move away, and they did it surprisingly quickly. Even Robert seemed taken aback.

"Maybe he called them away," he said, sounding genuinely confused.

She frowned. "Who?"

"The demon king; the one who seemed so bewitched by you."

Donna shivered. "Don't say that."

He shrugged. "Come on, let's get out of here."

"Wait a minute—" She wanted to say how it seemed too easy. Too fast and convenient.

But Robert had already touched the wall of light that encircled them, and it disappeared. He took three steps forward and was immediately engulfed by shadows. It looked like someone had poured a huge vat of oil over him, only the oil was moving.

Donna screamed as she lost sight of him in the crush of bodies.

"Run!" he shouted. His voice was muffled.

Oh God, how many of these things are there? She glared at her tattoos glinting in the night, cursing herself for how useless she was. She counted five, six . . . no, *seven* of them. Seven demon shadows. Robert didn't stand a chance.

She ran toward the writhing mass of darkness, trying to catch a glimpse of the young alchemist she was already tentatively thinking of as a friend.

"Get out of here!" Robert called, but she could hear pain in his voice. *"Run, Donna, and don't look back."*

Her heart stuttered. He'd done it again—those had been her father's words to her, that awful night in the Ironwood all those years ago. At least, those were the words her father spoke in her nightmares. It was a truly bizarre coincidence that Robert had twice echoed Patrick Underwood.

Was it an omen? Donna wasn't normally superstitious,

but maybe Dad was trying to send her a message. Yet she couldn't imagine he'd be telling her to run. She had never run from a fight in her life, and there was no way she was about to start now—not even when facing demonic shadows she hadn't even known existed until today.

What can I do against them?

"Do *something*. Anything!" She hadn't meant to scream it aloud, but it made her feel better for a moment—at least until seven inky heads lifted in unison and glanced in her direction with empty eyes.

What had Robert said about them before? They're hunters. *Think, Underwood!* she told herself fiercely. *Use your damn brain.* The shadows followed movement—the quicker the better. Surely it wouldn't be too difficult to make herself a more attractive target than the fallen alchemist.

She was moving before she even had a chance to be afraid. Robert hadn't hesitated when it came to helping her, and she owed it to him to do the same. If it wasn't already too late.

Donna ran faster than she'd ever thought possible— cold air sang in her throat and her chest felt stretched too tight. She pumped her arms and legs, barely looking at the scattered earth as it flew beneath her. As badly as she wanted to return to the clearing with the doorway to Hell, she knew that it was hopeless. Too much time had passed, and she didn't really know what she could do to re-seal the gate anyway. Especially considering it was now probably fully open, letting demons and their shadows into this side of reality in even greater numbers.

Not to mention the fact that Demian, the king of the demons, would undoubtedly be there.

Cold wind whipped her hair about her face as the lightning-lashed sky lit her way through the trees. An idea was taking shape in Donna's mind, but the shuddering ground and the hiss of the shadow men behind her made it almost impossible to think clearly. At the moment, all she could do was to try leading them away from Robert, but she couldn't outrun them indefinitely. Far from it. She'd probably only managed it for this long because she'd kept darting around tree trunks and circling back the way she'd come. These particular creatures seemed to do better when moving in a straight line. Perhaps there were no zig-zags in Hell, she thought, clamping down on the strained laughter that was bubbling up from a dark place.

Her throat burned and she knew she couldn't keep going. She was also pretty certain she was circling back to the pathway where Robert had fallen. In a sudden wave of regret, she cursed herself for running in the first place; she should never have left her new friend behind, no matter how good her intentions had been.

Bursting from the undergrowth, Donna hit the trail at an exhausted run. Her pursuers were only seconds behind her; she could hear them whisper-gliding through the Ironwood.

She could make out a figure lying cold and still on the hard-packed earth. Dream-memories of her father threatened to drive her to her knees, but Donna kept moving. *This isn't Dad*, she told herself firmly. *This is Robert Lee*. Her throat tightened as she reached him, wondering if it was possible to survive being overrun by demon shadows. Wondering if she had drawn them away in time.

"Please," she whispered to nobody in particular. *Please, let him be okay*. Let her not have cost a good man his life.

Before she could even crouch beside Robert to check for a pulse, the shadows flowed out of the trees and onto the path. This wasn't the first time Donna had looked death in the eye, but it wasn't exactly something you were ever prepared for. Violent slashes of lightning rent the night sky, a dramatic portent she could have done without.

She stood in front of Robert's body and waited for the first monster to reach her.

Twenty-two

*And then she isn't running anymore because she's
lying flat on her back on the hard ground. The
darkness, like hundreds of cold hands, is pressing
down on her. She can't breathe. She will drown
in all this blackness if she can't get back on her
feet.*

Donna felt like she'd been here before, only that
wasn't possible . . . was it? Then she remembered

that she sort of *had*, in that weirdly realistic, almost lucid dream just before she was woken up by Ivy's hand across her mouth. It seemed so long ago.

The shadows had engulfed her so quickly it was like she was, once again, in her bedroom and Ivy had cast the Wood Queen's charm to make the blackness *absolute*. The brutal darkness was so complete she might as well have been blind. Donna knew that if she took too deep a breath, she would inhale the demon shadows—somehow take them inside her soul and become one with the dark.

Her chest ached from the constant shallow breathing, and her skin hurt from the obsidian coldness. She couldn't hear anything, and all she could feel was the earth at her back as she lay on the ground. She turned her head and saw Robert's body on the other side of the pathway.

Robert! That thought brought a spark of warmth, something to hold onto. A glowing thread in the starless tomb she'd somehow fallen into.

Then Donna remembered that a thread could be more than a metaphorical thread of hope . . . it could connect her to her power. That spark she felt was the piece of *prima materia* she'd been born possessing, that shard of the first matter so revered by alchemists as the mystical building block of all material things. It was what gave her the ability to open gateways in the very fabric of reality—what had marked her as different even before she'd been bound with magical iron.

Donna reached out with her consciousness and

latched onto that inner brightness. On one level, she knew that her body was still in the Ironwood, dying under the weight of shadows. But on another . . . she knew she could travel through doorways that only she could open. She just had to remember how.

This time, with only the single glowing ember as her guide in the dark, she focused everything she could on the *thought* of pulling herself out, hand-over-imaginary-hand, along a line of pure white light. Everything inside screamed at her to give up. To just let go of the thread and surrender to the encroaching oblivion. To let the demons win.

But Donna was tougher than that, and she had a mission: saving her mother was more important than anything else. If she gave up now, all her efforts—all her *mistakes*—would have been for nothing. And that was absolutely unacceptable.

It was with that final thought, accompanied by a blast of radiant energy, that Donna Underwood activated the power inside her and literally burst free from the overpowering horde of demon shadows.

The explosion was nothing short of cataclysmic, and Donna was vaguely conscious of the trees that lined the path catching on fire. Her tattoos were writhing around her hands and wrists, and their bright glare dazzled her so badly she had to turn away. It was too much, even for her.

The shadow men had gone.

Gasping for breath, Donna crawled along the path until she reached Robert. His face was white and still, but his chest was moving and she almost cried with relief. He was alive. Somehow he was hanging in there. Bowing her head and resting it, for a moment, on Robert's shoulder, she struggled to understand what she had just done.

She'd been trapped by the demons in a dark and suffocating realm, and then she had escaped by using her increasingly scary and yet familiar abilities. Perhaps it really was as simple as opening the "door" of wherever the shadows had sent her and getting the hell out. And yet . . . she knew that her physical body had been lying in the forest the entire time she'd been fighting to free herself. Had she freed her *soul*?

Donna shivered and decided that now wasn't the time to think about it.

She touched her jeans pocket unconsciously, checking that her mother's elflock was safe. Strangely, the action steadied her and helped her to focus. Just as she was trying to figure out what to do next—and how she was going to get Robert out of there—she heard a familiar voice calling from between a burnt copse of nearby trees.

"Donna! Are you out here?"

"Xan!"

Donna staggered to her feet and waved her arms, grateful for once for the shimmering tattoos that seemed

313

like they'd never stop moving. She felt like a living distress beacon.

Xan appeared at the end of the path, his long black coat flying behind him like a cloak as they ran to each other. He was moving swiftly, and she remembered that his part-fey blood gave him agility and speed beyond the limits of ordinary humanity.

He swept her into his arms and held her tightly, crushing the air out of her as though he thought he'd lost her forever.

"I can't believe I found you," he muttered into her hair.

Donna made a sound of protest and managed to get him to release her.

He ducked his head, dark blond hair flopping into his eyes. "Shit. Sorry, I was just so happy to see you. I feel like I've been running around this place for hours."

"How did you find me?" she replied, trying to regulate her breathing.

His viridian eyes met her. "How could I *miss* you, don't you mean? True, at first I thought I was never going to reach you in this place—I even started thinking I must've somehow wandered onto one of the Old Paths, because it felt like I was walking around in damn circles and the Ironwood is *not* that big." He shook his head. "Then there was a flash of light that reached beyond the tops of the fucking trees! That's where I knew you'd be. Donna, how the hell did you do that?"

She shrugged, not ready to talk about any of it. She was truly glad to see him, but there was still so much to worry about. Still so much to *do*. And yet . . . she had one question of her own before they made their next move—one that couldn't wait.

"Xan . . . I meant, how did you know that I was in the Ironwood?"

He had the grace to look vaguely shifty. "Ivy told me you were in trouble."

Donna was so astonished she actually took a step back. "She *did*?"

"Yeah. When I saw her, she started babbling a whole load of what I honestly thought was nonsense. I finally got her to calm down so I could make sense of it. Figured I had to head out here and find you for myself."

Wow. Navin had been the one to alert the alchemists—and therefore Robert—about where she'd gone, and Ivy had told Xan. Donna was intensely grateful for such good friends. *Surprising* friends, in some cases, but no less welcome for that.

She gestured at the young man lying on the ground beside her. "Will you help me get him somewhere safe?"

"Of course . . . who *is* he?"

Donna swallowed another surge of emotion. "The Order of the Crow alchemist I told you about. Robert Lee. He's a good guy; he saved me."

"Sure. Let's do this." Xan hoisted Robert's body over his shoulders, his knees almost buckling. "Does he have to be so damn tall?" And that coming from Xan, who was hardly what you'd describe as short.

If Donna weren't so thoroughly shattered, she would have laughed.

Twenty-three

Donna leaned on the railing of the old iron bridge and watched the ashes of her mother's hair fall into the dark water far below. She rubbed her gloved hands together, just to make sure she'd gotten all of it.

Holding her breath, she waited to see if anything would happen—something dramatic, maybe, that would tell her if the Wood Queen's curse was truly broken.

Nothing. Just the gray water winding through the city

of Ironbridge, taking her hopes along with it. Shouldn't it have been instantaneous, like magic?

She pushed away from the railing and checked the time on her phone. She needed to get to Ironbridge General and see if the ritual had worked.

Whatever might happen, she wanted to spend the little time she had left in town staying as close to Mom as possible. Donna knew she was running on borrowed time, and couldn't help but wonder what the alchemists would do to discipline her for this latest incident. They'd already exiled her to London—what more would they dream up to punish her for everything she'd done, everything she'd risked to save Mom? Aunt Paige had barely even been civil to her, though Donna was finding that less upsetting than she would have just a week ago.

She could also visit Robert. He'd spent the past two days close to death in the room next door to her mother's, in the alchemists' Special Care Unit at the hospital.

Thanks to her.

The alchemists were waiting for Robert's condition to stabilize before moving him back to England, where the Order of the Crow could care for him. Swallowing away the sudden pain in her throat, Donna tried to ignore the guilt gnawing at her like a pack of hungry rats. She turned away from the dark water and began to walk across the bridge.

She stopped and stared.

Oh, crap. That couldn't be good.

A thick white mist had formed at the very end of the bridge, right where she was headed, like it had sprung up with the single purpose of blocking her exit. But that was crazy, right? Fog didn't have a mind of its own.

Spinning around, she checked where she'd just come from, only to see more of the swirling mist. It had become impossible to see beyond the very beginning of the relatively short bridge.

Was this some kind of trap? Aliette would know exactly where Donna had scattered the remains of the elflock.

Maybe she could open a gate—a dimensional doorway—again. Maker was already trying to show her how to control her abilities. If she didn't get a handle on them soon, the Order would bind her again—she didn't doubt that for a minute. But if she could try tapping into it now, she might be able to step through the fog and arrive at Ironbridge General.

Taking a moment to compose herself, Donna tried to reach the tiny shard of first matter embedded within her very soul.

But a tall figure in a black suit was already striding toward her, out of mist which seemed to curl away from him as he passed through it.

And then she realized who it was, walking so purposefully in her direction. All she could do was to wait for him to reach her, unless she chose to dive into the river instead. She considered this for one crazy moment, looking into the no-doubt freezing depths flowing fast beneath the bridge, but decided that if she was going to die this day, she'd far rather do it facing down a demon than drowning in winter-cold water.

Maybe she was still in shock—that could be the only explanation for how bizarrely disconnected she felt.

Demian met her in the center of the bridge and bowed slightly, his silver hair shifting around his face. "Donna Underwood, I offer you greetings."

"Hey," she muttered. Why was everyone so damn formal?

"Are you . . . well?"

What do you care? she wanted to ask. Biting back that less than ideal response, she opted for something less inflammatory. "As well as can be expected, under the circumstances."

The demon's cruel mouth curved into a smile that made her knees turn as watery as the river rushing below. She hated the effect he had on her, but she knew it wasn't real. Maker had assured her of that. Powerful demons had the ability to affect human emotions, and Demian seemed able to manipulate hers with ease. Yet she doubted that he even knew what he was doing to her—the books she'd been reading late into the night for the past two days said that some demons gave off pheromones the same way that humans breathed. In any case, Demian seemed to have taken a shine to her and, to be perfectly honest, it gave her the creeps.

He stretched out his hand and plucked a single black rose out of the air. He pressed it into her hand.

If she hadn't been wearing gloves, the wicked-sharp thorns would have drawn blood. Donna wondered if Demian realized that; she had the feeling that he wasn't used to interacting with humans. Well, he *had* said the demons had been locked away in their realm for two hundred years.

She tried not to show how afraid she really was. "A flower? For *me*? I don't think you should be giving me roses."

His face tightened, whether in confusion or anger she couldn't say. He shrugged in a disturbingly human gesture. "It is just a flower."

"But aren't we at war?"

His face relaxed. "We're demons, not savages."

She nibbled her lower lip, wishing she knew what to say to end this—all of it. "What are you going to do?"

He blinked his eyes, the flickering blackness making her feel vaguely sick. He didn't pretend to misunderstand her. "Do? We will take back this world, when the time is right."

She began to tremble. "And when will that be?"

"When it is." He smiled enigmatically.

"That doesn't tell me anything."

"I have work to do; many of my people are scattered throughout this realm."

Donna thought of Newton trapped in the bronze

statue of a head, rotting forever in Simon's laboratory. She swallowed. "Will you . . . rescue them?"

Demian's pale eyebrows lifted. "You know something of this?"

Oops. "Not really. Just something I heard." She said it too quickly, and she was sure he must have noticed.

He moved toward her until she could feel the heat radiating from his body. Demian was totally invading her space, but she refused to step back.

"You are lying. I can smell it on you," he said.

Donna made herself stand still, although every instinct screamed at her to run. "I'm a child of the alchemists—I've read about demons before. That's all."

Should she tell him about Newton? What would that mean for Simon? Not that she cared about the Magus, of course. But perhaps it would bring worse repercussions for Quentin.

Demian either believed her or decided to let it go. He shifted his stance to something less deadly.

"I'll see you soon," he said. "Go and visit with your mother—she is waiting for you."

How did he—? Donna stopped herself from asking the question. What would be the point? Demian spoke in riddles.

She turned her back on the king of the demons and ran all the way to Ironbridge Hospital. Nobody stopped her when she got there; everybody knew who she was, and word had come down from Quentin himself that

Donna was to be admitted to her mother's room any time, day or night.

Nurse Valderrama greeted her and ushered her into the waiting room, a wide smile spread across her pretty face. Her brown eyes were sparkling under the bright hospital lights.

Donna tried to catch her breath, holding onto the edge of the tall desk at the nurses' station. "Is she—?"

"Go see for yourself."

❦

Rachel Underwood opened her eyes and smiled at her daughter.

The bed sheets were crisp and white, and for once her face didn't look like it was blending into the pillows—there was a faint glow of color in her cheeks.

"Hey, Mom." Tears streaked Donna's face, but she didn't wipe them away. She was too busy holding her mother's hands.

"Darling, it's so good to see you again—to *really* see you."

Mom still looked like she'd been very sick, but there was a definite improvement. A few good meals would help, Donna thought, as would coming home the first time in years.

But what she noticed most was her mother's hair. It had been brushed until it shone, and now lay in a single red braid almost the entire length of her back. The white streak in front had disappeared.

Donna swallowed, feeling as though her heart might burst with happiness. "You're okay? You really are okay?" She had to know for sure; there had been too much disappointment and false hope over the years.

Rachel's smile was gentle. "I really think I am. Thanks to you."

No mention was made of what Donna had done to get this far—what she had sacrificed in order to bring her mother back from the very edge of madness—but the knowledge passed between mother and daughter in a silent communication. The look they shared, in that fleeting moment, held no judgment.

Light glinted on her mom's wrist, and Donna saw that she was still wearing the charm bracelet. Seeing it there made her throat tighten all over again, though she wasn't entirely sure she could say why.

"I think," Rachel said, "it might be a good Christmas."

"And a Happy New Year?"

"I hope so."

And maybe it really would be. At least, in this one infinitely precious thing.

My mom is okay, Donna thought. *The world might be going to Hell and I'm being exiled, but Mom's okay.*

That counted for something, didn't it?

What have I done?

The Wood Queen might have manipulated me, but I'm the one who did it—it was my untested and barely understood power that opened the gateway to the demon realm. I feel sick just thinking about it, just writing it down in these pages.

Hell on earth. Potentially. Although Demian doesn't seem in too much of a hurry to do anything. Quentin says he's gathering his army, rebuilding after the centuries of imprisonment.

I have to face the consequences of my actions—the choices I've made. Yet again.

There are still things I don't understand, but of this much I'm almost certain: I think I've brought down war on everybody in Ironbridge. Maybe even on the world beyond our boundaries.

When I remember that night, though, all I can see is Robert's stillness as he lay on the ground.

They don't know if he'll be okay, but he has a chance—Nurse Valderrama told me that, and I have to hold on to that tiny thread of hope. They've taken him back to England, so maybe I'll see him again. Because that's where they're sending me: London. I get to spend this last month with Mom, while also finishing up my schoolwork and saying my goodbyes to Navin and to Xan.

Mom's doing okay, which is just about the only good thing to come out of this mess. The Order is pretending to be happy to have her back, but it's so obvious they don't know what to do with her. She told me that I should go along with their plans to apprentice me to Miranda Backhouse—for now. I am beginning to think that London and the Order of the Crow might not be such a bad place to be, but the thought of losing Mom so soon after getting her back hurts more than I can say.

And leaving Nav breaks my heart; he's being so brave about it, but I know how much he'll miss me. If it's even half as much as I'll miss him . . .

Xan, who has so many more secrets than I'd even guessed, says he could come with me. He told me, "Just say the word, Donna, and I'm there. You and me on that plane. It's been too long since I visited my mom."

His smile had been filled with hope, but I'm still not sure how far I can trust him. I know people say stuff like that all the time, but I really mean it. Sure, he came through for me in the end, when it mattered—helped me to escape the demons and carried Robert out of the Ironwood—but he's just kept too much from me. I did learn that the secret visits to Maker were the reason for his strange behavior; it was nothing to do with Ivy at all.

I'm truly happy that Maker says he's going to help Xan—maybe even build him new wings—but I'm not sure that Xan fully understands what he's letting himself in for. When it comes to the alchemists, nothing is given freely; everything has a price. But Xan is intent on bargaining for the wings he wants so desperately. He won't listen to me when I tell him to take things slow, check the fine print and make sure he's not signing himself up to be a new weapon in the Order's arsenal.

I was at his house just yesterday, and things between us were the most uncomfortable they've ever been. We both made an effort, but it was clear there are major things we need to figure out if our . . . friendship is to continue. But we don't have time for that. Not now that I'm leaving.

What does any of this matter, anyway? Aunt Paige says that war is coming to Ironbridge—and I won't even be here to see it. To help. I tried to tell her—to make her believe that I would stand with the alchemists and do anything I could—but all she said was, "You've done enough."

They say that a Reaper Storm of demons is on its way. I don't know what that is, but it sounds like an apocalypse. The echo from my nightmares is enough to tell me that things are going to get bad—as bad as they could possibly get.

And amid all of this fear, flowers arrive for me every day at the Frost Estate. Simon turns away each delivery, but they keep on coming. Roses—dozens upon dozens of them. Each flower is absolute perfection.

Black roses.

The Council of Alchemists

Official Hearing

Case Number: 1/61803
Location: The Frost Estate
Accused: Donna Underwood
   (Order of the Dragon)
Accuser: Simon Gaunt
   (Magus of the Order of the Dragon)
Defense: Maker (Order of the Dragon)

Alleged Crimes: fraternizing with the dark elves (dealing with the Wood Queen); destroying the remaining drops of the elixir of life; sharing alchemical secrets with a commoner; conspiring with a half-fey outcast; other matters yet to be determined.

Alchemists Present:
Order of the Dragon: Quentin Frost (Archmaster), Paige Underwood, Maker, Simon Guant (Magus).
Order of the Crow: Miranda Backhouse, Robert Lee.

329

Excerpt from hearing transcripts prepared by the Order of the Rose.

Witness: Navin Sharma (Commoner)

SHARMA: This is my job, dammit. To support her; to protect her. To be there for her in the same way that she always is for me.

SHARMA: Next question, please.

GAUNT: Why were you in the Ironwood?

SHARMA: I wasn't just out for a walk, dude. I was kidnapped.

GAUNT: You will address me as Mr. Gaunt, boy.

SHARMA: Only if you address me as Mr. Sharma.

MAKER: Navin, please.

SHARMA: Fine. He can call me Navin.

GAUNT: How were you . . . kidnapped?

SHARMA: I'd just gotten a call from Dad to say that my grandfather was sick and had been rushed to the hospital. I was out on my bike so rode home as quickly as I could—that meant using a few shortcuts I know. One of them is this footpath, sort of an alleyway between streets, with high fences on both sides and tree branches overhanging everything.

GAUNT: Is this relevant?

SHARMA: Look, I'm either telling this or I'm not. You asked how I got kidnapped and this is what happened.

MAKER: It's all right, just carry on in your own way.

GAUNT: Maker, I am dealing with this witness—please wait your turn.

MAKER: He's my witness, Simon. Stop badgering him.

SHARMA: Um . . . So anyway, I was riding pretty fast along the path only about five minutes from home, and that's when I was attacked.

GAUNT: By elves?

SHARMA: Yeah, but at first I thought they were monkeys.

GAUNT: Monkeys?

SHARMA: Right. Because they were in the trees and they were all sort of jumping down on me.

GAUNT: Because monkeys are certainly an indigenous species of Ironbridge.

SHARMA: Was that sarcasm? That wasn't bad, coming from an old guy like you.

MAKER: Navin . . .

SHARMA: Sorry. I only thought they were monkeys for a second. I soon realized they were wood elves, but by then I had three of them surrounding me and I'd been knocked off my bike.

GAUNT: And how did you know what a wood elf was?

SHARMA: I'd seen one in Maker's workshop while I was in there with Donna.

GAUNT: Ah! So you admit that you broke into Maker's workshop?

SHARMA: The place had already been broken into. We were investigating.

GAUNT: You're saying that Donna Underwood willingly took you to a place belonging to the alchemists?

SHARMA: Well . . . I wouldn't say willingly. Not exactly.
GAUNT: Then what would you say? Exactly.

SHARMA: I sort of followed her.

MAKER: Simon, I thought you wanted to keep this witness's testimony relevant? We were talking about how Navin Sharma was abducted. Shouldn't we return to that point?

GAUNT: Very well. But later, I would like to revisit the matter of exactly how many of our secrets Underwood shared with a commoner.

MAKER: Noted. Navin, please continue.

SHARMA: Okay, so this *commoner* was lying on the ground with his bike on top of him. My leg was trapped and I was trying to get myself free when the elves started wrapping me up in vines.

GAUNT: Vines?

SHARMA: You know, like in Tarzan?

DONNA UNDERWOOD: [Choking sound.]

SHARMA: It was weird, man. I tried to fight them off, but they're strong little suckers. They were so fast, too—had me covered in those vines from head-to-foot before I knew anything—it was like being packaged up by a spider. A really big one.

GAUNT: You didn't cry out for help?

SHARMA: Of course I did! But for one thing they'd stuffed those damn vines in my mouth, and for another I thought maybe my leg was broken and it hurt like a ███████████████████ .

MAKER: Navin, if you could remember where we are? And Simon, please try to remember that this young man is a witness. He is not on trial.

SHARMA: I might as well be, the way everybody but Maker and Quentin have been treating me.

GAUNT: You will address Mr. Frost as "Archmaster."

SHARMA: Why? As you're so keen on pointing out, I'm not an alchemist. I'm not part of your freaky little club.

GAUNT: Mr. Sharma. After you had been . . . "wrapped

up" in vines and subdued by the dark elves, what happened then?

SHARMA: One of them smacked me in the head with something and the next thing I remember was waking up in total darkness.

GAUNT: They took you to Ironwood Forest?

SHARMA: To the Elflands, yes.

GAUNT: And where were you kept?

SHARMA: In a pit. A dark, freezing cold pit with insects and all kinds of shit down there. They'd untied me, but that was only because there was no way I could go anywhere. I thought I was dead for sure.

GAUNT: Why do you think they didn't kill you?

SHARMA: Is that a trick question? Obviously, they were using me as bait.

GAUNT: Because the Wood Queen, Aliette Winterthorn, she whom the alchemists know as ▓▓▓▓▓▓▓▓ , wanted to force a meeting with the Underwood girl in an effort to obtain the elixir. Is that correct?

SHARMA: Right.

GAUNT: How did you survive the dark elves, Mr. Sharma? It is highly unusual that once taken into the Ironwood a mere human would escape . . . intact.

SHARMA: That's because most other people don't have Donna Underwood on their side.

Transcript Ends.

ଈ

Acknowledgements

In the spirit of keeping things much shorter than last time, a big thank you to the following people who helped to make this book a reality:

To Miriam Kriss. An agent that any writer would be lucky to have. Thanks for talking me down, building me up, and everything in between.

To Brian Farrey, Sandy Sullivan, Lisa Novak, and the whole Flux gang. You made my book a hundred times better, yet again. Thank you for all your hard work.

To Jessica Clarke and everyone at Random House UK. For support above and beyond the call of duty, each and every one of you rock. Jess, you are an 'Authority Figure' I am more than happy to look up to!

To my friends and fellow writers. You help me to stay sane (mostly) and inspired (always), on this crazy writing journey.

To the Deadline Dames. For everything.

To my family. You all seem so proud of me for writing these stories; thank you for the love and support.

And last, but by no means least . . .

To Vijay Rana. Veej, without you there would be no books and no writing career. You're my favourite person. (Blanket!)

Read on for an exclusive extract from
Karen Mahoney's new novel,

Falling to Ash

Coming Autumn 2012

You can't choose your family. Living . . . Or dead.

I knew my morning was off to a bad start when I returned home from an all-night party at Subterranean to find two cops waiting at my apartment door.

Ordinarily, this wouldn't freak me out. Not too much, anyway. Once a police officer's daughter, always a police officer's daughter. It didn't take me long to figure out who they were despite the regular street clothes – I can smell a cop from a mile away.

For a split second I considered sneaking off before they saw me, but it wasn't like I had anything to hide.

Apart from being a vampire, I mean.

It's not as though I'd killed anyone. Lately.

No, I'm kidding. I don't do that – not unless someone makes me really angry.

OK, now I really am messing with you. I may be a member of Boston's underground undead (that nobody is supposed to know actually do exist, outside of colorful legends and the Twilight franchise of course) but I like to think of myself as one of the good guys.

Gals.

Whatever.

I took a moment to watch the man and woman as they knocked at the door again. One was white – the woman – the man was black, and actually the shorter of the pair, but I couldn't tell how old they were from where I was standing. My eyes are good, but even I can't see through the back of people's heads. Though now that I think about it, X-ray vision would be pretty cool.

The woman turned round and I tried to look like I hadn't been lurking. Nothing to see here, officer. Just your average teen vampire. Totally harmless.

"Hey," I said as I walked toward them. I flashed them a fangless smile (I'm well trained) and produced the door key by removing one of my chunky knee-high boots and shaking it upside-down.

I grabbed the key off the floor, replaced my boot and tugged down the short skirt of my black dress. "You want to come in?"

❧

I set about making coffee, putting my back to the detectives and measuring grounds, taking my time, adding water and trying to remember if there was anything vampire-y in the kitchen that would give me away. The clock on the microwave told me it was 8:05 A.M.

Noticing that made me think guilty thoughts about the microwave. That's where Holly and I heat up the blood we drink when we can't stomach it cold from the bag.

Pushing that thought hastily away, I swung round to face my unwelcome guests.

Detectives Alison Trent and Denmark Smith had introduced themselves and showed their I.D. before following me inside the North End apartment I share with Holly. They seemed surprised that I could afford such a nice place, but I wasn't about to tell them about all the interesting ways that the vampire Family of Boston finances their affairs.

Trent was probably in her late thirties and had shoulder length blonde hair tied back in an untidy ponytail. Her face was make-up free and her blue denim jacket looked well worn, kind of like the rest of her clothes. Her wrinkled pants and fitted sweater were black, and she looked vaguely familiar in that really annoying way that sort of itches at the back of your mind. Maybe my dad knew her and I seen her at some kind of police social event, back before he'd been quietly retired off the force.

Trent's intelligent blue eyes took in everything around her, cataloguing and filing it all away for later examination. Way to make a girl feel nervous.

Detective Smith on the other hand, the younger of the pair, was everything that his partner wasn't – at least in the sartorial stakes (no pun intended). He was dressed in a beautifully cut charcoal gray suit, and his shoes were shiny enough that you could see your face in them. If you actually had a reflection, that is. His black curls were close-cropped and perfectly sculpted – even his fingernails were neat and tidy. He was obviously handsome, but a little too handsome for me. I wondered that he even had time to solve crimes, what with all the personal grooming he must do.

I turned back to the counter and pulled down the only two clean mugs I could find. They were large and decorated with comic book characters; one was Wolverine and the other Batgirl. I splashed coffee into them both and shrugged as I offered Batgirl to Detective Trent.

Smith raised his eyebrows but accepted Wolverine without a word.

Trent stirred sugar into her coffee and watched me. "You live here alone?"

"I have a roommate."

"She wasn't out dancing with you?"

Dancing? I smirked, but let the old-fashioned term slide without my usual snarky commentary. "No, she works nights."

Of course she works nights. She's a vampire.

Smith took a sip from his mug. "What does your roommate do?"

Drinks blood! "She's a motorcycle courier."

I hoped the questions about my home life were over and that we could now get down to business. "Do you think maybe we could get to the point? It's been kind of a long night . . ."

"I should have thanked you sooner for seeing us so early, Marie," Trent said. "I realize what an imposition this is, but when we saw you coming in at this time I figured you're either an early bird or a night owl so maybe you wouldn't mind talking to us." This was said in a no-nonsense kind of tone that made it quite clear that she didn't care whether I minded or not.

I nodded, schooling my face into an expression of polite interest. I'd already gotten them to assure me that they weren't here with bad news about my family, but that didn't mean there wasn't bad news of a different kind.

And I have more than one Family. Theo will never let me forget that.

Smith tried a tentative smile. "We're hoping you can help us with an investigation."

The cops were taking up the only two chairs at the table, so I moved to the windowsill and sat down.

"OK," I said.

Trent leaned forward. "Do you know a boy named Richard Doyle?"

Who? My mind raced and I searched my memory. Life since being turned, a little over a year ago, was becoming more blurry as each day passed. Especially when I was tired or anxious.

I slowly shook my head. "I don't think so."

"You don't think so?" Trent gave me a cop stare I recognized well from my father. "You either know him or you don't."

"Sorry," I replied. "Can you tell me anything else? Something that might help me to place him?"

"You mean, something more than his full name?"

Smith's tone dripped sarcasm.

"I don't have a great memory," I replied, smiling sweetly.

He didn't respond to my feminine charms. I was tempted to show him my fangs; perhaps that would get a reaction.

"Miss O'Neal," he said. "Are you on any substances at this time?"

"What?" I didn't blush – couldn't blush, at least not until I fed properly – which was a good thing considering how guilty I felt, and probably looked. "What kind of substances?" Like, blood? Do you mean *blood!*

Trent pushed Batgirl away and scowled. "Don't play us for fools, Marie. We're talking about narcotics. Do you take drugs?"

"Of course not, officer," I said sincerely.

"Detective."

"Of course not, Detective." I cringed. This wasn't going well. I already knew they were detectives, but I was suddenly nervous and couldn't think straight.

Authority figures do that to me.

Trent stared at me. "Richard Doyle is dead, Marie. He was murdered, that's why we're asking you about him."

I leaned back against the winter-chilled glass and shivered.

"He attended the same art course at U/Mass that

you dropped out of last year," Smith said. "Maybe that'll help you place him."

I resisted the urge to give him the finger. Not because I have oh-so-much self control, but because suddenly I did know who they were talking about. Of course I did. It's just that a lot can happen in a year (like, for example, being turned into a monster against your will) and sometimes those things take up a lot of space in your head and heart.

Sometimes, it's hard to remember your own name, let alone the name of someone you only knew briefly as the skinny dude with the shock of red hair who worked at an easel on the other side of the room from you.

"I'm sorry, detectives, I really am. When you called him 'Richard' I got confused. I knew him as Rick." Which was true enough. "Or Red." Also true. "Some of the guys called him 'doily'."

Trent raised blonde brows. "Why would they call him that?"

"Um . . . his surname? Doyle? And the whole Irish thing. You know." I shrugged.

Smith looked at me like I was from another planet. "The 'Irish thing'? You're going to have to explain that one to me."

I tried to look like I wasn't from Planet Vampire. "Irish lace, you know. Doilies. Doyle."

Smith's blandly handsome face was blank.

I sighed. "I guess it made sense at the time."

His partner came to my rescue. "Marie, we need you to tell us everything you know about him."

"I don't know much, I swear."

Smith snorted.

I glared at him. "I mean it. We just took the same class for a couple of months. We were hardly BFFs."

He still didn't look convinced and I wondered what else was going on here. For some reason these two cops thought I knew more about Rick than I was telling.

I licked my lips. "How was he killed?"

"I'm afraid we can't share that information at this time. There wasn't much evidence at the scene, so we were really hoping you'd be able to give us something to go on."

"But why would I be able to do that? I keep telling you, I hardly knew the guy."

"Because we found this on his body."

Detective Trent produced a small, clear plastic bag from an inside pocket. She laid it on the table and I could see a scrap of white paper inside.

On the paper there was a hastily scrawled note in crimson ink that, to my suddenly feverish brain, looked like it could have been blood.

A note that consisted of my name and address.

Well, that can't be good, I thought.